The Catalogued Corpse

Doro Banyon Historical Mysteries-Book One

D.S. Lang

Book Cover by Karen Phillips

Editing by Alyssa Colton

ebook ISBN: 979-8-9867318-9-6

paperback ISBN: 978-1-962039-03-1

Chapter One

D orothea Banyon pulled her coat collar up, put her head down, and dashed into the swirling rain. The towering oaks and maples dotting the area between Wheaton Hall, the women's faculty apartments, and College Hall were barely visible. She loved passing the familiar red brick building, the campus' centerpiece, with its clock tower and ivy-covered walls. Most days, Doro took the winding path to the library, where she served as the first assistant. As a little girl, she had dreamed of being a student here. Then, after graduation, her goal had been to be a faculty member. Now, she was, but whether or not she could continue in that role remained to be seen.

This blustery Tuesday, she planned to cut through the main building and get a brief respite from the storm. Sidewalks made slippery by wet leaves and numerous puddles impeded her progress. While galoshes kept her feet dry, they did not improve traction. Maintaining a professional appearance was mandatory, something the college president had emphasized at her recent evaluation. At twenty-five, she was the youngest faculty member at Michaw College, a small school in a rural Ohio town. Looking and acting older was wise. Slipping on the wet walkway and getting muddy was to be avoided.

A sigh escaped Doro as she darted inside. For a moment, she savored being sheltered from the storm. The autumn storm, at least. Another type of tempest continued to blow.

Yesterday, she and the head of the English department had clashed, and not for the first time. Since Professor Hemet Corlon planned to bring his senior seminar to the library this morning, she was heading to work early to ensure not one item was out of place, which was often one of his nitpicking complaints. Even a pencil laying on a table could evoke his wrath. So could a card catalogue drawer not neatly pushed into its nook. More than once the man had asserted that "*girls your age ought to be married*," but the previous day's contretemps had involved her role as the faculty advisor to a women's group on campus.

The bell in the building's tower chiming seven-thirty shook Doro out of her ruminations and sent her back into motion. She rushed down the corridor, back outside, and almost made it to the library entrance before running into anyone. Unfortunately, that someone was Dr. Samuel Winwood, Michaw's president. He was as critical as Corlon, and both had strong opinions about a woman's place, which was far away from a college campus. "Good morning, sir."

His gray gaze swept over her. "Good morning, Miss Banyon. You seem to be in a hurry."

Doro smiled and hoped it looked genuine. To her way of thinking, Winwood was a poor replacement for Thomas Adams, who had retired a year-and-a-half earlier after a ten-year stint at the college's helm. Winwood's sharp features always made Doro feel like he saw her as prey. Short and wiry, with coal black hair slicked back from his face, he resembled a panther that was ready to pounce. "I'm eager to start my workday." Not exactly true, especially when facing Corlon was near the top of her agenda.

Winwood's bushy black eyebrows lowered as the man emitted a harrumph. "I was not aware you started your day an hour early."

"I don't always." As she studied the president's stern expression, Doro wondered how much he knew about her run-ins with Corlon. Probably more than she would like, since the pair—along with two others—had come to Michaw together. The quartet, not fondly called the *Fearsome Foursome* by some faculty members, wanted to turn back the hands of time and return the college to its original all-male status. Doro was among the many Maples, alumni nicknamed for the school's mascot, who disagreed. She fought her knee-jerk reaction to the man and his cronies. When Doro responded, she tried not to sound defensive. "I want to make sure things are in good order. Occasionally, some resource materials are moved from the reserve table to a nearby shelf. I want to ensure they're all accessible to students and professors. Of course, I always want to be right on time at the reference desk."

"I should hope so. Now, I have a meeting to prepare for, so I'll be on my way." With that, he strode off.

Briefly, Doro chastised herself for making such a paltry assertion. Of course, she was never late, because tardiness would be noted in her file, along with other reprimands from the past year. Petty complaints from Corlon mostly, and a few from Provost Otto Pottiger. Both men had mentioned her habit of having her students pull their desks into a circle instead of keeping them in rows. Doro found discussions flowed more smoothly that way, but Corlon and Pottiger criticized the set-up as too informal. Another criticism was directed at her bobbed hair. Both men referred to it as *flapper style*—a ridiculous observation, since women of all ages and levels had cropped their locks.

She shook off the gloom and rushed on. When she reached the library door, Doro was surprised to find it ajar. Had her boss come early, too? That was odd. Floyd Quartine would work late today, so she didn't expect him until noon. Besides, if he was in the building, why hadn't he secured the door? With rain blowing inside and creating a puddle, Doro moved forward. After she got out of her coat and galoshes, she would have to wipe up the floor. Otherwise, Professor Corlon would issue more complaints than usual. Annoyance filled her before she was ten feet into the building. Wet footprints created a trail in front of the circulation desk and toward the card catalogues, which were behind tall bookcases. Who had created such a mess? Surely not her boss, who held the library in high esteem and worked hard to maintain the space.

Fresh anxiety hit Doro. On Monday evenings, she locked up. Surely, she had secured the door. The mechanism was tricky, so perhaps it hadn't engaged. Or the janitors had exited that way and left it unsecured. Doro hated to think about the building being open all night. What if some mischief makers had come along? Most of the students were pleasant young people, not prone to vandalism. But an open door might be too much to pass up, and some would see no harm in moving books around, yanking out drawers, and such. Doro braced herself for a mess. At least, she had time to get things restored to normal.

Nothing was out of order in the first section, so she moved on. After a few more steps, Doro froze in place. Lying on the floor near the tall card catalogue, with a plethora of cards scattered around him and one drawer near his head, was Corlon. Doro croaked out his name. "Professor Corlon. Professor Corlon." When the man failed to respond, she closed the distance between them and bent over for a closer look. A tiny trickle of blood ran from his temple to his cheek. Had he taken a tumble and dislodged the drawer?

After several deep breaths, Doro took a better look. Abruptly, she realized the man wasn't breathing. His slack jaw and arms akimbo sent fresh waves of shock crashing over her. He couldn't be dead. Not from bumping into the catalogue. Could he? A mystery aficionado with a vivid imagination, Doro's mind whirled as fast as her heart raced. Was this an accident? Or a murder?

Almost as soon as the questions arose, Doro pushed them away. If her parents were here, they would chuckle over her fanciful thinking. Her history professor father would say, "*Read some nonfiction instead of so many whodunits,*" while her mother would provide an alternative, "*Why not try the classics, dear?*" But they were no longer in Michaw. They were hundreds of miles away in Colorado. Before she got lost in how and why they had left, Doro focused on the scene before her. The drawers, constructed of solid oak, were heavy due to the many cards jammed into them. Just last month, a student had dropped one on his foot and suffered a broken bone. But had the drawer fallen on Corlon? Or had he tripped and tumbled against it? Or had someone used it as a weapon?

As she continued her perusal, Doro noted a stain on one corner. The sharp edge had the potential to do significant damage, and it clearly had.

After long moments and more deep breaths, she gathered herself together and went to the circulation desk. Professor Corlon had probably met with a tragic accident. She would not let herself think otherwise. Knowing it had to be reported, she reached for the candlestick telephone. Her hands shook as she picked it up and waited for the town operator to come on the line. In a quavering voice, Doro asked to be connected to the president's office. When his secretary answered, Doro said, "Mrs. Jones, it's Doro, and I need to speak with President Winwood right away."

"I'm sorry. He's getting ready for a big meeting. May I take a message, dear?"

Hearing the voice of her mother's old friend eased some of Doro's tension, but the response reminded Doro of her earlier encounter with Winwood. She would've liked to wait, but that seemed like a poor idea. Corlon's students might come early, and they shouldn't see his lifeless body by the card catalogue. "I'm sorry, but it's an emergency. I really need President Winwood to come to the library right away."

A pause preceded the woman's reply. "He won't like the interruption, but I know you wouldn't insist if it wasn't important, and you don't sound like yourself."

Doro didn't feel like herself, either. When the tremors in her hands spread through her body, she leaned against the desk. "No, I can't wait." Mrs. Jones had worked on campus for several years. Prior to that, her husband had taught science at the college. When he had suffered a heart attack and passed on, his widow had needed a job. Dr. Ebediah Banyon, Doro's father, had made sure she got one.

"Of course, dear. I'll make sure he comes right away."

Ten minutes later, President Winwood, his expression taut with fury, stomped into the library. "What in the world would make you insist I be called away when I am preparing for a Board of Trustees meeting tomorrow evening? President Adams might've jumped to your tune, since he and your father were friends. I will not. Keep that in mind, Miss Banyon. You may have a degree in library science, but you've got little experience. Considering how little, I would not have hired you."

His tirade took Doro aback. The statements revealed what she had long suspected—the man wanted her gone—but now was not the time to argue. "This is an emergency, sir. If you'll follow me, that will become clear." Her voice still shook, but she got the words out.

His eyebrows rose. "Lead on." The two words, clipped and cold, hit Doro like ice pellets. Without responding, she headed to the card catalogues. Before turning to them, she relented and provided a succinct warning. "It's Professor Corlon. Evidently, he came early and had an accident." Or encountered a killer.

"What?" Winwood shot Doro a sidelong glance before pushing past her.

She knew the moment he saw the fallen figure, because Winwood gasped in shock. Within a moment, he dropped to his knees and put his fingers against Corlon's neck.

"He's dead." His usual rough voice trembled.

"That's why I called your office. I was afraid he was." Almost certain of it, but she had hoped the man was simply out cold.

The president's eyes became slits as he stared at her. "Did you two argue again?"

The question, an accusation really, stunned Doro. "He was here when I arrived." She gestured toward the trail of muddy water leading from the front door through the library to where the professor lay dead.

"Hemet would wipe his feet," Winwood said.

The response opened a new avenue of consideration. Professor Corlon was fastidious, something Doro had forgotten in the shock of seeing him prone on the floor. His penchant for neatness led to him checking out every nook and cranny of the library whenever he visited and was probably a reason for his dislike of classroom desks being moved. Due to those facts, the man was unlikely to leave a mess in his wake. Had someone followed Corlon into the building? The idea made her heart skip a beat. "Maybe another person was with him."

A harrumph escaped Winwood. "Someone who yanked a drawer loose, hit Hemet with it, and disappeared? That hardly seems likely." His gaze narrowed on Doro, as if she was a specimen under a microscope. "You've been a thorn in our sides ever since we arrived on campus a year-and-a-half ago."

For a moment, Doro stood in shocked silence. Was President Winwood suggesting she had clobbered Corlon with a catalogue drawer? "Surely, you don't think I had anything to do with this..." Her voice trailed off as she gestured toward the body.

"That's neither here nor there." Winwood waved one hand in the air as he stood. "Our new security officer is on campus, even though he doesn't start until Monday. I'll have someone go to his quarters and get him."

"Aren't you going to contact Constable Lammers?" Doro asked in surprise.

Winwood's nostrils flared with a sharp intake of breath. "Another friend of your father. One who should also retire. No. I don't trust him to do an impartial investigation."

Doro ground her teeth to hold back a sharp retort. "Mr. Lammers isn't as old as Dad, who hasn't retired himself. He's teaching in Colorado. Wade Lammers has only been on the job here for a couple of years, but he has experience as a security man."

"I understand about it being a second career for Lammers, but he's only up to mundane tasks and then, only during daylight hours."

Winwood's comments were harsh—typical of him. "Wade has three young children to raise alone, which is why he left his railroad job. After his wife died, he couldn't be gone for days on end. Besides, he provided security on trains. He'll know how to proceed with this accident."

"Accident," Winwood repeated in a mocking tone. "We shall see. I'll call the man, but I also want our new officer on the case. I'm going back to my office to contact them both. You need to come along."

"Professor Corlon's class will be here soon. I have to explain..." How was she going to do that, when she did not know exactly what had occurred?

"Put a note on the front door that class is canceled. I don't want you staying here alone and tampering with evidence. Let's get going."

Doro wanted to protest that she had no reason to ruin evidence, but the president stalked off before she could. When he paused at the exit to scowl back at her, she rushed to the circulation desk, scribbled a missive, tacked it by the door, and reluctantly followed Winwood to his office.

⁂

While Winwood holed up, Doro sat in the reception area with Mrs. Jones, who maintained a casual conversation. Doro was too shaken to fully respond.

Within twenty minutes, a tall man with dark brown, close-clipped hair strode into the office. His stern expression and squared shoulders gave him a military bearing. He had to be the new security officer, so Doro watched as the secretary greeted him.

"You got here quickly," Mrs. Jones said.

"The person sent by President Winwood made it clear I needed to hurry," he said in a breathless baritone. "The little apartment is nearby, but I needed to change clothes. I don't have any uniforms yet."

Doro studied his attire. Dark gray pants, a white shirt with a navy tie, and a fitted jacket all looked freshly ironed. Had he actually pressed his clothes before coming? If so, he'd been quick and thorough.

"Your uniforms should be here before your actual start date," the older woman said.

"Thank you, ma'am," was the man's reply.

Before further conversation could ensue, Winwood stepped out of his office and thrust his hand at the newcomer. "Mallow, I'm glad you're here. Let's speak in private." The president glanced at Doro. "Do not leave yet."

Doro released a long sigh. She had not been in favor of hiring a campus policeman. The town of Michaw had a constable, which was more than sufficient since few crimes occurred, and even those were minor—occasional thievery was the chief complaint. As far as the college, the biggest case had been a stolen examination a few years back. Doro had helped to find the wrongdoers, which had not involved the local lawman. Solving the mystery had been challenging and intriguing. She would've liked to crack other cases—but none had occurred. Until now. And finding a dead body wasn't intriguing. It was disturbing. Deeply disturbing.

Mrs. Jones's voice broke into Doro's thoughts. "Try to relax, dear. You look done in." Sympathy glowed in the secretary's gaze.

Upon their arrival, Winwood had provided the basic information to Mrs. Jones. His words had not been a blatant accusation, but the man had mentioned Doro knowing Professor Corlon would arrive early, and Winwood had highlighted a recent argument between the pair.

Doro, shaken to her core, had added nothing. Now, she said, "The professor and I have had cross words a few times. As for being aware of his early arrival, I was. But he was dead when I went to work." Even to her own ears, she sounded defensive.

"Of course, he was. President Winwood is upset because they've been friends for years. He doesn't think you hit Professor Corlon with a card catalogue drawer."

Doro wasn't so sure, since Winwood had been more accusatory than distraught. "I wish Constable Lammers would get here. The new guy seems...well, stiff and solemn." She paused briefly. "I assume he's the security officer."

"He is," Mrs. Jones replied. "The constable is probably making his rounds. He'll undoubtedly be in his office by nine-thirty, as usual. I'll contact him then."

"Good." Wade Lammers would investigate without bias. Doro wasn't sure the same could be said for this new man—Mallow—who had been chosen by President Winwood, Professor Corlon, Dr. Vincent Jerritt and Provost Otto Pottiger. Winwood had hired the other three, who were old friends of his. Each one did the president's bidding.

"Don't look so worried, Doro. President Winwood likes to bluster and seeing his old friend and longtime colleague dead...well, that's enough to upset anyone."

The comments made sense, so Doro nodded. Her relationships with Professor Corlon and President Winwood had not proceeded smoothly because both found fault with her. She had long suspected why, and the president had confirmed it. He wanted to get rid of her, and probably other female faculty members. At least that was the grist ground out in the campus gossip mill. Her hands tightened into twin fists. Despite Winwood's assertions, Doro was highly qualified for her job—more qualified than her supervisor because she held a master's degree in library sciences while he had been an English professor.

"Miss Banyon," Winwood's voice cut into her reverie. Doro looked up to see the new security man, still looking solemn, behind the president. "We're going back to the library. Wait a few minutes before you come along." He turned to his secretary. "Keep trying the constable's office. The man ought to be at work soon."

"Of course," Mrs. Jones replied in her usual cordial voice.

Doro figured the woman wanted to ease the situation and, while she appreciated the effort, it didn't work. At least, it didn't for Doro, whose insides were in tight knots. She jumped to her feet, but Winwood and Mallow were already in the hallway with the door closing behind them. "I don't see why I can't go along."

"President Winwood must have his reasons. It would be best to wait like he wants you to do."

Following his orders rankled her, but Doro sat back down and passed the next few minutes chatting with Mrs. Jones. Later, she had no idea what they had discussed. Her head was filled with Corlon's death and Winwood's accusations. After repeated glances at the wall clock, she saw five minutes had passed and rose again. "It's been enough time, I think."

Mrs. Jones nodded. "Take a few deep breaths on your way, dear. And remember, you're a valuable faculty member at this college. President Winwood hasn't been here long enough to realize that fact. When he and his colleagues see how much you and other women contribute to the school, he'll change his stance."

She didn't point out that Winwood had been at Michaw College for more than a year, which was plenty of time to notice Doro's qualifications and contributions. Nor did she think the man would change his mind about higher education being wasted on women, who belonged at home—according to him and the rest of the Fearsome Foursome. "Thank you."

Doro breathed deeply as she hurried back to the library but overcoming her anxiety was impossible. President Winwood had accused her of murder. Was he now convincing Officer Mallow of her guilt? A shudder ripped through her as she rushed on.

Chapter Two

W hen she arrived, the two men were at the circulation desk.

As she drew alongside them, President Winwood spoke. "This is Officer Everett Mallow, who will investigate the crime. Officer, Miss Banyon found the body."

Doro bit her tongue to keep from asking about Constable Lammers, who should be in charge instead of this young usurper.

Mallow nodded as he retrieved a notepad and a pencil from his jacket pocket. "I want to hear what happened from when you walked into the library until you saw the professor, Miss Banyon. The exact time of your arrival is important, too."

"Perhaps we could sit down in my office," Doro said, "instead of standing in front of the circulation desk."

The officer shifted from one foot to the other, but his expression remained solemn. "I don't have all that many questions, miss."

Didn't the man understand her shock and uneasiness? Should she admit to feeling shaky? Not to Mr. Starched Shirt. And his shirt, peeking out above his jacket, was starched. The material looked stiff enough to stand upright on its own. Details about the newcomer had not reached her. But he was nothing like Wade Lammers, the town constable, whose shirts were clean but rarely ironed. But Wade was always relaxed and affable. Officer Mallow appeared to be his exact opposite. Was that part of the reason Winwood and company had chosen him?

"I've alerted the provost, along with the head librarian, who should arrive soon. It might be best if you availed yourself of a quiet place to interview Miss Banyon," the president said.

"Of course," Mallow said.

"My work area is over there." Doro pointed to the corner. The space afforded to her was tiny, but private.

Mallow turned his head to follow her gesture, revealing his strong profile. Without his gaze on her, Doro noticed his good looks—dark brown hair that might have waved if it wasn't so short, slightly tanned skin, crystal silver eyes, and ebony lashes any woman would envy. Too bad arrogance rolled off him in waves. Not that she was interested in flirtation or courtship. She planned to be a career woman.

Mallow turned to the president. "I want to talk with anyone else who was in the area this morning. Witnesses can lead to a quick solution."

"I'll arrange for them to come here, Everett," President Winwood assured him.

Using the officer's first name indicated a level of familiarity that only escalated Doro's anxiety. Had Mallow worked at the president's previous institution? How well did they know each other? Was the new officer beholden to him?

"Thank you." Mallow pointed to Doro's desk. "Lead the way, miss."

Doro picked up her voluminous leather bag, a high school graduation gift from her parents, which was still on the counter. Before she took a step, Mallow spoke again.

"What's that?" he asked.

"My bag." Wasn't that obvious?

"I'll need to go through it," Mallow replied.

The idea set Doro's teeth on edge. "Student papers are in it. I need to grade them."

"You teach along with being a librarian?" Mallow inquired.

"I do," Doro said.

For a moment, he waited, as if expecting to hear more. "What do you teach?" he asked.

Doro released a pent-up breath. "A course on the mystery novel."

A harrumph left Winwood. "The former president held a loose rein and approved classes that lack substance. Miss Banyon teaches one of them."

Mallow's attention riveted on Doro. "Do you fancy yourself an armchair detective?"

The question ignited her anger, which she held in check with effort. "We examine the structure of novels, assess the plots, review character development, and evaluate the mysteries."

"The books are hardly classics," Winwood put in. "Students would be better off studying Shakespeare, Chaucer, and the great poets like Robert Browning and Lord Tennyson."

Doro noted the absence of women writers but withheld comment. She didn't need to draw more of Winwood's fire.

"I'm not in a position to judge the content of courses," Mallow said, before turning back to Doro. "But I'll need the bag."

She thrust it at him before pivoting on her heel and stomping to her office. Once inside, she pointed to one of the two chairs facing her desk. "Please sit down." After settling in herself, Doro folded her icy hands in her lap. Officer Mallow, his handsome features schooled, offered not a jot of commiseration or compassion. Maybe he was accustomed to seeing dead bodies, although he was too young to have served in the Great War, which had ended in 1918, ten years earlier.

"Miss Banyon, what time did you arrive for work?" Mallow asked.

"Shortly after the tower clock chimed seven-thirty."

"I see. The library doesn't open until eight-thirty. Why so early?" His gaze riveted on her.

The query sounded accusatory, which had Doro shifting restlessly in her hard chair. Surely, the man did not suspect her. Or had Winwood slanted information to make Doro look bad? The possibility increased her anxiety, while she also wondered about being forthright. Her main reason for arriving early was to ward off criticism from Professor Corlon by ensuring every nook and cranny of the library was in pristine order. If she admitted as much, would the officer ask if Doro and Corlon didn't get along? Not that Winwood probably hadn't bent Mallow's ear. Since she did not want to reveal the extent of their conflict, Doro formed her reply with care. "A class was scheduled to be here shortly after opening, and I wanted everything to be ready for them."

He jotted a few notes before looking directly at Doro. "Do you come over an hour early for every class visit?"

His tone and expression revealed doubt. Since Mallow could easily discover she didn't, or maybe he already knew, Doro answered honestly. "Not always."

"Only for certain professors? Ones who don't think unqualified young women should be on the faculty?" His deep voice held an edge.

The two questions hung like a dense fog between them. Evidently, the president had shared details. Mallow's tone and expression gave away nothing of his own perspective. "I have a master's degree in library science from the University of Michigan, Officer Mallow. I completed the program in one year, because I worked hard. As for being young, I'm twenty-five and I doubt if you're much older."

Color formed two splotches on his lean cheeks. "I'm twenty-six."

His candor surprised Doro, who found herself at a loss for words.

Mallow did not suffer the same issue. "Professor Corlon sat in on my interview and made no objection to my youth. Neither did the others on the hiring committee."

The admission did not ease Doro's mind. If anything, her trepidation escalated. The Fearsome Foursome had hired this man. Would he be their stooge? "Did you know President Winwood before being hired?" Although the question might seem impertinent, she wanted to know.

For a moment, Mallow looked baffled. "No. I never met anyone on the hiring committee until I was interviewed."

"Just curious," she murmured. "President Winwood is relatively new here, and he brought several others with him. Professor Corlon was one of them."

"I know," he replied.

When Mallow said no more, Doro wondered what else he knew. Or what he had been told by Winwood, Corlon, Pottiger, and Jerritt. A period of silence ensued before the officer broke it.

"From what I've heard, you grew up around campus."

"I grew up in Michaw. My father was a history professor here for almost two decades. He left for a job in Colorado several years ago."

"And you stayed."

Doro lifted her chin. Was he so old-fashioned that he thought young women belonged at home with their parents until marriage? "I was a senior, so I finished here before going to library school. Only a handful of colleges offer advanced degrees for librarians. When I completed mine, I was offered a position at Michaw. Since my grandmother lives in Sylvania, which is only a few miles away, I took the job. We have no other family in the area. If I left, she'd be here alone."

"And she doesn't want to leave her hometown," he suggested in a softer tone.

"Not after seventy years," Doro replied.

Mallow nodded. "Understandable. As for the case, President Winwood said you and the professor often clashed."

"I wouldn't say often," Doro replied. Only whenever they crossed paths.

"What would you say?" he asked.

Doro stared at the top of Mallow's head as he bent to scribble more notes. Queasiness had roiled inside of her since running across Corlon's body. She had barely held it at bay when President Winwood levied his veiled accusations. Now, it churned into biliousness. How could she explain without sounding callous? "Professor Corlon and I have disagreed on a few matters. For one, he didn't like that the library meeting rooms are booked up for the rest of the term."

Mallow's brow furrowed as he looked back at her. "Why did that bother him?"

"He formed a committee to review all of Michaw's long-standing policies. The group has three members, so they could get together many places. But he insists college business should take precedence over student organizations. I've repeatedly told him we make reservations at the beginning of the term. He didn't ask until three weeks later." Doro squared her shoulders. "I will not banish students for a handful of disgruntled employees."

His frown deepened. "Disgruntled?"

Wishing she could substitute another word was futile, so Doro plunged ahead while silently admonishing herself to think before speaking. "As I mentioned, a few folks want to review college policies. I don't know how familiar you are with Michaw, but it became a progressive institution under President Adams. Women were admitted and employed in significant numbers. That's been the case for over a decade."

"I'm aware of those facts."

Did he agree with Winwood and his followers about taking the school back to its roots? Founded in 1880, Michaw College had been "men only" for over thirty-five years. When Thomas Adams took the reins in 1916, after being a Michaw professor for many years, he had wanted to move the institution in a more modern direction. While a few professors had objected, most—like Doro's father—were enthusiastic about the change. After war was declared in 1917, the idea became popular as many students and employees went into the military, leaving empty spaces across campus. Dr. Adams found almost no opposition to his plan when the school was on the brink of closure. "Most alumni, students, and employees want things to stay like they are now. I'm not alone." Doro knew she was babbling, but what she said was true.

"I didn't say you were." His tone matched hers in terms of defensiveness. Mallow cleared his throat. "Let's get back to the case. I assume the library was locked last night, but Professor Corlon got in. I didn't note any forced entry. Did you when you arrived?"

"No, but he has a key to the library. All the department chairs do. You can ask any of them."

Mallow looked up. "I'll speak with them."

Eager to end this interview, Doro asked, "What other questions can I answer, Officer?"

He looked back at his notepad. "You followed the wet footprints to the bookcases and made some of your own."

"I wiped my feet on the doormat, so I left very few prints and no water," she replied. "But yes, I went toward the puddles. The front door was ajar, which is unusual. It's never happened before today."

"You laid your bag on the counter, right?"

"I did because it's heavy. I didn't want to haul it along while I looked to see who sloshed water and mud around." Why was he asking about something so mundane? Doro did not have to wait long to find out.

"From the wound on Professor Corlon's head and the position of his body, his attacker snuck up behind him, most likely from the circulation desk side of the library, but maybe from the other way, which I understand leads to a back door."

The last observation surprised Doro. "I didn't look beyond his body. Were there muddy prints that way, too?"

A moment's hesitation preceded his reply. "There were."

"As I said, I wiped my feet," Doro repeated, "and I didn't go toward the back door."

Mallow looked up from his notepad to study her face. After a long moment, he continued. "What did you do after putting your bag down?"

Hadn't she made her actions clear? Or was the man trying to trip her up? When Doro replied, her voice trembled. "I followed the footsteps and found Professor Corlon. At first, I thought he was unconscious. When I couldn't rouse him, I realized he was dead."

"Take your time, Miss Banyon. I understand how difficult this must be for you."

Her gaze shot to his face, where sympathy softened his handsome features. Mallow might be stiff and starched, but he wasn't completely devoid of empathy. "I was stunned when I realized he wasn't just out cold. For a bit, I wondered if he'd accidentally hit his head."

For long moments, his steady gaze stayed on her. Finally, he jotted something down and spoke again. "The catalogue drawers are all easy to pull out from what I could tell."

"They are. Students take them to tables for sorting. Otherwise, a jam can occur in front of the cabinets."

"That makes sense. Do they ever fall out on their own?"

The question seemed odd, but Doro answered. "No, never that I know about."

"So, accidentally dislodging one isn't likely."

"It isn't," she admitted with reluctance, "which means someone used the drawer as a weapon." Would he confirm her supposition?

Silence echoed in her small office before the officer replied. "If you teach a course on the mystery novel, you know a blow to the head has to be forceful to kill someone."

She leaned back in her chair and wrapped her arms around her waist. "Fiction writers sometimes play fast and loose with the facts."

"Sometimes, they do," he replied, "but wouldn't you point those instances out to your students?"

"I do. So, I guess it was wishful thinking that Professor Corlon suffered an accident."

A shrug lifted one shoulder. "I'm still very early in my investigation, so I won't rule anything out yet." He tapped his pencil against the notepad. "Let's go back to the student groups using library rooms, so Professor Corlon couldn't."

Doro yearned to say the college existed because of students. She resisted. "All right."

"What organizations got preference over faculty members?"

The question annoyed Doro, who had already explained library policy. Once again, her stomach churned. Doro was the faculty advisor for the chief women's group on campus. President Adams had approved the organization, but Winwood wanted to disband it. His friend Corlon was in the same camp. Doro, and some other female faculty members, believed it was a step toward returning the school to its original men-only status.

"Miss Banyon? The meetings?"

Doro cleared her throat and stared directly into his silver-gray eyes. "The Young Women Voters for Equality and Justice." She thought his gaze widened before the thick, dark lashes swept down and his focus went to his notepad.

"Never heard of it."

"No, I don't imagine you have." Doro didn't keep the antipathy from her voice. She didn't even try. Many men looked askance at the group and others like it.

He looked back at her. "I don't have a college education, miss, but I read widely, and I was a policeman. I'm aware of many ladies' groups who fought for the vote, and others who are devoted to female rights. Just don't know about yours."

Doro studied his face. Reading his schooled features proved difficult, as difficult as figuring out how he felt about women's rights. Prior to the Nineteenth Amendment being passed and ratified, many suffragettes had been harassed, beaten, and arrested at peaceful marches. Had Mallow been one of the policemen involved in harming the women? The officer would have been young, but he could have been a lawman when the voting rights movement was in its final swing. "It was formed on campus for students and female faculty. We haven't marched elsewhere, so you wouldn't have seen us in your work."

His brow furrowed. "In my work?" Confusion filled his voice.

Was he feigning ignorance or making fun of her? "The police were at all the suffragette marches. Most groups had banners and sashes with their names. This entity didn't exist until a couple of years ago."

"Women have had the right to vote since 1920, which is the year I graduated from high school. I wasn't a policeman until I turned twenty-one. I left the department a year later to work for the Prohibition Bureau."

The comment surprised her. "You were a federal agent."

One corner of his mouth lifted a fraction. "Technically, I still am. My resignation won't be effective until Monday, when I officially begin work here."

Surely, he couldn't be about to smile. Doro gazed at him. "I see." The two words came out sounding like criticism, but she had only meant to make an observation. She opened her mouth to explain, but Mallow reacted first.

His amusement faltered. "If you see me as someone who plans to break up campus parties or search for leftover bottles of booze, you're wrong. I'm done with hunting bootleggers, raising speakeasies, and..." His voice trailed off. "Anyhow, I was hired to ensure the campus remains a safe place."

"It always has been," Doro put in.

"So, I've heard, but many schools have hired security officers lately. Michaw isn't the only one." He cleared his throat. "Now, this group meets regularly?"

"Yes, weekly. As I said, YWV is relatively new, and we only concern ourselves with campus issues."

Mallow opened his mouth, but quickly shut it. Before he spoke again, the officer made more notes. "YWV is your abbreviation for the group?"

Doro nodded.

"And you discuss issues like President Winwood and others debating whether to keep the school as a co-educational institution."

"We discuss a wide range of topics." Doro had no intention of providing specifics to this man. The group had nothing to do with the murder, and she would not allow the members to become scapegoats.

"Are the meetings open to everyone?" he asked.

"Every female on campus, yes."

"No men?"

"No. As I said, it's the Young *Women* Voters."

"And all the attendees are young."

The observation laid like a trap, so Doro carefully sidestepped it. "We don't ask for proof of age."

This time, his lips twitched enough to signal a repressed smile, but he hastily glanced down at his notes. "Interesting." He released a slight cough, which might have been a smothered chuckle. "Professor Corlon objected to this group of young women taking precedence over his committee. Is that right?"

"He did. More than once." Since others would say the same, Doro saw no sense in lying. Perhaps, revealing other details would be wise. Then, Officer Mallow could not accuse her of covering up. "In fact, he's the one who asked President Winwood to remove official status for YWV."

"Why?"

The single-word query merited a complete explanation. Before Doro replied, she considered how to present the group, and herself, in the best light. "Professor Corlon didn't see any reason for women to have their own group."

"There aren't any all-male organizations on campus?" Mallow asked.

His question played right into her ballpark. "There are a few." Several seconds of silence ticked away. Something in Mallow's eyes telegraphed disapproval. Toward whom, Doro did not know.

"Corlon didn't want the men's groups to lose their official status, though."

Since his statement revealed the target of the disapproval, Doro let some of her tension drain away. "No, he doesn't, and President Winwood seemed to take his side."

Mallow skimmed his notes before looking back at Doro. "President Winwood explained that he and Corlon worked together at another school, and the two of them came here a little over a year ago."

"That's right. Dr. Adams retired in June of last year, and the board hired Winwood, along with Corlon and two others, Provost Otto Pottiger and Dr. Vincent Jerritt."

"Did Professor Corlon take the place of someone else who retired?"

"He did," she replied.

After jotting more notes, Mallow again focused on her. "The two others sat in when I was interviewed. I had the impression they were close to Winwood and Corlon before coming here."

"President Winwood created a Provost's position and hired one of his college fraternity brothers, Pottiger, who has taught at a couple of universities." Doro failed to keep her nose from wrinkling. Every time, she thought about the provost, she recalled the stench always clinging to him: sweat, cigar, and Limburger cheese. "The other man, Jerritt, was added to the mathematics department, as chair." At least the math professor was always nattily dressed and well-groomed. Tiny points in his favor.

"What happened to the former chairman?" Mallow asked.

"She was demoted to regular faculty status," Doro replied. The woman had been among the first females hired and had gained tenure under President Adams.

"How do others on campus feel about the changes?"

"Several professors deserved a chance to be the chairman ahead of a newcomer, and the same is true for the provost job. At least three faculty members deserved consideration. I'm not the only one who thinks so." Doro kept her voice well-modulated and her words non-accusatory.

The officer looked thoughtful. "Which means there are plenty of people on campus who may hold a grudge against the professor."

Since Doro figured he was dangling bait to get her to bite, she simply shrugged. "No grudges. Just a strong difference of opinion on changes at this school. Professor Corlon is—was—outspoken in championing President Winwood's agenda."

"Interesting."

An all-purpose vague word, but Doro did not comment on it. Instead, she waited for another question to come her way.

"How many faculty members have argued with Corlon?"

Did he expect her to present suspects? If so, he'd be disappointed. "I don't know details about any arguments. Perhaps other faculty members do."

He nodded. "I'll be talking with many people. As for this morning, did you see anyone else on your way to the library?"

Doro took no time to wonder what he meant. Instead, she answered directly. "Only the college president, which I'm sure he told you."

"You saw no one on your way to campus?" Mallow inquired. "Other than President Winwood."

"I live on campus, Officer Mallow. All female faculty members do."

"That's right," he murmured. "I heard that in passing when I came for an interview, but I got a lot of information that day and since being hired. I haven't absorbed it all. Anyhow, you didn't run into anyone in your residence hall?"

"No, I didn't. Most of the women don't leave until closer to eight o'clock. Since we all have kitchenettes, we eat breakfast in our quarters. Sometimes, we share a meal downstairs because that kitchen is larger."

"All right. Let's go over your trek from your apartment to the library."

With a sigh, Doro slumped back in her chair. "As I said, I live in the women's faculty apartment building, Wheaton Hall. It's only a hundred yards from the library, but on the opposite side of College Commons, the front lawn. You probably saw it when you got to campus. The structure is a duplicate of Madden Hall, the men's residence, on the opposite side of the commons and behind the library, to the side of College Hall. The faculty residences are miniatures of the main building—red brick with white pillars and trim."

"I've seen it. When there's space, I'll have rooms in Madden. It looks nice from outside, but all the buildings do. It's a lovely campus." He ran his fingers through his hair. "Getting back to your walk here."

The edge of impatience in his deep voice set Doro's teeth on edge. If he only wanted the bare facts, that's what he would get.

"I walked out of my building and took the sidewalk to College Hall. Then, I cut through there to get out of the rain. I ran into President Winwood on my way. We spoke briefly, and I continued to the library. The door was ajar, so I came in. I saw puddles and mud on the floor, laid my things on the counter, followed the trail to the bookcases, and on to the card catalogues. I found the professor, checked to see if he was breathing, discovered he wasn't, and called the main office." The statement repeated what she had already said, but the officer might still be trying to find a discrepancy. Doro took care to avoid presenting any.

Officer Mallow's pencil flew across his notepad and continued moving when Doro stopped talking. When he looked up, his gray gaze was intent. "You already said what happened here."

A pent-up breath escaped Doro. "I thought you wanted a complete recitation of my trip this morning."

He ran a hand over his face. "And this was right after you arrived at seven-thirty?"

"It was." The man's reaction revealed her terse account had annoyed him, but hadn't he wanted only facts? All the facts? A repeat of facts?

"Did the professor usually come early when his classes met in the library?" Mallow asked.

"Somewhat early." How else would he inspect the main areas of the library? Doro wondered but did not say.

For a moment, Mallow looked as if he might ask for more details. Instead, he posed another query. "How many folks would know his class was meeting here today?"

Doro shrugged. "All his students. Probably some of the other English professors. My boss and our student worker."

"And Professor Corlon lives on campus?"

"No, he rents a duplex in town."

"So, his neighbors might know he left early."

"Possibly," she replied.

Another frown formed on the officer's face. "Would you know where he lived? Even the street name would help."

His weary expression chipped away at Doro's defenses. The man was trying to do his job. In actuality, he wasn't supposed to start work until next week and had probably planned for some time off. "Over on Oak Avenue."

"Is that close to campus?"

The question further highlighted how new Everett Mallow was to Michaw—the college and the town. Because Doro had spent most of her life in the area, she usually welcomed strangers. But she had not done so with him. A jolt of chagrin hit her. Just because she and the campus security officer hadn't met in the best circumstances—which was putting it mildly, since she still seemed to be in the suspect category—didn't mean she shouldn't be more hospitable. "If you turn right at the entrance to campus and go two blocks east, you'll run into Oak. Professor Corlon lived on the upper floor of a white frame cottage a few houses from the corner. The porch has trellises across the front with a few late roses still blooming."

After making a note, Mallow smiled. "Thanks. I planned to get acquainted with the school and town before my official start date, but things changed."

The boyish grin nearly disarmed her. He was handsome when stiff and stern. Smiling, he was striking. Doro glanced away and cleared her throat. "When did you get here?"

"Yesterday afternoon," he replied. "I worked a shift with the Bureau the night before. We're short-handed, and my resignation isn't official until Monday. That puts me in the on-call category."

No wonder he looked weary. "President Winwood shouldn't expect you to investigate this case. Constable Lammers can handle it."

The charming grin disappeared. "I'm as capable as the constable. Maybe more capable, since I've been an agent for three years."

Loyalty drove Doro's response. "The constable is quite capable, and he's a mature man with security experience. He worked for the railroad as a safety officer. I'm sure Winwood belittled him, but he does that to many longtime locals. It's unfair." Doro had known Wade Lammers all her life. His family went back in Michaw even farther than her own, and they were good people. Not having college degrees didn't make them dumb, despite what Winwood and his three associates thought.

"Quite a lot in life is unfair, Miss Banyon." Mallow stood up and flipped his notepad closed. "I have to talk with several others. For now, you need to stay in the library." Then, he turned on his heel and left before Doro could form a response. The young officer had thawed until she mentioned Lammers taking over the case. Then, Mallow had gotten defensive. Interesting, although Doro wasn't sure what it meant. And she certainly shouldn't care.

Chapter Three

At four o'clock, Officer Mallow wrapped up the interviews. Doro got word when President Winwood spoke with her and her boss to inform them not to return to work until Monday. Classes were canceled at least that long.

As soon as the administrator left, Doro turned to Floyd Quartine, the head librarian. "Students may want to use the library before next Monday," she said. "Hours have already been cut." As had staff jobs. Prior to Winwood's arrival, there had been another librarian, a secretary, three student aides, and a page. All women. Now, it was only Doro and Mr. Quartine with a student to help re-shelve books once a week. Because the tomes piled up long before then, Doro ended up doing the task daily.

Quartine's gray brows went down as a frown formed on his angular face. "I can't subvert the president's orders."

"Of course not," Doro agreed.

A long, rumbling sigh escaped Quartine. "Take some time for yourself, Doro. You work hard, and you deserve to relax."

Her boss was a good, kind man. Doing Winwood's bidding did not come easily to him, because Mr. Quartine put students first. Next came his staff, so seeing some put out of work upset him. Doro knew he disliked the changes, probably enough to retire at the end of the school year. The thought saddened her. He'd been the head librarian for as long as she could recall. "Thank you."

He nodded. "You go along. I'll be leaving soon myself."

With reluctance, Doro gathered her things. Since Mallow had not returned her bag, she reluctantly stopped at the table where he and Constable Lammers were going over notes. They both stood.

The constable, a muscular man of middle height and years, offered a rueful smile. "I'm so sorry I didn't get here sooner. Davey fell out of a tree at recess and broke his arm. I was still making my rounds when Dr. Silton found me. My boy was at his house with Mrs. Silton and their maid fussing over him. They were kind enough to keep Davey for the day, but I needed to finish checking all the businesses. I didn't know about Professor Corlon until noon."

"I hope Davey is all right," Doro said.

"He's hurting now, but keeping him from climbing and such for the next month will be hard," the constable said. With one hand, he pushed an errant lock of hair off his face, but it fell back almost immediately.

For as long as Doro could remember, Wade Lammers' stick-straight hair had given him the same trouble. The only difference now was that his nearly coal black locks were shot with bits of gray. "I'm sure it will," Doro observed. The eight-year-old was active, to say the least. "Will he be able to go back to school tomorrow?"

"Doc thinks so," Lammers replied. "If not, Mrs. Silton assured me the boy could stay at their place while I'm working."

"That might be best," Doro murmured.

Mallow broke into the conversation. "We have a lot to go over, Miss Banyon. Did you need something?"

She pulled her attention away from the constable. "I'm sorry to bother you, but we've been told we should leave until Monday, and I'd like to take my bag."

"That's not possible," Mallow replied.

When the security officer did not continue, the constable offered a smile. "Officer Mallow wants to go over all the evidence again, but you'll get it back as soon as possible."

"Evidence." Alarm ballooned inside Doro until she could hardly draw breath. The officer's previous suspicions had put her on edge. After a few hours, she had relaxed. Now, all her anxieties rose full-force. The urge to argue with Mallow hit Doro hard, but she swallowed it back.

"Nothing to be alarmed over," Lammer said. "I can drop it off at your place later."

A scowl darkened Mallow's face. "I doubt I can ascertain if it contains important information that soon."

Annoyance pierced Doro's anxiety. She turned to Lammers with a smile. "Thank you, Constable. I certainly don't want to stand in the way of justice, but student papers are in my bag. I'd like to grade them."

Mallow's expression softened. "As the constable said, we'll get it to you soon. We not only talked with many people, we needed to examine the muddy footprints, such as they were."

The revelation piqued Doro's interest. "I didn't notice any clear ones."

"Unfortunately, they weren't true prints, just muddy splotches and puddles. Nothing that will help solve the case," Mallow admitted.

His disclosures encouraged Doro to ask for more details. "Did others know anything to help?"

"Bits and pieces," Wade replied.

Mallow nodded. "Most sang your praises."

Since Doro couldn't read the sentiment behind the words, she made no reply. At this juncture, silence seemed sensible.

"You're a favorite of many folks on campus," Mallow observed.

"And in town," the constable added. "I remember Doro from when she was born. I'd just left school and hired on with the railroad, but when I got home, my mother was over the moon about the new baby at the Banyon place."

Warmth spread through Doro at the image created by his recollection. "How is your mother?"

Lammers grinned. "Pretty well. If she gets stronger, she'll be able to help with the children. Then, I can respond to crimes quickly. Not that we need more big cases around here." Color rose in his ruddy cheeks. "How about your momma? How is she doing?"

"The dry air in Colorado agrees with her," Doro replied.

"So, she and your pops won't be moving back," Lammers said.

"No, they won't. Her health is better in a dry climate, and Dad loves his job at Colorado College." She touched the locket beneath her blouse. When her mother had left over seven years ago, she had given the piece of jewelry to her only child as a talisman and said, "*We may not be in the same place, but I'll always be with you.*" Doro, deeply touched by the sentiment, rarely took it off.

"We'd hate to lose you," Lammers put in.

His sincerity touched her. "I'm not departing soon." As long as her grandmother was alive, Doro planned to stay put. Later, she might move to Colorado. Only time would tell.

"Good," the constable replied.

Once again, the new security officer interrupted. "Before you go today, I have a couple more questions," Mallow put in.

"I'm happy to answer them for you." Not true, but Doro fought to remain impassive.

The officer gestured toward a chair across from him. "Please take a seat."

Although Doro wanted to escape as soon as possible, she followed his request, or order, depending on the interpretation. Both Mallow and Lammers returned to their chairs.

"As the constable said, we've spoken to many people. You indicated, Professor Corlon didn't get along well with more than a few folks," Mallow observed. "Miss Agatha Darwine made a point of telling me that, too."

His attention never left Doro's face, which made her feel like a specimen in one of the science department's microscopes. "She did?"

Mallow nodded. "Are you friends?"

He made the question seem accusatory, another reaction that upset Doro. She wasn't privy to the other interviews, but surely someone other than Aggie had revealed the professor's run-ins with multiple people. "We are."

"Close friends?" Mallow asked.

"Does it matter if we're close or not?" Doro heard the irritation in her voice and hoped he did, too.

"It might." His steady gaze remained on her.

"Aggie is as honest as the day is long. So is Doro," Lammers said.

Although his expression remained congenial, an undercurrent of authority laced his tone. Doro could have hugged the man for supporting both her and her friend.

"I wasn't suggesting otherwise," Mallow said.

When the silence became oppressive, Doro asked, "What's your other question, Officer Mallow?"

He cleared his throat. "A couple of people mentioned the president of YWV...sorry, I forgot the rest."

"YWVEJ. Young Women Voters for Equality and Justice," Doro put in. "But YWV is fine."

"Right," he said. "Anyhow, two professors said Miss Kitty Tenseng is president of the group. Evidently, she and Corlon have clashed."

Doro brushed off his failure to remember the group's name and concentrated on the case. Since Mallow had not asked a question, Doro took care with her response. "Professor Corlon doesn't support the group, as I already said."

"What about Miss Tenseng's clashes with him?" Mallow asked.

Anxiety hit Doro as she wondered what Aggie had revealed. Hopefully, not much. "She was in his class last year, and that exacerbated the problems." So had Corlon failing Kitty's beau, but Doro kept that to herself. Maybe Mallow already knew. If not, he could ferret the information out on his own.

"I'd like to speak with the girl," Mallow said.

"She's probably in her dormitory room, since classes are canceled until next week," Doro suggested.

"No, she isn't," Mallow said. "I had someone check. Her roommate reported Miss Tenseng leaving very early this morning or late last night and not returning. The girl can't be sure exactly when, because she woke up to find Miss Tenseng gone."

The news made Doro's stomach clench. Only yesterday, Kitty had been in tears over Corlon threatening to have Pierce

Dudley, the girl's beau, expelled. Before stomping out of the library, Kitty had vowed to get even with the instructor. She would never have killed the man, but her words—along with her absence—would put Mallow hot on her trail. "I'm sure there's an excellent reason. Kitty has family in Toledo and in Richfield Center, a little town a few miles away, so there may be an emergency."

"How would she get word of an emergency? My understanding is that the college operator is off-duty from nine at night until eight-thirty the next morning. According to her roommate, Miss Tenseng left before then," Mallow said.

"Not all students reside on campus." Doro began to feel her way along to a sensible, safe answer. "Kitty has been stepping out with a boy who lives in one of the boarding houses. He might've gotten the message and passed it along somehow." But how? If he had pelted Kitty's window with pebbles, wouldn't her roommate have heard? Uneasiness filled Doro. Kitty's beau had lost his basketball scholarship after failing Corlon's class the previous year, which meant Mallow would see the girl as having two motives...if Doro revealed the details. For several seconds, she debated what to do. Then, the officer interrupted with another question.

"Have students always been allowed to live off-campus?" Mallow made the question seem accusatory.

Beneath the table, Doro clenched her ice-cold hands together. "For some time, yes."

Mallow looked suspicious. "For how long?"

"Since President Adams took over as president, although only seniors can live in a boarding house. There are two. Both are run by lovely women who mother their tenants." Doro didn't reveal Winwood's intention to end the practice, which would hurt the widows who owned the establishments.

"I'm sure they do," the officer said with a trace of asperity.

"I'll testify to that fact," Lammers replied. "One landlady is my mother, and the other is my aunt."

Dark color surged into Mallow's cheeks, which had Doro fighting to withhold a chuckle. "Your sister has been in town helping your mother, hasn't she?" Wade Lammers' aunt was closer to his age than she was to his mother's, but the family was close-knit.

"She was, but Ma is strong enough now to handle her boarders. They're all fine young folks, who pitch in around the house and in the yard. But Kitty's suitor boards with my aunt," Lammers said.

The red in Mallow's face intensified as he shifted in his chair. "I see. Perhaps, you would speak with the young fellow, Constable."

"Sure thing," Lammers agreed in his usual amiable voice.

"Was that your only other question?" Doro kept her tone well-modulated. Withholding her amusement at Mallow's discomfort was more challenging. Insulting local folks, especially the constable's family, was not a good way to garner respect.

"It was," he replied, "so you're free to go. But not away from Michaw. We're borrowing a fingerprinting kit from the county sheriff. A deputy will bring it out. When I get it, I'll be printing various people."

He didn't need to say she would be one of them. After that, Doro wasted no time in bidding the men farewell and heading toward Wheaton Hall. Although the rain had ended earlier, a chilly dampness continued. Doro hurried along the path to her quarters. When she reached the main door to the building, it opened before she retrieved her key from her pocket. Her friend, Agatha Darwine, stepped back to let Doro enter.

"Come in and get warm," the other woman said. "You must be cold and exhausted. The walk from the library nearly froze me to the bone. Such unseasonably nippy weather, and the rain made it worse. I have the kettle simmering, so I can make tea in a jiffy."

Since she was both weary and chilled, Doro didn't argue. Instead, she followed Aggie to the second floor and into a cozy apartment. Aggie had made the small suite into a haven. A colorful quilt laid over the end of the loveseat and two armchairs framed the small fireplace, where flickering flames provided warmth and cheer. Some of Doro's tension drained away. "Thank you. I'm sure my place is cool by now, and I haven't been warm since I left it this morning."

"Sit down by the hearth. I'll be right back with tea and cookies."

While Aggie rushed into the adjoining kitchenette, Doro slipped off her coat and hung it on a hook by the front door before settling into a chair. As the soft cushions cradled her, Doro sighed with relief. After several moments, she leaned forward to warm her hands.

Soon, Aggie was back. After placing the tray on a tiny table between the chairs, she sat opposite Doro, poured a cup of tea, and handed it to her friend.

"This is wonderful," Doro said after taking a sip.

Aggie prepared her own tea, took a cookie, and leaned back to enjoy both. "Did you have lunch?"

Doro shook her head. "After Officer Mallow interviewed me, I tried to catch up on paperwork but kept getting distracted. There was a parade of people in-and-out of the library until about an hour ago. Besides, I wasn't hungry." The knot in her stomach had gotten worse ever since she saw the body. It still had not completely loosened. Even now, she felt residual tension and distress.

"I could see the stream of folks from my office window. When I returned to the English department, we were told we could go at noon. Since things were quiet, I stayed and caught up on grading. With no classes until further notice, I wanted to be free to write."

Doro smiled. Her friend not only taught several literature classes, she was a gifted poet. "You'll likely have several days free. Before I left the library, I was informed not to plan on coming back until Monday, at the earliest." Her good humor faded, and with it, her smile. Mallow had also ordered her to stay in the area. Had he issued the same directive to everyone? Doro took another sip before asking Aggie, "Were you told to stay close to campus?"

Her friend's eyes widened. "No. Were you?"

"Yes." Because she wanted another opinion, Doro voiced her fear. "Officer Mallow sees me as a suspect."

"That's ridiculous." Aggie finished her cookie and laid down her cup. "He's rather brusque, but he probably wants to get off to a good start in his new job. Investigating the murder of a professor, one who's close to President Winwood, can't be easy. Especially when Officer Mallow should've had a few more days to settle in."

Doro mulled over her friend's assertions. Maybe she was being too hard on the man. "True, but he asked a lot of questions about me not getting along with Corlon. I'm sure Winwood shared that information, and their two buddies, too."

"Professor Jerritt is out-of-town this week," Aggie said. "From what I heard, he left on Sunday and won't be back until Saturday."

"Then, only Winwood and Pottiger can cause trouble right now," Doro said. "Mallow kept my bag, and he mentioned fingerprinting people as soon as a county sheriff's deputy brings a kit."

Aggie's gaze widened, but she shook her head. "That doesn't mean he thinks you did it. He'll weigh all the facts. If nothing else, Constable Lammers will be sure Officer Mallow does."

Doro laid her cup and saucer down. "I suppose so, but you're right about Mallow being brusque. He's as starched as his shirt."

A low laugh left Aggie, and her eyes sparkled. "He was nattily dressed and good looking."

Denying the assertion was impossible, so Doro focused on her dilemma. "It doesn't matter how he looks or dresses. He wouldn't even let me bring my bag home because it needs to be examined. Like there's evidence in it. But there are only class papers. How will I grade them? Midterm reports are due next week."

"Don't worry about that. Everything is topsy-turvy. Many students will go home for a few days, and the rest will gossip about the murder. Same with faculty and staff."

Doro shifted in her chair. Would some gossip be about her? Maybe it was already. "I suppose people are talking now."

Aggie rolled her eyes. "Of course, they are. A murder is big news."

"Are they discussing suspects?" Doro's voice trembled, along with her hands. Her friend briefly looked down at the small table between them. When the silence expanded, Doro asked another question. "Are people saying I did it?" Her heart thundered so loudly, she could scarcely hear her own words. Other suspects existed, but Doro didn't want to be among them. Didn't people know her better?

"No one with sense believes such a thing," Aggie hurriedly replied.

"Which means a few are talking about me killing the professor." The knot in Doro's stomach doubled. Only a handful of faculty members, all new since the departure of President

Adams, found fault with Doro being outspoken. So far, they had been careful about airing their preference for a male-only school, but they supported the Fearsome Foursome.

Aggie lifted her cup and took a long swallow. "Only a couple, as far as I know. I overheard two talking in the department conference room. They said you found the body and sometimes that person is guilty. Which is ridiculous."

"It is, because I didn't kill him." Doro gripped the cup tighter. "Both you and I are avid mystery readers, and we know that sometimes happens in stories."

"Pshaw. Those are fiction. In real life, I doubt that's true."

"But how much do either of us know about real crime?" Her friend's failure to quickly respond telegraphed the answer, so Doro supplied it herself. "Very little."

"Maybe we don't, but we both know you didn't kill Corlon," Aggie said, "and most everyone else does, too. I'm sure other suspects will be discovered in short order. They probably have been already." Aggie offered a reassuring smile.

Although she realized her friend was trying to be positive, Doro felt no uptick in her emotions. "True, but Officer Mallow has me on his list."

Aggie's brow furrowed. "He showed his list to you?"

"No, but his attitude revealed as much, although I may not be at the top." Her mind returned to Mallow's mention of Kitty Tenseng.

"You look worried. Who else is under scrutiny?" Aggie asked.

Doro replied with what Mallow had revealed about Kitty and finished by saying, "I'm sure there's an explanation for her disappearance."

"Since Constable Lammers said he'd check with her beau, she could be eliminated soon. Pierce probably got a call at the boardinghouse about an emergency and drove her to the train station in Sylvania, since Kitty doesn't have her own vehicle."

"I hope so."

"Officer Mallow asked me about Professor Corlon's dealings with faculty and students. Of course, I told him the truth. The man had run-ins with a few folks."

"You mentioned them by name?" Hope flared in Doro's heart. Mallow had not asked her for such information, but he had wondered about the number of people who argued with Corlon.

"I certainly did," Aggie replied. "Just last week, Corlon had a shouting match with Professor Gibling. That was after their meeting. Stanley was yelling that he better not get passed over for tenure, and Corlon said he should be more collegial, if he wants to stay."

Doro put one hand to her mouth. "You didn't tell me about overhearing them."

"I didn't want to upset you. Stanley Gibling is vocal about more women being hired as faculty and staff. He's been supportive of the YWV group, too." Aggie paused for a moment. "He even supported Coach Ayers when he argued with Winwood and his cronies. Stanley is a big supporter of the athletic teams."

"But the Fearsome Foursome isn't."

"Stanley thinks they want to cut sports, and Coach Ayers does, too," Aggie commented. "Professor Corlon talked about making Michaw College a more academically oriented institution, which is ridiculous. It's always been a fine school."

Doro wondered how often Aggie and Stanley, who had been stepping out until a few months ago, chatted. Personal matters could be discussed at a future point, not now when so much else was on her mind. "I've heard Winwood say the same thing, but they stop before actually stating sports should go."

"True," Aggie agreed. "Stanley accused Corlon of wanting to end intercollegiate athletics. Of course, Corlon denied it, but I'm sure the entire Fearsome Foursome believe a truly elite, scholarly school has no sports teams or women. All of them talk about how institutions of higher education operated a century or more ago. That's their standard."

"They're backward beyond belief."

A slight chuckle left Aggie. "Stanley told Corlon as much at a department meeting. His candor hasn't done him any good, but he hasn't stopped."

Doro studied her friend's troubled expression. "Which worries you?"

"It does," Aggie admitted. "After the last meeting, Stanley was furious with Corlon. On his way out of the department, he saw me."

"What did he say?"

Aggie stared into her cup. "He said the entire campus would be better off if Corlon was dead, and his buddies, too."

Doro gasped. "Stanley said that out loud?"

"He didn't say he'd kill the professor," Aggie hurried to reply. "And I'm sure he didn't. But others heard him. Officer Mallow interviewed some of them before me. Since the exchange was revealed, I couldn't deny it." A soft sigh left her. "But I wish I could have."

"Stanley won't hold it against you," Doro assured her friend. Aggie looked and sounded like she hoped to reconcile with Stanley, who had been the one wanting to step out with others. As far as Doro was concerned, Aggie deserved better.

Her friend's voice sounded again. "Maybe, maybe not. But he'll probably leave Michaw since it's out that Corlon planned to block his tenure."

For a moment, Doro pondered the situation. "Stanley's situation is similar to mine, since he teaches American literature, not British classics. The Fearsome Foursome all think Mark Twain, Stephen Crane, Louisa May Alcott, and others are not worth studying."

"They feel the same about some of the poetry I include." Aggie grabbed another cookie and began munching. "In any case, someone as smart and good-looking as Stanley will move on and not look back."

The expression on her friend's face echoed in Doro's heart. "There are other fellows around." Stanley's heated exchange with Corlon bothered Doro almost as much as his treatment of Aggie.

"Probably so, but I'd like a family of my own. I miss not having one."

"You have me and my family. My grandmother anyhow, since my parents are in Colorado."

"She's been lovely, and I appreciate being invited to her house for holidays and summers."

Doro's heart went out to her friend. "I wish you'd come to Colorado with me sometime."

A sigh left Aggie. "Maybe I will, but working in the summer helps me put money in my France fund. I've only seen my brother once since the war. He and Monique have three children now. All under seven. It'd be difficult for them to get here, so I want to go there again soon."

"I understand." Her friend's parents were both deceased, and her only brother had married a French woman during the Great War. The couple now made their home near her family in Paris, which left Aggie mostly on her own.

Aggie laid her cookie on her saucer. "I shouldn't be having another one. I'm already too chubby."

"You are not. You're fine just as you are," Doro assured her.

A half-shrug lifted one of Aggie's shoulders. "Easy for you to say. You're slim and can wear the latest styles." She looked down at herself. "I look ridiculous in them."

"Fuller skirts are becoming fashionable again, and none of the female faculty wear flapper-style attire. Very few women do."

"Maybe not, but you look lovely in the long straight tops and matching skirts. And your hair suits the shorter cut. With my curls, a sleek bob is out of the question. On the top of that, it's red."

Doro shook her head. Her friend lacked self-confidence, which was a shame, because Aggie was an accomplished poet, a sweet person, and a cute girl . "Your hair is a gorgeous shade of auburn. As for curls, I wish mine had some wave. It's straight as a string." A few years back, Doro had convinced Aggie to get a bob. When long, the waves were nearly impossible to control, even in a braid, which had been her friend's preferred style when they met.

A rueful smile touched Aggie's lips. "We always think what others have is better, I guess."

"Maybe so," Doro agreed.

Aggie waved one hand in the air. "We've gotten away from the case," she said with a trace of asperity. "Others have clashed with Professor Corlon."

"They have," Doro replied. "We could make our own list."

"We could." Aggie rose, went to the keyhole desk on the far side of the room, and took out a notepad. She retrieved a pencil and took both to Doro. "Getting the names down is a good idea, and your handwriting is neater than mine."

A chuckle escaped Doro. "Yours is fine, when you don't have writer's cramp. Of course, you're constantly creating poems in your vast array of journals." She pointed to a bookcase crammed with notebooks. "It's no wonder you can barely hold a pen after your hours and hours and hours of scribbling."

Aggie laughed along with her friend. "You exaggerate. I wish I could write all day, but other duties impinge upon my poems."

"Which is a shame," Doro said with sincerity, "because you're talented."

"Thank you," her friend replied before saying, "we should get back to suspects."

Since Doro concurred with the last assertion, she took the supplies and jotted down Stanley's name. "I'm putting Stanley on the list, even though I don't see him as a viable suspect." Or maybe she doesn't want to see him in that light.

"Neither do I, but Mallow probably will."

"Probably so," Doro replied.

"Who else clashed with Corlon and might've done it?" Aggie asked.

Doro met her friend's inquisitive gaze. "Myself. We know I didn't kill the man, but Mallow is suspicious." An image of his handsome features, as rigid as a statue's, came to mind. Since she didn't know many law officers, Doro didn't know if his demeanor was typical. Constable Lammers was affable, but Doro had known the man all of her life, so his behavior wasn't a sound yardstick.

"He listened to me about the others," Aggie said, "so he's probably being thorough is all. I'm sure he wants to make a good first impression."

"I suppose," Doro replied, but she didn't like the new security officer being handpicked by President Winwood. "I'm glad we're making our own list. Since we have time off, we can ask around campus and town. Discreetly, of course."

"Very discreetly would be best," Aggie put in. "Getting in the way of lawmen isn't a good strategy."

One of Doro's questions rose to her lips. "I haven't heard many details about Mallow. He mentioned being a policeman for a year before taking a job with the Prohibition Bureau. All I knew before today was hiring him was the president's idea."

"Winwood and his cronies were all supportive of a campus security officer," Aggie added. "Evidently, there was one at their previous school. Somehow, they convinced the trustees having someone here was a good idea. If you'd listened to campus gossip during the hiring phase, you'd know more." When Doro started to speak, Aggie put up both hands. "I know you don't like to engage in tittle-tattle. Nor do I. However, on occasion, information is gleaned that way."

"I can't deny that, but I don't understand how Winwood has so much sway. Except that he and two of the current trustees went to college together. There's been a turnover on the board since President Adams left." One longtime member had died, and another had suffered serious health issues. Two additional seats were left vacant when terms ended. Now, four of the seven had served for less than a year-and-a-half. "But that has little to do with the murder."

Aggie grimaced. "I hate to think about a colleague or student being guilty."

"But you named a few to Mallow."

"Under duress," Aggie said, "although I didn't think of Kitty."

"She may be removed as a suspect soon." Doro tapped her pencil against the notepad. "Who else came to mind?"

A look of contrition tightened Aggie's features. "I didn't want to tell Mallow, but you've likely thought of the same people."

"I'll let you know as you reveal your list." Doro made the statement with a smile, a smile that wavered when she thought about Kitty.

"Who is on the list so far?" Aggie asked.

"Kitty, although I'm sure she didn't do it." *Sure* might be too strong a word, but such an action would be out of character for the young woman. "Stanley and me."

"We know you weren't involved," Aggie voiced a hasty objection.

"To be fair, we need to list anyone who might've had opportunity and motive. The means is already clear," Doro commented.

"Hitting someone over the head with the drawer from a card catalogue has to be unusual. I certainly never considered one as a weapon."

"Because you're a scholar and poet. I suppose someone angry enough to kill might use whatever was readily available." Doro made some notes before leaning back in her chair. "Which goes back to motive, in a peripheral way."

Aggie's auburn brows rose a fraction. "How do you mean?"

"The killer didn't follow Corlon with a weapon, so maybe they argued and the person acted without forethought."

"Good point. But that doesn't help us generate leads. Anyone who was upset with Corlon and company might've been pushed to the point of no return."

"That's true," Doro agreed. "Still, we know the murder wasn't planned. But opportunity means the killer was up and out early." Doro refined the point. "Stanley has a ten o'clock class, with office hours before it, right?"

"He does on Tuesdays and Thursdays." Aggie sighed. "I hate to say it, but he might've been on his way to his office and seen Corlon go into the library. After their argument, another confrontation seems likely."

"Even though we don't want to believe he did it, I put his name down," Doro said as she made another notation.

"I know. Even if he isn't the killer, Stanley always gets to his office early. Any number of folks might've seen him."

The observation increased Doro's edginess. "And they probably shared that detail with Mallow."

"I imagine so."

"Let's concentrate on people who are usually out on campus early, since not many would know Professor Corlon's class was coming to the library this morning."

"His students would," Aggie said. "I know several are struggling in his class, because they came to me wondering what to do. Two basketball players and Coach Ayers wondered if the boys could transfer to my class, but it's too late. Ayers already clashed with Professor Corlon over eligibility. Pierce Dudley isn't the only one off the team due to grades, and Coach was furious. He accused the professor of grading his players' papers much harder than he did other students' work." Aggie ran one forefinger around the rim of her cup. "You know many female students have the same complaint. Kitty is only one of them."

"I've heard a lot of terrible stories. At first, I thought the girls were exaggerating. It's gotten worse and worse, according to the members of YWV. At the last meeting, one broke down and sobbed. Another told me Professor Corlon not only gave her a failing grade on an essay, he humiliated her in class and refused to explain what was wrong with her writing."

A scowl darkened Aggie's face. "He's done that to other coeds. Several left school last year due to his nastiness."

"The topic comes up at our group meetings. Only two shared their stories. They asked others to do the same, but the rest refused. Afraid of repercussions," Doro said. "I wish you could come to the gatherings."

"Maybe next term. Now that Corlon won't be making course assignments, I might not have such a heavy course load, which gives me a motive," Aggie said. "I complained to him many times."

"You were still in your apartment this morning when I left for the library," Doro commented.

"But I could have gone out and come back."

The comment set Doro to thinking. "Did Mallow say that?"

Aggie grinned. "He mentioned it."

"Awful man. He is so suspicious."

"He's a lawman," Aggie said with a shake of her head.

"As is Constable Lammers, and he isn't accusatory and officious," Doro pointed out.

"You've known the constable all of your life," Aggie said. "Besides, he never worked as a city policeman like Mallow has. I'm sure they see more crooks and killers. Especially since Prohibition started. And remember, Officer Mallow is an agent. I hear there are plenty of speakeasies and bootleggers around Detroit. Toledo, too. Dealing with them had to put him on guard."

The suggestion gave Doro pause. "Do you know if Officer Mallow is from Detroit?"

"That's what I heard, but he's been living in Toledo." Aggie stared at her friend. "Evidently, not much campus gossip gets to the library."

"If it does, I'm too busy to hear it."

"You're more overburdened than I am. You're teaching a class, advising a student group, and doing three more jobs at the library. Winwood ought to be ashamed for cutting positions there."

"He isn't. As far as I can tell, the man is shameless, but so are his cronies." Doro didn't keep the censure from her voice.

"Professor Jerritt isn't as vocal as the others, but he supports whatever Winwood, Pottiger, and Corlon do or say. Winwood will move Heaven and Earth to find his friend's killer, and Pottiger will be at his side."

"Jerritt will be, too, when he gets back. All the more reason for us to work this case."

A smile kicked up one corner of Aggie's mouth. "You've waited a long time for another investigation to come along."

Although Doro couldn't completely disagree, she shrugged. "We found out who pilfered an exam ages ago. I haven't thought much about it lately." The statement was valid, because Doro now had many other concerns and interests filling her mind. "I still love reading whodunits, but more to get material for my class and as a form of escapism, not as a pattern to sleuth around myself."

"You seem set on cracking this case." The amusement stayed in Aggie's voice and expression.

Warmth rose in Doro's cheeks. "I can't deny that I'd like to find the killer and prove it's not me."

Aggie readily agreed before asking, "What about the two girls who spoke up at the last meeting?"

Doro mulled the question over. "I don't think either is a good suspect. They both work in the dormitory cafeteria from six o'clock to eight-thirty. Mrs. Fields has rousted tardy helpers out of their rooms, so she would know about where they were and why."

"So, I've heard," Aggie said with another grin. "It's one of the reasons I didn't seek employment in the kitchen when I was a student."

"Very wise." Doro chuckled as she spoke, but the humor left when she asked, "Anyone else come to mind?"

"Not right now."

After scanning her notepad, Doro made an observation. "We have Coach Ayers, Stanley Gibling, Kitty Tenseng, Pierce Dudley, and me. All of us have a motive. As far as opportunity, I was in the library. We don't know about the others. Coach always gets out early for a walk. Sometimes, I see him if I happen to be looking out my window to check the weather. But I didn't this morning since I was in a hurry."

"I suppose we need to ask others who are out early what or who they saw."

"Good idea," Doro replied.

"We know President Winwood was near the library before you saw him." Aggie frowned.

"He takes a daily constitutional, although not usually quite so early," Doro replied. "But he had to prepare for a big meeting, so he might've walked sooner than normal."

"In the chilly rain?"

Doro shrugged. "You know how he is. Regimented to the extreme."

"I suppose."

The lack of certainty in her friend's voice, and the observation itself, gave Doro pause. "Professor Corlon and President Winwood were close friends, so he has no motive." She tapped her pencil against the notepad. "At least he has no obvious motive."

"Exactly." Aggie nodded. "Are you going to put him down?"

"I suppose we should include anyone with opportunity." Doro made a note in her book.

"Did you see anyone else?"

Doro shook her head. "No one."

"What about Mrs. Jones? Wasn't she in the office when you went there?"

Again, Doro felt a stab of alarm. "Surely, you don't think she killed Corlon."

"No, but I don't believe you or Kitty did, either. In fact, none of the people we've discussed strikes me as a killer," Aggie replied. "But someone murdered the man, and we both know the guilty party isn't necessarily the most obvious suspect."

"You're certainly right on that count." With reluctance, Doro jotted the secretary's name down. "But it's possible someone else, someone we haven't considered, did it."

A long moment of silence filled the room before Aggie spoke. "I suppose so, but we aren't close to the railroad tracks, and the campus is south of town, while the main road is north."

Doro tapped the pad with her pencil. "Although I agree a stranger isn't the likely killer, let's keep the idea on the back burner."

Aggie nodded.

"Now, we have a list, but how are we going to expand or shrink it?"

"An excellent question."

The trace of amusement in her friend's voice made Doro smile. "Do you expect me to answer it myself?"

A half-shrug lifted one of Aggie's shoulders. "You're good at unraveling whodunits. And you teach a course on the mystery novel. Think about how the amateur sleuths in them get information."

Doro took little time to respond. "They pry around. As carefully as possible, with a few exceptions. And there are always gossips ready to tell all they know. Or think they know."

"And this campus has more than its fair share of big mouths."

A chuckle escaped Doro. "I can't argue with that." After again scanning the list, she glanced back at her friend. "Mrs. Jones is a lovely lady..."

"But she falls into the gossipy group."

"She does and has as far back as I can remember. Mrs. Jones and my mother were good friends, but Mother couldn't abide the tittle-tattle."

"I can't, either, but I'll listen in this case. We'll surely learn a little from her."

"True. Mrs. Jones might've seen someone we haven't considered. Or she might know if Corlon had a recent run-in with another professor."

"Someone other than Stanley."

"Of course." Although Doro expressed agreement, she wondered about Coach Ayers, who could be volatile. His altercation with Corlon was only one example. The man had shouted down more than one colleague at faculty union meetings.

"You don't sound convinced." Aggie shifted restlessly in her chair. "Coach is opinionated and argumentative at times, but he's harmless."

"I'm sure he is," Doro replied. But how sure was she? Not one-hundred percent. "As far as talking with Mrs. Jones, we may have to go to her house. The library is closed and all classes are canceled, so President Winwood might've told her to stay home for a few days."

"Maybe so," Aggie agreed. "Can you call the office and find out? She might be the best person to interview first, since she sees all the comings and goings in the administrative office."

Doro rolled the pencil between her hands. "I don't want to call Winwood's office. If Mrs. Jones went home, he'll answer, and I'd rather not speak with him again. I'll make a call to her home later."

"Good. Now, who else is an early bird?"

Doro rolled her eyes. "If you mean, who is out at the crack of dawn like Coach Ayers, I have no idea. I like to wake after sunrise, especially when the days are quickly getting shorter. I rarely leave for the library until eight-fifteen. Mallow asked about me coming early because of Professor Corlon's class, and he knew about my run-ins with the man."

"Stop fretting. It's a minor point. Plenty of others argued with Corlon, and a whole lot more people disliked him."

"All true." A soft sigh escaped Doro as she laid pad and pencil aside before pouring herself another cup of tea. After a long sip, she spoke again. "We have a list, and a plan of sorts."

"Who, other than Mrs. Jones, should we interview?"

Doro grinned. "Interviewing makes us sound like serious detectives."

"We are, aren't we?"

The amusement left Doro. "We'll have to be, because I don't trust Officer Mallow not to do Winwood's bidding. Wade Lammers won't succumb to pressure, though." She studied the list in her lap. "I made a separate column for people to interview and put Mrs. Jones in first place. Maybe we should go to her place in the morning instead of me calling tonight."

"I agree. We don't need anyone listening in."

Her friend made a solid point, so Doro nodded. "To-morrow morning, we can walk uptown. I'm allowed to go that far." Mallow's admonition rankled far more than was sensible. She wasn't guilty of anything. Facts would show as much. She rose from the chair. "I appreciate the snack and conversation, but I am exhausted. I think I'll go to my place, take a hot bath, and get into bed."

"You need to eat something more nutritious than cookies."

"I'm not starving. If I am later, I'll fix a sandwich."

"All right," Aggie replied. "Why don't we plan to have breakfast here tomorrow morning? Since the campus is vir-tually shut down, we can sleep late and meet at nine o'clock."

"Let's make it nine-thirty," Doro said. As tired as she felt, a long snooze sounded wonderful. With luck, she could escape her troubled thoughts. And Mallow's accusations.

Chapter Four

Wednesday morning, Doro woke with a feeling of foreboding. Before she even opened her eyes, a dark shadow hovered over her. For several moments, she struggled to focus on its source. What was wrong? Something serious. Something disturbing. Then, she remembered, and foreboding became angst. Professor Corlon had been murdered, and she was among the suspects.

Doro turned over, buried her face in the pillow, and yanked the covers over her head. How she wished the clock could be rewound to the previous day—before she found the body. Corlon had vexed her, but the man didn't deserve to be killed. No one did.

A rap at her apartment door cut off further rumination. Faint light permeated the room. As she lifted her head, Doro noted the time: seven-thirty. At this hour, only another resident would visit, probably Aggie. Maybe she had some new insight into the crime and couldn't wait until their scheduled meeting. Although Doro considered feigning sleep, she knew her friend would not give up easily. Besides, they needed to move forward with their investigation. The sooner the killer was caught, the sooner innocent suspects like Doro would be in the clear.

After rolling out of bed and donning her wool robe, she padded to the door, where more knocking had ensued. She took a glimpse in the wall mirror and sighed. Her brunette hair normally fell neatly into a bob, but now it stuck out in every direction. If she had taken a hand mixer to it, Doro could not have gotten every lock less tidy, but Aggie had seen Doro looking almost this disheveled. Not that her friend would care, so Doro opened the door only to see Officer Mallow in the hall. "Men are not allowed in this building," were the first words out of her mouth.

His lean cheeks colored. "The president gave me permission to come in." After a quick perusal of her attire, he focused on Doro's face. "He said you'd be up and dressed long before now. He also gave me keys to all campus buildings. When I tried buzzing from the lobby and didn't get an answer, I came up."

"The buzzers aren't working," she shot back, in case he thought she'd been ignoring the summons. "They haven't been for over two weeks." Another repair pushed to the bottom of the list by Winwood, but Doro withheld that observation.

"I see." Mallow cleared his throat as he shifted from one foot to the other. "I saw a reception room downstairs, so I'll go there now. You can get ready and meet me." He avoided looking at her as he spoke.

Although the man was clearly uncomfortable, Doro felt no sympathy for him. The previous day, he had been officious and accusatory. Undoubtedly, he planned to take up where he'd left off. "How long will the interrogation take today?"

"I only have a few questions. I-uh-I..." His voice trailed off. Mallow cleared his throat and glanced back at Doro. "Would you take a little time to answer them?" His tone was restrained.

Saying *no* wasn't an option, so Doro nodded. Besides, he sounded less overbearing at the moment. But not a lot less. "I'll be there shortly." Then, she saw her leather bag slung over his shoulder. "Can I have my belongings now?"

The color in his face deepened. "Sure." He thrust it toward her.

"Thank you." Without waiting for a reply, she shut the door in his face. Aggravated by the man and wary about more accusations, she dawdled. Making the bed, performing her ablutions, straightening her hair, and choosing her clothes took a full half-hour. Even then, Doro did not rush to the reception room. Let him wait.

When she got downstairs, the room was empty, save for the officer sitting in a leather wing chair—one of four grouped around the massive brick fireplace—at the far end. His profile was clearly visible, but he seemed to be intent on the flickering flames. Evidently, he had started a fire, because no one else was up and about.

If he was aware of her arrival, Mallow gave no sign. After a deep breath to calm her nerves, Doro crossed the forty feet to where he sat. He didn't look at her or speak, so she sat across from him and waited. When he still failed to respond, Doro glanced his way. Surprise struck her. He was dozing. For several moments, she gazed at his face. His ebony lashes rested against the purple smudges beneath his eyes. Had he not slept at all? Surely, he hadn't been out questioning local folks overnight. When he suddenly awoke, more evidence of a wakeful night was clear—red-rimmed and bloodshot eyes looked back at her. She knew as soon as he was fully awake, because pink tinged his face.

"Sorry. I nodded off, I guess." As Mallow shifted to sit up straight, he turned to look at the hearth.

Doro sensed he was regrouping, so she left him to it for a moment. "I slept later than usual myself." When the words were out, she chastised herself. He was a lawman, and she was a suspect. Injecting pleasantries into their exchange wouldn't change that. But his embarrassment about being caught snoozing earned a modicum of understanding.

Mallow ran one hand over his face before looking at her again. "I wish I'd slept a little," he admitted, his voice rough, "but I didn't get a single wink."

Anxiety again hit her. "Working on the professor's murder?" Was that why he had sought her out this morning? To say she was at the top of his suspect list? Or worse, his only suspect.

He shook his head. "No, I haven't officially left my other job yet. Last night, we raided a speakeasy in downtown Toledo.

We hit the place after midnight. It was filled, so we ended up arresting over a hundred people. Of course, some ran out the side doors. I was one of the coppers who got to chase them down." His voice lacked enthusiasm and energy.

The revelations surprised her. It was like they were having a common conversation. Because that felt better than interrogation, Doro followed up with a pertinent question. "Did you catch them?"

A rueful smile tugged at one corner of his mouth. "Not all of them, but we usually don't if there's a sizeable crowd. We got the owners, which is important."

"So, the place is closed down," she said.

"It is, but two more will open in its stead." Weariness and frustration echoed in his voice. "It's a never-ending cycle, but that's not why I'm here."

"Of course not," she murmured. Back to business. "I know nothing more than I told you yesterday, Officer. I'm aware you don't believe me, but that's the truth."

Something flashed in his gaze before he spoke. "I believe you, but I can't go on gut feelings. I need corroboration. Before I left campus yesterday, I got it. That's one thing I wanted to say this morning. Along with asking some new questions." He extracted paper and pencil from his jacket pocket.

"Dare I ask what confirmation you got?"

A full-fledged grin lit his face. "Plenty enough to make me feel bad for grilling you. President Winwood saying he saw you at seven-thirty was already an issue. But someone—even you—could've killed the professor earlier, gone home, waited a bit, and headed back. Later, I talked to Corlon's downstairs neighbor, who saw him leave home before seven o'clock. It's a five-minute walk to campus from there. That puts his arrival around ten before the top of the hour, which tightened your timeframe. When I came in this building late yesterday, two ladies who live on your floor were over there eating supper." He jerked a thumb at the table in the far corner. "They said you're quiet, but your door always squeaks loudly, so the lady across from you hears it opening and closing. She was up and sitting in her parlor early yesterday morning. She didn't hear you leave until almost seven-thirty. The other woman was sitting at her window from seven until well after you left the building. All that eliminates you."

Doro mulled the information over. "My door is noisy, but I haven't been able to get the problem fixed. A janitor used to be assigned to our building two days a week. Now, he comes once a month." Another reduction, courtesy of President Winwood.

He shrugged. "In any case, I have plenty to clear you."

Doro wanted complete certainty. "I'm no longer under scrutiny?"

"You've dropped off the list."

Doro slumped back in the chair with relief. "I'll be happy to help in any way I can."

His lips twitched. "Good, because I need assistance. Professor Corlon clashed with a few people, as you already know."

"I wasn't privy to all the encounters," Doro said, "but Michaw is a small college in a small town. Gossip travels far and fast. Others will tell you the same."

"But you grew up here and spent time on campus all your life. Plus, you're highly involved in campus activities. Quite a few people mentioned that."

Although the officer didn't look or sound critical, his true opinion remained murky. "My father was a Michaw professor, and he took part in many campus activities. My mother did, too. They thought it was important to be part of the school's community. As do I."

"I've heard as much from a few people." He tapped his pencil against the notepad. "Anyhow, folks said you have close connections with students, staff, and faculty. The constable and I spoke with some yesterday. Before the raid last night, I had a little time to go over my notes. This morning, I met with Lammers, so we could prioritize our work and arrange more interviews."

"You have a new list of suspects?" Doro wondered if the officer's list would be the same as the one compiled by Aggie and herself. Probably not. After all, Mallow and Wade were lawmen. While Constable Lammers was acquainted with folks on campus, he did not know them as well as the two women.

"We went over possibilities and developed one with updated details. It's tentative and short, but I'm hoping you can offer some insight."

"I'll try." And maybe learn something, as well.

"That's all I ask." Mallow flipped open the notepad. "We heard about Professor Corlon and Coach Ayers arguing more than once. I'm wondering if the issue is festering."

"They seldom speak to one another, and Coach keeps his players out of Corlon's classes now. That's what started the trouble between them last year. A couple failed and lost their scholarships."

"So, I've heard."

His level gaze had Doro shifting restlessly in her chair. What else had Mallow heard? Probably a lot. Unable to form a quick response, she bowed her head and studied her clasped hands. "You have their names then."

"I do. One left school and moved to Iowa, so he's out as a suspect. However, Pierce Dudley is still here, and he is Miss Tenseng's beau. Him losing his scholarship gives her two reasons to dislike Professor Corlon."

With reluctance, Doro again looked at the officer. Some of the starch was gone, but he still seemed stiff. "Kitty isn't a killer."

"That remains to be seen, since we haven't found her or young Dudley and, as far as motive, he's got two himself. His loss of scholarship and Corlon picking on Miss Tenseng."

The phrase *picking on* was interesting, but Doro didn't ask if Mallow was sympathetic to Kitty and Pierce. Even if he was, the officer was unlikely to let sentiment sway him. Nor should he. What bothered Doro most was the young couple's absence. "Pierce lives in a boardinghouse just off campus."

"As you said yesterday. Constable Lammers and I went over there last evening before I got called to my other job. I returned this morning. The landlady hasn't seen Pierce since Monday evening. He didn't show up for breakfast yesterday morning, which is highly unusual. According to her, the kid has a hollow leg and gobbles up whatever she puts in front of him. Missing a meal is something he's never done before. Now, he missed three yesterday and one this morning. No one has seen Miss Tenseng during the same time period."

Doro cleared her throat. "Did his landlady say if he got a telephone call? Perhaps, either he or Kitty had a family emergency. Pierce owns an automobile, so they could've left town in a hurry without telling anyone."

"Or maybe without wanting to tell anyone," Mallow pointed out.

Because that seemed all too likely, Doro sidestepped a direct response. "I'm sure they'll contact someone on campus soon."

"We'll see." Mallow's expression could only be construed as skeptical. "Dudley was angry over losing his scholarship, but Coach Ayers was, as well. What's your opinion of how angry?"

Clearly, Mallow had gathered many details. Denying what others had said would be foolish, but how should she respond? Briefly, she considered what had occurred the previous year. "Coach Ayers was furious. He'd already lost one player due to failing Corlon's class last fall. That boy and Pierce were two of his best players. With a failing grade, Pierce also lost his scholarship, and he isn't eligible to play this year. His senior year.

What's really wrong is that Pierce is an excellent student. He's gotten mostly *As* with only a few *Bs*. And just one failing grade."

"From Corlon."

Doro nodded. "Both boys got low scores on papers. Grading them is subjective, unlike scoring a test. They did fine on Corlon's exams. Just not the essays, which count for most of the grades."

Mallow frowned. "Why would the man fail students who were doing well? It makes no sense."

"Some people on campus think President Winwood and his group plan to do away with intercollegiate athletics."

"Is there a basis in fact for the gossip? Or is it speculation?"

Doro rested her hands on the chair arms. "The basketball team won the league championship several years in a row. Supporters and alumni expect a winning team. Losing a star player mid-season put them in second place for the first time in nearly a decade." Her response did not completely answer his query, but some background details were important. At least to Doro, they were.

"And without Dudley, they aren't apt to win this coming season," Mallow observed.

"Very true, so Coach Ayers was upset. His anger simmered over the summer, and the rumors haven't helped."

"I haven't spoken with the coach, since he wasn't on campus yesterday." Mallow ran one hand over his face. "Did you ever hear Dudley threaten the professor?"

"Never. All Pierce said to me was how unfair Corlon was to athletes and coeds. That was last spring right after the semester ended." Doro didn't add her own view—that Corlon singled out those two groups because they didn't fit into how the Fearsome Foursome envisioned the new Michaw College.

"And you agreed?"

She clasped her hands again. "Yes, but I didn't say so, because that might've made matters worse. I told Pierce we all run into unpleasant people and unfair situations. Dealing with them is part of being an adult."

Mallow nodded. "A valid observation and sound advice. How did he react?"

"He promised to let it go. I'm sure that wasn't easy."

"Will him failing a course make any difference in the future?" the officer asked.

"Perhaps, since Pierce wants to go to law school. Another few years of school will be costly, so he'll need to work. Being at a law firm would be ideal, and the attorneys will look at grades. He may have to teach for a while instead."

"He was lucky to have a scholarship for college, even for a short time."

The officer had garnered plenty of details, but it was the first part of his sentence that intrigued Doro. Few lawmen had degrees or wanted them, but Mallow had previously mentioned his lack of a college education. Had he wanted to attend a university? The question remained in her head, because being too personal wasn't wise. While he had eliminated her as the killer,

Mallow was working, not socializing. "The school should offer more scholarships," Doro said. "President Adams had planned to do so, but Winwood ended the initiative."

The officer didn't react to her statement. Instead, he posed a query. "What do you know about Coach Ayers?"

"He came to Michaw four years ago. He taught and coached at a high school before then. We exchange only passing pleasantries. It's no secret that Ayers was unhappy with two of his players losing eligibility."

He laid his pencil down and rolled it over the notepad. "If sports are eliminated, he'll lose his job. Others told me about his family. He supports his wife, her mother, and five children. I doubt if his salary is high, but he lives in college housing, doesn't he?"

Doro nodded. "There's a big old farmhouse on the southern edge of campus. The college bought it years ago, along with the acreage. It was divided into two residences—one for the football coach and one for the basketball coach."

Mallow jotted down more notes. "I hadn't heard that, but we stuck mostly with asking people about basic information yesterday. We followed up on a few leads before I had to leave town. For one, Lammers and I talked to the football coach. He's a bachelor, so no dependents to support. Also, he's planning to retire at the end of the current season. He's not a fan of Corlon, but he wasn't upset, either. Yesterday morning, he met with his assistant coaches at the diner. Plenty of alibi witnesses to that."

"Good. He's been coaching at Michaw for almost three decades. I'll be sorry for him to leave, but he deserves to enjoy more free time." Since the new officer sounded more open, Doro posed a question in semi-statement form. "You and Constable Lammers are working together."

Several seconds of silence ensued before he shrugged. "He's a good man, and I was wrong to dismiss him as inexperienced."

The concession made Doro smile. "I'm glad you realize that."

For a long moment, he studied her face. "Not every small-town constable is equipped to do the job properly."

"I'm sure," she agreed but didn't point out the same would be true in big cities. Or any place in any job. Some people were incompetent, and others were careless. Instead of voicing those observations, Doro delved for more about Mallow. "Since you haven't officially left the Prohibition Bureau, you must still have authority to question people and make arrests."

"I have authority, but not particularly due to that," Mallow replied. "I've been given status as a deputy constable of sorts. Having a campus security officer is new at this point, but the town council and mayor are happy to have another lawman around."

The news reasserted Doro's uncertainty about Mallow. "The whole job seems unusual to me. How many universities employ lawmen?"

He frowned. "I don't know numbers. Not a lot yet, and most are retired coppers. In the current situation, it'll be good.

Constable Lammers has to fulfill his town duties, which makes it hard for him to conduct interviews, gather evidence, and all."

His mention of evidence jogged Doro's memory. "Were you able to get the fingerprinting kit?"

"Yep. Since I was called into work last night, I picked it up instead of having a deputy drive out here. I already got prints off the drawer and card catalogue. One set was partial, but two others looked sharp. A good analyst should be able to make matches, since there weren't as many prints as I figured."

The final phrase gave Doro pause. "No one told you about the library undergoing a thorough cleaning Monday night."

Confusion clouded Mallow's gray gaze. "How thorough?"

"The janitors dusted and wiped all the tables, counters, and card catalogues. Some places, they waxed, as well."

Mallow put the heel of one hand to his forehead. "They're thorough in their cleaning?"

"Very thorough. The two of them came early, while I was still working, so I saw a lot of their efforts."

After jotting down a few notes, Mallow leaned back in his chair. "That's helpful. I won't have to get fingerprints from dozens of people, which I feared needing to do. And the scarcity of prints made me wonder if the killer cleaned the surfaces or wore gloves."

His obvious relief led to another question from Doro. "How will you get prints to match? Ask everyone who's on your list to give them? Or make them do it?"

"I'd rather not force folks to provide fingerprints until I have more solid evidence," Mallow replied. "As you know, there's a long list of people with a grudge against Professor Corlon. I need to sort out the ones with a profound motive from those who simply didn't like him or his policies. To that end, I'd like to find out more about Stanley Gibling. He's been stepping out with your friend, Miss Darwine."

Doro nodded before saying, "They were for a couple of years, but he wanted to take a break last spring. They haven't gone back to courting since then." She withheld her feelings about Stanley's treatment of Aggie.

"Several folks said Gibling's run-ins with Professor Corlon stemmed from denial of tenure."

"It hasn't actually happened yet," Doro put in before halting. "The final decision on his tenure won't be until next month."

"Gibling said as much, but he acted like it was a done deal. He seemed furious about it."

"Furious is a strong word." Not that it didn't fit Stanley's past reactions. Had he been foolish enough to let Officer Mallow see the depth of his ire? Her stomach knotted.

"According to President Winwood, it's accurate."

"You spoke with Stanley. Did he seem full of rage to you?"

A half-shrug lifted one of Mallow's shoulders. "He's a smart man. Too smart to let me see if he wanted revenge."

That answered one of Doro's questions. At least Stanley hadn't lost his composure with Mallow. While she disliked him dropping her friend, Doro didn't think he was a killer. "Any professor who's denied tenure would be upset, especially when the refusal is personal. Others can, and probably have, told you more about the situation. From what Stanley revealed to Agatha and me, he was singled out for criticism and mistakes that others made, too. He believes his support of females on campus led to Corlon being against him. And Winwood."

"Women were first admitted in 1917, eleven years ago. That's a long tradition to overturn."

His knowledge of the school's history impressed her. "It is. President Adams, who retired last year, was supportive. Many other professors were, too." Doro's father had been one of them, but she withheld the personal detail. She didn't comment on upending a policy dating back more than ten years, either. Let Mallow get more information from others. At the moment, they were dealing well with one another. She wanted the camaraderie to continue, so she could stay up-to-date on the case. "About two dozen entered that year. Numbers have increased each term since then."

"How many coeds are there in all?"

"One hundred and one, so they're about a third of the student body."

"Does the entire group attend the YWV meetings?"

"We have thirty to forty coeds dedicated to our mission. We have another couple dozen who attend sporadically. Only a handful aren't interested at all." Or they were afraid to show enthusiasm for fear of upsetting their parents or some male faculty. But Doro kept the suppositions to herself. Mallow remained an unknown quantity. While he wasn't as stiff and pompous as the previous day, he might agree with Winwood and his cronies, or be pressured by them to accuse one of their detractors. In any case, Doro planned to proceed with caution. As the old saying went: *Discretion is the better part of valor.* "Why are you asking about the young women? As you already pointed out, others clashed with the professor."

With one hand, Mallow rubbed his neck. "I'm not targeting them or anyone. I just want to be as thorough as possible. As the faculty advisor, you know the members best. Kitty Tenseng is still at large, but I wondered if there were others with grudges against the professor."

Doro did not wish to argue about Kitty holding a grudge, so she said, "None of the girls would follow Corlon and hit him with a card catalogue drawer. Few are strong enough to do damage, either." Why was he digging into this area again? Had someone targeted the group during an interview? As soon as Mallow was on his way, she planned to talk with Aggie. They not only needed to see Mrs. Jones, they should stop by the constable's office and dig into what the two lawmen had learned. Lammers was more apt to share knowledge than the man currently across from Doro. Not that he hadn't divulged bits and pieces. But scraps weren't enough to crack the case.

"Duly noted." He flipped his notepad shut. "I haven't been here long enough to get a handle on things. I'll keep my ear to the ground, though."

A long moment of silence passed before Doro responded. "Campus gossip isn't always accurate, Officer Mallow. You'll discover as much when you're here longer."

Some indefinable emotion darkened his gaze, but it passed quickly. "I'm sure I will."

"Do you have other questions?" Doro asked.

"Not now." He tucked his pad and pencil into his jacket pocket before standing up. "I appreciate your help." He hesitated before continuing. "Please keep a low profile while we investigate. With a killer on the loose, I don't want anyone playing armchair detective. Good day."

His order aggravated her, as did his use of the term *armchair detective*. Since he quickly strode off, Doro didn't respond. Instead, she left the reception room as soon as he was out of sight and went straight to her friend's apartment, where she found Aggie still in her robe and nightgown. Her friend had yet to adopt pajamas as her nightwear. "Sorry. I hope I didn't wake you."

"No, you didn't." Aggie swung the door wide and gestured toward the chairs by the fireplace. "I was puttering with a poem, because I thought you might sleep later than planned."

After sitting down, Doro grimaced. "I might've still been dozing, but Officer Mallow woke me by knocking on my door."

Aggie's auburn brows shot up. "How did he get inside?"

"As the campus security officer, he has keys to all the buildings. Since our buzzers aren't working, he came up."

"That had to be a surprise." Aggie flopped into the chair across from Doro.

"It was. I figured you or another resident was knocking, so I went to the door in my pajamas and robe."

Aggie grinned. "How did Officer Mallow react?"

Seeing no humor in the situation, Doro pursed her lips. "He said he'd meet me downstairs and hurried off."

"You thought he was detached and stiff yesterday. Perhaps, he's shy instead."

"Piffle. Besides, I don't care what he is, as long as he doesn't help Winwood and his crew railroad an innocent person."

The amusement drained from Aggie's features. "You aren't usually so quick to judge people. Why are you suspicious about Officer Mallow's motives? Because Winwood and his three pals were on the hiring committee?"

Guilt swept through Doro. "Probably so, but doesn't the Fearsome Foursome selecting Mallow give you pause?"

A chuckle left Aggie. "You didn't refer to them that way with him, did you?"

Doro shook her head. "Of course not. He's an unknown quantity, so I'm careful in what I say." When Aggie opened her mouth, Doro put a hand up. "I know. I'm not usually so judgmental or suspicious. But we're dealing with a murder investigation."

"As is he," Aggie pointed out. "I'm guessing he wants to catch the right person. I'm sure Constable Lammers does."

"Good points." Lammers would do the right thing. Maybe Mallow would, too. Doro hoped so.

"You're upset because Mallow has you on his suspect list. However, that won't last long."

Once again, her friend made a valid statement. "It hasn't lasted. I'm already off." She shared the officer's observations about her alibi and corroborating witnesses.

"Your noisy door is a good thing," Aggie said with a grin. "I don't suppose he named his current list."

"Not in so many words, but he mentioned Kitty, Pierce, Stanley, and Coach Ayers. He knows everything we do and more." After she finished going over what she and Mallow had discussed, Doro offered her new plan. "Let's talk to Constable Lammers after we see Mrs. Jones. He'll surely share more than Officer Mallow did."

"Probably, but I'm concerned about Kitty and Pierce." Concern darkened Aggie's gaze. "Where could they be? It isn't like her to simply leave town and not tell someone."

"It has to be an emergency. They might've left before Corlon was killed." Doro wanted that to be the case.

"Perhaps," Aggie agreed, but her tone was tentative. "When we're in town, we might find someone who saw them leave late Monday night or early yesterday morning, someone who knows why. I'm sure you're right about an emergency coming up."

"We should get going. The sooner we gather clues, the better." At least Doro hoped any extra details would clear Kitty and Pierce. And Stanley. Not that she wanted Coach Ayers to be the killer, either, but someone had done it. And that someone was most likely a person known to her, maybe well-known and liked. The thought did nothing to lift her spirits.

⁂

An hour later, Doro and Aggie were on the front porch of the Jones house. The compact cottage, set on a side street, was only two blocks from campus. A few late-blooming roses climbed the trellis at one end of the porch, while a colorful array of wet leaves covered the tiny front lawn and walkway.

When Mrs. Jones answered the door, she smiled and ushered the young women inside. "Sorry, the boy who rakes for me didn't come yesterday due to the rain. He's in school now, but he'll be here later. I hope you girls didn't get your feet soaked in all those wet leaves."

"We're fine," Doro assured her. "We should take our shoes off, so we don't get your floors dirty. That's if you don't mind us coming in for a while."

"Of course not," the older woman said. "I'm happy to have company. I baked biscuits, and I surely won't put a dent in them. Why don't I get a plate and bring coffee? It's fresh brewed."

"That sounds wonderful," Aggie replied. "Our kitchenettes are too small for much baking."

"I've seen them," Mrs. Jones said. "I'd be hard-pressed to cook in one. Go into the parlor. Doro knows the way."

Doro preceded her friend into the comfortable room. As a child, she and her parents had often visited Professor and Mrs. Jones. "I've always loved this house," she said, after sitting in one of the fireside chairs.

Aggie sat across from her and looked around the room. "I want to have a place like it someday. It's pretty and homey." A wistful note was in her voice.

"Thank you," Mrs. Jones said as she entered the room.

Doro hurried to take the tray and put it on the low table in the middle of the seating arrangement. "This looks wonderful. I didn't take time to eat this morning."

After pouring coffee and handing a cup and saucer to each of her guests, Mrs. Jones took one for herself. "You need more than this. I could cook ham and eggs. It wouldn't take long."

Both young women demurred. "This is perfect," Doro said. "We wanted to chat with you."

The older woman perched on the loveseat with her own coffee and biscuit. "About yesterday morning?"

"Yes, if you don't mind," Doro replied.

"Of course not. I'm sure you won't ask anything Officer Mallow didn't already," Mrs. Jones replied.

Before speaking again, Doro exchanged a long look with Aggie. "He surely didn't accuse you."

A chuckle left the older woman. "Not exactly. Naturally, he asked if I saw anything unusual on my way to work. He already knew I was there earlier than normal to help President Winwood prepare for his meeting. It's been delayed now, but he was planning to work all day yesterday. Anyhow, my typical path takes me right by the library, but I got a ride from my next-door neighbor because of the heavy rain. He dropped me off behind College Hall, so I didn't see anyone."

"What time did you arrive?" Doro asked.

"A few minutes after seven, maybe a little later," their hostess replied.

"How did you get into the building?" Aggie posed the question.

"President Winwood unlocked the outside door. You know, the one closest to the offices," Mrs. Jones said. "He always does when he wants me to come early. Since he likes to take a daily jaunt around campus, he does it then."

After another swig of coffee, Doro considered when she had seen the man. "He was already there?"

The older woman shook her head. "I didn't see him when I arrived. Later, he told me about losing his pocket watch on his way to school. The chain broke when he pulled it out to check the time. Anyhow, he retraced his steps to find it. The timepiece is a family heirloom."

"I saw him near the front of College Hall shortly before the clock chimed seven-thirty," Doro observed.

"He passed that way earlier, I'm sure. In any case, he went back and found his watch," Mrs. Jones said.

The explanation made sense to Doro, who continued with her queries. "You didn't see Pierce Dudley or Kitty Tenseng late Monday night or early yesterday, did you?"

Mrs. Jones shook her head. "No. Why do you ask?" She glanced from Doro to Aggie.

Doro nodded to her friend, and Aggie made the response. "Officer Mallow can't find them, and he wants to interview both."

Dismay darkened Mrs. Jones's eyes. "I don't need to ask why. Kitty and Pierce have plenty of reason to dislike Professor Corlon, but I can't believe either would harm the man. Or anyone else."

"We don't believe it, either," Doro supplied. "One of them must've had an emergency."

"Isn't her family in Toledo?" Mrs. Jones asked.

"Her parents are. They own Tenseng Grocery Store, which is near downtown. When we get back to Wheaton Hall, I'll place a call," Doro said.

"You'd have to wait by the telephone in the main hall. Why not try from here? Perhaps, our operator will connect you quickly. You know where the little nook is, don't you?" Mrs. Jones backed her invitation with a smile.

"I do, and it's kind of you to offer," Doro said.

"Nonsense. It's no trouble."

With that, Doro headed to the main hall where a telephone sat in an arched wall recess. She picked up the candlestick base, lifted the earpiece, and wound the crank. In moments, the local operator came on the line. After being assured the woman would ring back as soon as the call connected, Doro returned to the parlor. "It'll be a few minutes."

"Is there anything else you'd like to know about my interview with Officer Mallow and Constable Lammers?" Mrs. Jones maintained a pleasant expression as she spoke.

"I don't suppose Mallow mentioned the suspects?" Doro asked.

"He posed questions about various people, so I suppose they're being scrutinized." Mrs. Jones laid her cup and saucer down. "He didn't mention Kitty and Pierce, but I was one of the first interviewed. He brought up Stanley Gibling. I know he and Professor Corlon had more than one heated exchange, because three happened in President Winwood's office. Their voices were loud enough for me to hear every word."

"I had to admit hearing a similar confrontation between Stanley and Corlon in the English department," Aggie said in a somber voice.

"I couldn't deny knowing about Stanley's disgust with Corlon, either," Doro added. "Or about Coach Ayers clashing with Professor Corlon."

Mrs. Jones frowned. "Both Coach Ayers and Professor Gibling have been to the office to talk with President Winwood on several occasions. Not together, of course. I'm afraid neither one got far with their issues." She rolled her eyes. "I couldn't help but hear the exchanges. Sometimes, only words here and there, but loud and angry voices were always clear."

"I can imagine," Doro murmured. "I'm sorry you have to be exposed to the arguing."

A barely audible sigh escaped the older woman. "Working for President Winwood is different from being the secretary to President Adams."

"I'm sure it is," Aggie quickly agreed. "I miss President Adams."

"Don't we all?" Doro tacked on.

"I probably shouldn't say so, but I do, as well." Anything else Mrs. Jones might have said was cut off by the telephone ringing.

"Maybe it's Kitty." Doro darted out of the room without waiting for replies. After snatching up the telephone, she anticipated a response. Dismay filled her as she listened to the local operator's explanation, but Doro waited for the connection and asked several questions of the person who answered. After hanging up, she went back to the parlor.

"You don't look relieved," Aggie observed.

Doro again perched on the chair. "Our operator got through to the store clerk at home, and I spoke with him. He said Mr. and Mrs. Tenseng are away, but he wasn't sure where or why. He got a message early yesterday to put a closed sign in the window. They won't be back until Friday. No details, though."

Mrs. Jones put both hands to her face. "Oh, dear. There must be an emergency."

"Probably so. We'll check with Pierce's landlady about any telephone calls," Doro said. "I'll ask our local operator, too. Early calls go through her, not the campus operator."

"One of them will have information," Mrs. Jones said.

Doro got up. "We should be on our way, so we can head to the boardinghouse. After we talk with Pierce's landlady, we'll see Constable Lammers. He might've spoken with her already, since she is his aunt."

"You have a full morning," Mrs. Jones observed. "If I can be of assistance, let me know."

Chapter Five

The two young women bade their hostess farewell. Covering the few blocks to Pierce's residence did not take long. After Doro rapped on the door, the landlady, Angela Islington answered. "Come in, girls. I'm guessing you're here about the case."

Doro was not surprised at the woman's greeting. Mrs. Islington might have more details than most townsfolk, and if history repeated itself, she would enjoy sharing them. "Thank you."

Doro and Aggie followed Mrs. Islington into the front parlor. After the landlady gestured to the horsehair sofa, they sat down and murmured their thanks. When she offered refreshments, both demurred and Doro said, "You know about Professor Corlon's death."

"Everyone in town is talking about it." Mrs. Islington, a slender brunette in her early fifties, took the rocker at a right angle to the sofa. "I stopped by my sister's place on my way home from running errands. I wanted to see what she knew."

Doro wondered what Mrs. Lammers might have shared. "Did she have information?"

A rueful smile touched the landlady's lips. "Nothing that others don't know. Wade stopped to see her late last night on his way home. All he did was confirm the professor was murdered by a blow to the head with a card catalogue drawer." She shuddered. "Such a terrible thing. He can't share other details, though. The new campus security officer warned him not to."

Once again, Doro bristled. Mallow shouldn't bark orders at the town constable, who was older and more experienced. "Constable Lammers knows how to proceed as well as, or better than, Officer Mallow." Her tart tone revealed her annoyance. Although Mrs. Islington didn't appear to notice, Aggie clearly did.

Her friend turned to Doro with a frown. "Maybe they discussed the case and agreed to keep clues close to the vest."

Before Doro could respond, Mrs. Islington spoke. "That's what Wade told my sister. He's glad Officer Mallow isn't bossy. Wade feared he might be, because of being a federal agent and all."

Aggie grinned. "It's good to know Constable Lammers' opinion, since both Doro and I respect him so much."

Doro shot her friend a quelling glare, but nodded. "We do," she agreed before hurrying on. "But we wondered if we could ask you a few questions."

Mrs. Islington turned to Doro. "About what?"

The query made Doro realize an explanation was in order, since the landlady wouldn't know about campus goings-on, unless her boarders discussed the issues. Perhaps, a bit of background would suffice. "Did you know Professor Corlon?" The question could be a starting point.

The older woman shook her head. "I've seen him and the other new ones. At the diner or in a shop. None too friendly with us townsfolk."

"Not surprising," Aggie put in. "They aren't all that affable with many of us on campus."

A frown knit Mrs. Islington's brow. "I heard about them wanting to make big changes. It'd be terrible if girls couldn't come to school no more. My youngest is set on attending Michaw when the time comes. We can afford tuition, but not room and board somewhere else. I want my girl to have more opportunity than I did. More than her older siblings did, too."

"I hope we don't go backward, either," Aggie said. "It would hurt many women."

"It would," Doro agreed. "I'm not sure what will happen now." For a moment, she considered how to get the conversation back to where it needed to go. Before Doro hit on a strategy, Mrs. Islington continued.

"Since my boarders are students, chatter about the new regime is common at meals. Last evening at supper, they were all agog over who might've killed the professor."

Doro exchanged a quick glance with Aggie before turning to their hostess. "I bet there was speculation on who did it."

Mrs. Islington nodded. "Quite a lot. Only five of my boys were at the table. One had a meeting, and another had to go out of town."

"Who went away?" Doro kept her voice well-modulated, but anxiety flared inside her.

"Pierce and Kitty went to visit her family." The woman folded her hands in her lap and looked down at them.

Mrs. Islington's tone and posture indicated some level of discomfort, but why? "When did they take off?" Doro asked.

"I found a note from Pierce yesterday morning," Mrs. Islington replied. "He wanted me to know why he wasn't here." A slight smile touched her thin lips. "My boys know I fret over them."

Doro grappled with the information. Mr. and Mrs. Tenseng were away, according to their employee. Had Kitty and Pierce gone with them? If so, where and why? "Did he say if there was an emergency?"

Mrs. Islington glanced at her. "No details. Just that I shouldn't worry." A knock on the front door interrupted. "Excuse me," she said before rushing to answer. In a moment, she returned with Officer Mallow.

"Good morning, Miss Darwine." As the lawman looked from Aggie to Doro, he scowled. "Good morning again, Miss Banyon."

Aggie responded with a smile and a cheery *hello*. Doro simply nodded.

"Please sit down, Officer," Mrs. Islington said with a smile. "My nephew said you'd be here to talk with me. Can I offer you refreshments? I keep a pot of coffee going, and I made biscuits for breakfast. A few are left."

"Thank you, ma'am. That sounds wonderful," Mallow replied. After Mrs. Islington was out of earshot, he sat in the vacant chair next to Aggie, but his gaze was on Doro. "What brings you here?"

Not a trace of curiosity or doubt was in the question. Clearly, the man knew exactly why Doro and Aggie had stopped. "We're visiting. I've known Mrs. Islington since I was born."

His jaw set hard. "That isn't an answer, Miss Banyon. When we spoke earlier, I suggested you keep a low profile for a few days. Obviously, my advice went in one ear and out the other."

"You didn't tell me that," Aggie put in, as she turned to her friend.

Doro glared at her friend. Aggie loved mysteries as much as Doro, but the other girl would be content with reading or talking about them. Maybe Doro should have left Aggie in Wheaton Hall while she interviewed people and dug for clues. The two of them could have discussed her findings later.

After several moments of silence ticked away, Mallow spoke again. "Why am I not surprised?"

"I'll help Mrs. Islington." Aggie jumped to her feet and rushed out of the room.

"Nothing to say for yourself, Miss Banyon?" Mallow asked.

A low huff escaped Doro. "I'm allowed to talk with old neighbors."

His nostrils flared with a sharp intake of breath. "You didn't come here to chit-chat, and we both know it. As I already told you, I know you're an armchair detective. You not only teach a course on mystery novels; you solved some minor case a few years back."

Surprise rippled through Doro. How had he learned about that? "It wasn't minor to Aggie, who could have lost her scholarship if we hadn't found out what really happened to the examination." Doro had been a recent high school graduate visiting her father when she overheard a professor berating his student assistant for not locking the office door. After discovering a final examination was missing, Doro had joined forces with Aggie, who was being blamed. The two of them, another student, and Doro's father worked together to unravel the mystery. And save Aggie's scholarship.

"I'm sure it was crucial to Miss Darwine, but you weren't chasing a killer." Mallow paused for a heartbeat. "What if you and your friend make the murderer uneasy? He or she has already committed one murder. Committing another would come easier. It usually does."

The last comment reminded Doro that Mallow had several years of experience as a lawman. Chasing bootleggers and rumrunners had undoubtedly involved more than a few shootings...and some murders. Although Doro would have enjoyed brushing off his concern, she was no fool. "We don't plan to talk with suspects. We're just gathering information."

"Are you planning to share details with Constable Lammers and me?" he asked.

The query caught her off-guard. Revealing clues to the two lawmen had not been part of her plan, but Doro wasn't about to admit that. "Of course."

In the lingering silence that followed, his silver-gray gaze narrowed on her. Finally, he nodded. "Good. In that same vein, I'd like you to tell me where you're going ahead of time. Just to be on the safe side."

With no other option, Doro forced a smile. "I'll be happy to do that, Officer Mallow."

For a long moment, he scanned her face. "Thanks."

His single-word answer resonated with skepticism, which made Doro shift restlessly. Did he realize she planned to avoid alerting him? Relief filled her when Mrs. Islington and Aggie returned with refreshments. Four cups and saucers, along with a coffee pot, rested on the tray in Aggie's hands, while the older woman carried a plate of biscuits, butter, and jam. Although Doro had hoped to escape, she took her coffee and a biscuit before settling back in her chair.

"You said you had some questions for me, Officer Mallow," Mrs. Islington said with a smile.

When a look of discomfiture crossed the lawman's face, Doro had to repress a grin. He clearly didn't want to conduct the interrogation in front of the two younger women. Suddenly, staying for a snack seemed like a fine idea.

Mallow grabbed a biscuit and took a big bite before following it with a gulp of coffee. Then, he finished the roll.

Doro repressed a chuckle at his efforts to kill time. When her gaze caught Aggie's, she saw her friend was similarly amused. After Mallow gulped down another biscuit, Mrs. Islington spoke.

"I could cook ham and eggs, if you're hungry." The landlady studied him. "You're too thin. I suppose you don't eat regular meals. Did you have breakfast?"

Before Mallow replied, his stomach growled. Color swept into his face. "Not today, ma'am. I didn't have time, but please don't go to any trouble. I can't stay too long, since I'm meeting Constable Lammers at his office in a half-hour."

His response lifted Doro's spirits. Mallow would have to interview Mrs. Islington while she and Aggie were there.

"Go ahead with your questions," the woman said. "And have as many biscuits as you like."

Mallow pursed his lips. "Thank you, ma'am." After a moment, he extracted pad and paper from his pocket. "Your nephew said several students, including Pierce Dudley board here."

"That's right." Mrs. Islington's gaze went to Doro and Aggie before returning to Mallow. "I told the girls about him and his sweetheart going to see her family yesterday morning."

Once again, Mallow scowled. After a quick glance at Aggie, who bowed her head to select another biscuit, the officer focused on Doro before regaining an insouciant expression. "Why did they leave on a Tuesday? Surely, both had classes."

"It must've been an emergency," the landlady replied.

"Young Dudley didn't say?" Mallow's expression didn't lighten.

"I didn't talk with him," she explained. "He left a note. No details other than they were going to see Kitty's relatives. It was scrawled, like he was in a rush."

"He used the word *relatives*?" Mallow asked.

The older woman's forehead furrowed, as if she was trying to recall. "The note is still on my desk. Let me get it for you." Within a moment, she retrieved the missive and handed it to the officer.

Doro watched as Mallow scanned the paper. What difference would the wording make? She would love to snatch the note from his hand and see for herself.

"Do you mind if I keep this?" he asked Mrs. Islington.

"Of course not," she replied.

"Thank you," Mallow said as he tucked the paper into his jacket pocket.

The exchange whetted Doro's curiosity. When the officer's gaze met hers, she noted a glimmer of amusement. Clearly, he was enjoying his one-upmanship. Doro folded her hands in her lap and waited.

Mallow returned his attention to the landlady. "What time did you see Pierce last?"

"Monday evening after supper," she replied.

"Pierce isn't on the basketball team any longer, so he doesn't have practice. Does he have a class first thing in the morning?" Mallow inquired.

The mention of practice provoked another possibility in Doro's mind. Basketball practice had only started on Monday. Had that upset Pierce and Kitty?

"Not on Tuesdays." The landlady frowned. "Like I said, he wasn't here for breakfast. Sometimes, he and Kitty meet early and walk out by the pond, but Pierce usually grabs something to eat."

"There was chilly rain yesterday. Do they make a habit of going out in any weather?" Skepticism was in the officer's tone.

Renewed anxiety rolled through Doro. Last week, Kitty started working in the dormitory cafeteria, so the girl no longer had time to saunter around campus shortly after dawn. Not that she and her beau would do so in miserable conditions.

"No, I hadn't considered that." Mrs. Islington gnawed on her lower lip. "He might've met friends someplace."

Mallow posed another question. "Where might he do that?"

The older woman shrugged. "It was too early for the library to be open. I suppose he could've gone to the men's dormitory. The basketball players live there, and he's still friends with them."

"I'll check on that." Mallow murmured.

Doro felt sure he'd check on everything, which was his job. But still, she didn't like Kitty and Pierce being suspects. For several moments, she struggled to find some reason they shouldn't be. None came to mind, something that increased her determination to investigate the case more fully. The young couple could not be killers.

"I'm sorry I don't know more," the landlady said. "Maybe Pierce saw something that will help you solve the murder. Everyone in town is nervous."

"No need to be, ma'am. Constable Lammers is on the lookout for anything unusual, and so am I," Mallow assured her.

"Wade is a good man, but he's one person," Mrs. Islington said. "And you're working for the college."

"Nevertheless, I'm able to help him."

The answer reminded Doro that Mallow's authority extended beyond the college campus due to a special arrangement with the town. In addition, for a few more days, he was still a federal agent. How much power did that give him?

Mallow jotted more notes before asking another question. "Did any of your other boarders mention Professor Corlon's murder? Either yesterday or this morning."

She clasped her hands together. "Of course. Everyone in town is talking about it."

"What's being said?" the man asked.

The question sent a clear signal that Officer Mallow had never lived in a small town, where everyone knew everyone else's business—or thought they did—and passed it on. News of a murder would spread rapidly and, as it did, details would be tacked on. Details that might, or might not, be valid. Would Kitty and Pierce be scrutinized by the townsfolk? Fresh apprehension gripped Doro.

"My stars," Mrs. Islington said with a giggle. "What isn't being said? As far as my boys, every single one of them mentioned the professor being a hard grader, in general, and worse with some students. They all agreed Pierce was unfairly treated. Seems like Corlon cared little for sports. He mentioned more than once that money would be better spent on academics."

"Was Pierce the one who shared that?" Mallow asked.

"He wasn't the first to say so, but he agreed," Mrs. Islington replied.

"What about how he treated female students?" Doro blurted out the question. For a moment, she expected Mallow to chastise her, but he said nothing. Nor did he look in her direction.

"Pierce said the man didn't like Kitty or her group. Can't recall the name." The woman's brow furrowed, as if she was trying to remember.

"Young Women Voters for Equality and Justice." Aggie supplied the answer.

"Of course," Mrs. Islington agreed.

"Did Pierce give any details?" Mallow continued with the interview.

"Not really, although another of my boys, who's in one of Professor Corlon's courses this term, thought the man was backing off making the school all-male again," the landlady said.

Surprise hit Doro like a lightning bolt. A quick glance at her friend revealed Aggie had much the same reaction. "When did that come up?" Doro asked.

"Monday night at supper," the landlady replied. "Pierce said when people like the professor make trouble for others, it comes back on them. Another of the boys claimed Pierce had two reasons to dislike the man—losing his scholarship and Kitty maybe not being able to stay in school here, if girls are banned. That's when Phillip Nagel mentioned the professor saying times were changing, and a lot of schools admitted women now, which wasn't a bad idea."

"I haven't heard that at all," Doro admitted.

During the exchange, Mallow took more notes. "I need to meet with Constable Lammers shortly, but when will Phillip be back?"

"I'm not sure," Mrs. Islington replied. "He went with some other boys to play football at the field. The team practices are also off, according to what I heard at the market, so it's a pickup game."

"All organized college activities are on hold," Aggie put in.

"I heard that, too. People are saying President Winwood wants the murder solved quickly," Mrs. Islington said. "Of course, the rest of us do, too. It's scary to think we have a killer walking among us." A shudder rippled through the woman.

Mallow again looked tense. "I want it solved, too, and so does Constable Lammers. We're working hard to catch the murderer, but I honestly don't believe you or others should worry. It looks like Professor Corlon's death was personal, not a happenstance. I can't say more."

"Thank you for that much. It eases my mind," the landlady murmured. "My boys thought the same thing, since there's been plenty of criticism of him. They complain about other professors, too, but not like they did him." She glanced at Doro and Agatha. "None ever complained about either of you. Several have taken your mystery class, Doro. The only problem they've mentioned is that President Winwood wants to eliminate it."

Doro felt Officer Mallow turn toward her, but she kept her attention on Mrs. Islington. "He prefers more traditional courses."

"How long have you taught the mystery class?" Mallow asked.

Reluctantly, Doro faced him. "This is the third year. I suggested it to Dr. Adams when I was first hired in June 1926, and he agreed to put it on the schedule during both fall and spring semesters. It's always filled."

"Doro and I both love reading whodunits," Aggie put in.

Mallow nodded. "I see. Do you write them, as well, Miss Banyon?"

Only Aggie knew about Doro penning a mystery, and she planned to keep it that way. "Writing a book is a lot harder than most people think. And time-consuming, as well. I have my hands full with working at the library and teaching one class each term." Before Mallow might mention her failure to directly answer the question, Doro rushed on. "Aggie is a poet, though."

"Poems are much shorter than books," her friend said.

Mrs. Islington added a comment. "I've read some of your poetry, and you're very talented."

Aggie, her cheeks crimson, murmured her thanks.

"You must be published then," Mallow observed.

"Only in the local newspapers and our college annual," Aggie said. "Mostly, I write poems for my enjoyment."

"I see," Mallow said, but he quickly glanced back at Doro. "I'm surprised you don't write—for your enjoyment. I'd think writing a mystery would be a little like playing armchair detective."

His last comment didn't surprise Doro, but it annoyed her. The phrase *playing armchair detective* sounded dismissive. "As I said, I'm very busy."

"I'm sure you are." Although the officer's tone was placid, the words lacked sincerity.

Doro got to her feet. "We should go, Aggie." She doubted if the landlady had any other pertinent information, and getting away from Mallow seemed like a fine idea.

Her friend immediately stood, as well.

"I'm afraid I haven't helped much," Mrs. Islington said. "But I know nothing else."

Officer Mallow tucked away his pad and pencil as he rose. "I appreciate your time, ma'am. And the food, too."

Mrs. Islington escorted the group to her front door, where they all thanked her again. When they reached the sidewalk, Mallow stopped. "Like I told Mrs. Islington, the killing was likely personal, but you still need to be careful."

"We understand," Doro replied, but she resented being warned a second time.

"We do," Aggie agreed. "Neither of us wants to be targeted by the killer."

He gave a sharp nod. "Good, because a murderer can only go to the electric chair once." Then, he turned on his heel and strode away.

The color left Aggie's face. "He's right, Doro. We need to be careful."

"He wants to scare us off, but you don't have to come with me."

Aggie shifted from one foot to the other. "Talking with Constable Lammers won't be dangerous."

"No, but Mallow is headed there," Doro reminded her friend. "I'd like to talk with Phillip about Corlon's attitude toward coeducation. If he was mellowing, I didn't know about it."

"Neither did I." A sigh escaped the other young woman. "I'll go along with you, but let's hurry. I'm guessing Officer Mallow will head there next."

"Probably so." Doro linked her arm with Aggie's and turned toward campus. "Mallow's meeting with Constable Lammers will take a little while. We'll be finished long before Mallow gets to the field. After all, we only have a couple of questions to ask."

"All right."

Although her friend sounded less than enthusiastic, Doro continued down the tree-lined street and across campus. When they arrived at the field, the pair found a group of young men playing football. "There's Phillip Nagel." Doro gestured to a boy standing on the sidelines.

Aggie followed Doro to where Phillip was pacing back-and-forth along the out-of-bounds. He stopped as soon as he saw them. "Miss Banyon. Miss Darwine. What brings you out here on such a chilly day?"

Doro offered what she hoped was a bright smile. "We had a couple of questions for you."

His brows drew down as he looked from Doro to Aggie and back. "About what?" Wariness undergirded the words.

After clearing her throat, Doro replied. "We just spoke with Mrs. Islington, and she mentioned a conversation some of you boys had at meals yesterday and this morning."

He folded his arms across his chest. "None of us had anything to do with Corlon's murder."

"We don't think any of you did," Doro rushed to assure him, despite her misgivings about Pierce and Kitty taking off. "What we wondered about was Professor Corlon's change in attitude. Mrs. Islington said you mentioned him not being so adamant about returning the college to all-male status."

Some of the tension drained from Phillip. "I was in his class last year, and he made little digs from time-to-time. This term, someone said the females ought to go, and he objected. I was surprised, and so was everyone else who'd had him for another course. I debated about taking a class from him again, but I did okay before, and the later one fit my schedule. I work in town, so I need to be finished by three o'clock."

"Did he say why he'd changed his mind?" Aggie asked.

Phillip shook his head. "Not really. He made some remark about times changing. Then, he went back to his lecture."

"And the topic only came up once?" Doro asked.

"Yep. No one wants to run afoul of Professor Corlon. He's known for being a tough grader and, if you get on his bad side, he finds a lot of faults with your papers," Phillip asserted.

Since this did not come as a surprise, Doro nodded. "You didn't happen to be out early yesterday morning, did you?"

Phillip released a snort of laughter. "Miss Banyon, getting up to eat breakfast is tough enough. This term, I don't have a class until ten o'clock, so I have my meal and go back to bed."

"Was Pierce still there when you left for class?" Doro asked.

He nodded. "I'm not sure. I didn't see him, and everyone else was gone."

A male voice interrupted. "Hey, Phil. We need you back on the field."

"Sorry, gotta go." With that, the boy raced to where his friends stood in a huddle.

"I suppose we might as well leave," Aggie suggested.

"I suppose," Doro reluctantly agreed. The pair turned toward the main part of campus. "We learned very little."

"We got confirmation of what Mrs. Islington said," Aggie pointed out. "Honestly, I wondered if she'd misunderstood Phillip. Now, we know she didn't."

"That's a good point. But why the change of heart in Corlon?" Doro glanced at her friend. "Did you notice any softening in him?"

For several moments, the pair walked in silence. "I've only seen him at department meetings, and we don't engage in personal conversations. As far as his comments, he hasn't been so outspoken this term. Now that I think about it, Corlon had some cutting remarks at the first couple of meetings, but not since then. And last year, he was much worse."

"I wonder why," Doro commented.

"Who knows? He was still complaining to you about not being able to use the library meeting room whenever he wanted, wasn't he?"

"He complained as recently as this week." As Doro mentally reviewed his last few objections, she came to a stop. "But he used to rant about how women should be married and at home raising a family, not taxing their small brains with studying. His recent objections were mostly related to YWV, and how the group might wrongly influence female students."

Aggie paused next to Doro. "That's interesting. I wonder what caused the change, subtle as it is."

"I do, too. I also wonder if Pierce got a call." Doro released a pent-up breath. "I wish I knew exactly what he wrote in the note that Mallow took." Distracted, Doro did not see Everett

Mallow coming toward them. A gasp from her friend alerted her. "What's wrong?"

"It looks like our new campus security officer didn't meet with the town constable for long," Aggie said.

Doro followed her friend's gaze and felt her heart sink. Not only was the man quickly closing the distance, gray storm clouds darkened his eyes. She squared her shoulders and lifted her chin. "Good afternoon, Officer." The salutation sounded odd, since they had parted only a short time ago, but it was the best she could do on the spur of the moment.

His lips flattened. "I asked you to alert me about your—uh—travels regarding the case. You said you would and yet, you've been here to question a potential witness."

Doro exerted strict self-control to keep from making a sharp retort, mostly because Aggie's eyes had gone wide with dismay. Although Doro wasn't afraid of Mallow exerting authority, her friend clearly was. "You're making an assumption," she replied in a lighthearted tone.

Mallow's scowl only intensified. "Are you trying to make me believe the two of you came down to the field to watch a pickup game of football on a cold, blustery day?" He glanced at Aggie, who shoved her hands into her coat pockets and turned to Doro with a stricken expression.

If she had been alone, Doro would have put up a stronger defense. Not wanting to further upset her friend, who wasn't as outspoken or strong-willed, she shrugged.

"No comeback?" Mallow asked.

"What sense is there in pretending we didn't talk to Phillip? You'll ask him, and he'll say we did. Not that we learned much," Doro replied.

"Exactly what did you learn?" Mallow inquired.

"Just that Mrs. Islington was right about the conversation at the table. Phillip mentioned Professor Corlon being less hostile about women on campus." Doro shared the boy's story. "As I said, not much."

Mallow rubbed the back of his neck. "But it's something I want to pursue." His tone was thoughtful. "Did Phillip provide other details?"

Doro shook her head. "No, he didn't."

Immediately, Mallow turned to Aggie. "Is that right?"

The man's lack of trust annoyed Doro, although she had to admit—at least to herself—that he had little reason to rely on her.

"Yes, it is," Aggie replied.

Mallow's shoulders relaxed, and his hand fell to his side. "Thanks for your honesty."

Should the comment be taken at face value? Or was it a veiled criticism of her? Doro didn't know, and she shouldn't care. "We should be on our way."

He shifted to face her. "Where to?"

From anyone else, the short query could have been casual. Not from him, though. Admitting they planned to see Constable Lammers didn't seem like a sound strategy. She wanted to say that it was none of his business. When she looked past

Mallow, Doro saw her friend's worried expression and relented. "To speak with the local operator. She'll know if Pierce got a call at the boardinghouse." They could see Wade later.

The frown returned to Mallow's face. "I stopped at her house on my way here. She didn't want to divulge private information to a college employee."

Aggie's eyes widened. "She must know you're investigating a murder."

"She does," Mallow said. "She didn't believe I had authority beyond the campus, and my status as a Prohibition agent didn't move her, either. Neither was my special designation as a deputy. She'll talk with Lammers when he's back,"

"Back from where?" Doro asked.

"He took his mother into Sylvania, which is why our meeting was cut short. She sees a doctor there. Evidently, she was feeling poorly." Mallow ran his fingers through his closely clipped hair. "I'll get the details from him later."

Doro smiled. "Mrs. Lammers still doctors with an older physician in Sylvania. She considers Dr. Silton a young whippersnapper, even though he's in his mid-thirties."

Mallow nodded. "Wade said his mother is stubborn. He also said she's been struggling with heart trouble. That's why he took her. I'll manage on my own. Family comes first."

The sentiment increased Doro's regard for the officer, if only a tad. "We could let you know what we find out. I've known Cecelia Gardner all my life, and I think she'll share details. If there are any."

"I appreciate your help." His gaze went from Aggie to Doro. "Both of you."

Since he looked and sounded sincere, Doro responded in kind. "Of course. We all want the murderer found as quickly as possible. Now, it's cold just standing here. Good day, Officer Mallow."

Aggie also said her farewell, but the pair hadn't gone ten feet when he spoke again. "Can we meet later to discuss what you find out?"

The question indicated a mellowing in his attitude, but how much mellowing? Would he be willing to share his information? Time would tell. "Perhaps, we could meet in the reception area of the women's faculty residence? Seventy-five percent of the residents left until Sunday. The rest are planning to eat at the diner tonight, right?" she asked her friend.

Aggie nodded. "We were invited, but I said we were busy."

"Come around six o'clock," Doro suggested to Mallow.

A grin tugged at one corner of his mouth. "Sounds fine. Thanks again." After touching his cap brim, he headed toward the field.

Doro watched him stride away and wondered if she had made a major error. What if he expected information sharing to only go one way? From them to him.

"Why the gloomy look?" Aggie asked. "He's willing to let us gather information and meet with us."

"Because we can get details he can't, and he doesn't want to wait for Constable Lammers. We're doing Mallow a favor, and there's no guarantee he'll return it."

"I think he will," Aggie said with a grin. She looped her arm through Doro's and started walking.

Something about her friend's demeanor bothered Doro. But she couldn't determine exactly what. Or maybe she didn't want to know.

Chapter Six

The two friends got to Cecelia Gardner's home within a few minutes. After a second knock, the operator answered. "Hello," she said in a breathless murmur. With one hand, Mrs. Gardner brushed an errant lock of hair off her face. "This is a surprise."

"We're sorry to bother you," Doro told her. "Looks like it's a busy morning."

"It has been," the woman agreed. "Is there something I can do for you?"

"If you have a moment, we'd like to ask about yesterday's calls," Doro replied.

Mrs. Gardner stepped back. "Come along. I can't leave the switchboard, but we can chat between calls."

Doro and Aggie followed her down the narrow hallway to a tiny room at the back of the cottage. Mrs. Gardner took a seat in front of the call center, which resembled an upright piano with holes and wires to make connections. The two young women settled on the narrow bed pushed up against one wall.

A rueful smile touched the operator's lips. "I miss my boy, but it's good he's living in the city. I need his room for my equipment. When he visits, he has to squeeze in and not sleep late. Sometimes, calls wake him in the night. He says I ought to quit, but the money is handy and working from home is, too. Even with interruptions."

"I thought Mrs. Carson took over at night," Aggie observed.

"She does most of the time, but my boy comes for holidays and that's when she goes to see her own family," Mrs. Gardner explained. "She has equipment, which is useful. Especially earlier this week when I had an awful cold and could hardly talk. Now, while there's a calm spell, what are your questions?"

"We're wondering if anyone telephoned the Islington boardinghouse yesterday morning. Maybe Kitty Tenseng's family? Or were you still sick?" Doro made the query.

"No, I took over again yesterday very early. About six in the morning. No calls to or from the boardinghouse at all." Curiosity lit Mrs. Gardner's brown gaze. "That new campus law officer was here asking the same thing, but I didn't feel comfortable giving him any details. He said Wade Lammers is working on that murder, too. I'm happy to tell Wade whatever, but not no stranger."

"Officer Mallow is just doing his job." Aggie spoke in a pleasant tone. "But I understand your reluctance."

"As do I," Doro agreed with sincerity. "We also wondered if any calls went to Flanders Hall, the girl's dormitory. I know the college has its own operator, but connections are sometimes made through you, aren't they?"

Mrs. Gardner nodded. "Some out-of-town operators still don't know they can connect directly to the school's switchboard, but it's only been operating for a few months. Don't see why the school needed an operator. The town operator has done the job ever since telephone lines went in. Besides, their switchboard shuts down at nine in the evening and doesn't open again until the next morning at eight-thirty."

Doro didn't understand either, but she provided the explanation given on campus. "Dr. Winwood wants the college to be independent of the town. He was afraid important calls would be delayed." Privately, Doro figured he didn't want an outsider listening to conversations about the college's future. Gossip about moving back to all-male status had quickly spread from campus to town. Some hostile exchanges had taken place between local merchants and the Fearsome Foursome, because banning women, as students and as employees, would hurt businesses on Main Street. In addition, many townsfolk found Winwood and his buddies to be arrogant. Doro didn't disagree, but she was careful not to voice her opinion. "At least it takes some burden off you," she said.

A half-shrug lifted one of Mrs. Gardner's shoulders. "I suppose. Anyhow, if someone called the dormitory, I wouldn't know unless it was when the campus operator isn't working, although a long-distance operator could try to make a connection. I've heard from one that she was able to ring through to a dormitory without reaching me or the campus operator. New lines are going in, I guess. I can only say for sure that no one contacted the boardinghouse. At least not while I was on duty."

Apprehension clawed at Doro as she wondered if Pierce's note had been a lie. The young couple had disappeared early, but why? And where were Kitty's parents? Since Mrs. Gardner could not answer those queries, Doro focused on another avenue of investigation. "What about calls to Professor Corlon? Since he lived in town, you'd handle those connections."

"Of course," the operator agreed. She pressed one hand to her head, as if in deep thought. After a moment, she continued. "He gets a call once a month from his sister and niece in the Columbus area. The girl usually comes on the line first. I only hear the first bit, but she's always excited to talk to him."

The revelation modified Doro's opinion of the man. If he chatted with his young niece, Corlon must have had a softer side. "Children are often fascinated with the telephone."

Mrs. Gardner shook her head. "She isn't a child. The girl's in her last year of high school. I only know that because at the start of the last call, she mentioned coming to visit the campus here because she's looking at colleges."

That bit of information momentarily held Doro mute. When she looked at her friend, Doro saw a similar burst of interest on Aggie's face. Perhaps, this fact explained Corlon's change in attitude. "Did she specify the date of her visit?"

"Not that I heard. Like I said, I only catch a few words at the very beginning of calls."

"Of course." Doro planned to discuss how to get more information with Aggie but, for now, she asked another question. "Did the professor get other long-distance calls? Or local ones?"

"No other long-distance connections," Mrs. Gardner replied. "Occasionally, he'd hear from President Winwood about a meeting or appointment."

"What about Provost Pottiger and Dr. Jerritt? Did either of them telephone him at home?" Aggie asked.

"Very rarely," the operator replied, "and not recently. Both of them complained about needing to go through our town system. But hiring a college operator didn't change that. She has to ring me for town calls."

"But President Winwood called in the last month or so?" Doro made the inquiry.

The operator nodded. "Lately, he called a couple of times a week. Ever since Professor Corlon returned from summer break, six weeks ago."

"I see." The buzzing of the switchboard kept Doro from saying more. She hastily got to her feet, as Aggie did the same. Both young women expressed their gratitude for the operator's assistance. "We'll see ourselves out."

Once the front door shut behind them, Aggie turned to Doro. "Mrs. Gardner had some interesting information."

"She did. Not what we expected, but it may prove useful. We need to get details about Professor Corlon's relationship with his sister and niece. If the girl is planning to come here for college, she may have influenced him to alter his attitude."

"It certainly sounds that way," Aggie agreed. "Who would know more?"

"The rest of the Fearsome Foursome probably does. Unfortunately, confronting them isn't apt to help. None of them like me," Doro admitted.

"They aren't fond of me, either. None has much respect for Constable Lammers, but Officer Mallow might make headway with the group. Or what's left of it."

Although the observation seemed valid, Doro hesitated to agree. Mallow's stiff demeanor had softened, but he still seemed officious. Doro didn't like being told what to do. Not at all. Since that wasn't an excuse to impede an investigation, she reluctantly seconded her friend's idea. "We can let him know what we heard later."

Aggie's expression relaxed. "Good."

Her friend's reaction highlighted the difference between their attitudes. "I know you think I'm too headstrong, but Mallow is bossy. He has no authority over us asking questions, so we shouldn't have to report to him."

"But you will tell him where we're going and such." Aggie paused. "He made a good point about not knowing who's responsible. Professor Corlon had run-ins with more than a few people, and we may not be aware of everyone who argued with him. Chances are good that the killer doesn't want us identifying him."

"I'll let him know, and I agree we should keep him up-to-date. Wade Lammers, too. You're right about other suspects. Maybe we should talk with Stanley. He might have some ideas, and we'd be safe seeing him."

"All right. With classes canceled until next week, he's probably spending time on his book."

"Then, he'll be at home. Let's head to his boardinghouse."

⁓

A few minutes later, the two young women were inside the front parlor. Stanley's landlady ushered them to a pair of chairs in front of the fireplace before going to fetch her boarder. Within moments, he joined them.

Doro studied the man as he entered the room. Even frowning, Stanley Gibling was handsome. His brown hair was side-parted and swept back. Dark lashes framed tawny eyes, which had a brooding look. His usual attire included a three-piece suit with a dress shirt and bow tie. Today, he had foregone tie and jacket, making him appear more like a poet than a professor. No wonder he had caught Aggie's fancy. For a moment, she wondered if her friend still fancied the man. Aggie had said she was fine with their break-up, but Doro was not sure, and uncertainty made her feel ambivalent, at best, toward him.

"Good afternoon," Aggie said in her typical cheerful voice.

Doro added her greeting, but the professor's grim expression did not lighten. Nor did he return the felicitations. Instead, he said, "Not good for me. I've been applying for other teaching positions, but it's too soon for next year and too late for this one."

"Your tenure hasn't officially been denied," Aggie pointed out. "You may stay."

A snort left the man. "Winwood is the same as Corlon, and I'm sure he wants me gone. That's if I don't get arrested for a murder I didn't commit. Plenty of people told Mallow about my run-ins with the victim."

Aggie's hand flew to her mouth. "I'm sorry," she murmured.

He slumped back in the chair. "I'm not blaming you for telling the truth. I admitted saying I wished Corlon was dead, and I admitted not being sorry he is. He made my life miserable for over a year. Winwood undoubtedly pulled the strings, but Corlon danced to his tune. Often, with enthusiasm."

"He could be troublesome, for sure," Doro agreed.

Stanley turned toward her. "You two didn't get along, either. I suppose you're on the suspect list, too."

"Not anymore. My alibi has been confirmed," Doro replied.

"Lucky you." A dark scowl drew Stanley's brows down. "Mallow grilled me like a steak. I'm sure he's just like Corlon, doing Winwood's bidding."

"He's doing his job, and he's very new, so naturally he wants to catch the killer quickly. I'm sure he'll eliminate you as soon as possible." Aggie spoke in a serious, subdued tone.

"Or pin the murder on me, since I've got no alibi. I left here early on Tuesday, because I planned to meet with a student at the diner. The kid didn't show up, so I headed to campus. Corlon was going into the library when I passed there."

"Did anyone else see you?" Doro asked.

"Not right when I walked by him," Stanley replied, "but I ran into Winwood when I went into College Hall."

Confusion filled Doro. "What time was that?"

"A few minutes after seven," the man said.

"What was he doing?" As she made the inquiry, Doro thought back to Tuesday morning and tried to mesh Stanley's description with her own observations and Mrs. Jones' statements.

"Going to his office, of course. What else?"

What indeed? But she had seen him heading toward College Hall twenty minutes later. Searching for watch was a good excuse, but who could tell if he had actually lost it? "Did you tell Officer Mallow about seeing President Winwood?"

"Of course," Stanley replied, "because Winwood surely told him about seeing me."

Doro glanced at her friend. Aggie looked uncertain. Clearly, they would have more to discuss after this interview. "Did you speak with him?"

"No. He nodded and hurried on. I did the same," Stanley said. "I went to my office. No one else came until eight-thirty. You can bet Winwood told Mallow and Lammers that I must've seen Corlon and probably killed him. I didn't, but there's no one and nothing to back me up."

"I'm sure you'll be eliminated when more details come out," Doro said. "Both lawmen are working hard to solve the case, and Constable Lammers reports to the mayor, not President Winwood. He'll make sure no innocent person gets arrested. After all, it's the town that has a jail—not the college."

"True," Stanley agreed in a grudging tone.

"What about the student that didn't show up? Do you know what happened to him?" Aggie asked.

Stanley shook his head. "Not really. He should've been in my ten o'clock class, along with his sweetheart. But neither one showed up, which is unusual. It's the first class they've missed."

Doro sat up straighter. "Who is the boy?"

"Pierce Dudley," was the answer. Again, the two girlfriends exchanged a long look. Watching them, the professor went on. "Both he and the girl have reason to dislike Corlon, as I'm sure you know. Kitty because he wants women off campus. Pierce because the man picked on him and failed him. Without that scholarship, the boy may have to leave school. That's why we planned to talk. Not that my support would help here, but there are other schools."

The news served to further unnerve Doro. Surely, the young couple had not killed the professor. With determination, she fought down a rising tide of anxiety. "We've heard Professor Corlon was softening his attitude toward females on campus."

"I heard that, too, but I don't believe it." Stanley spat out the words.

"Why not? He seems to have reason," Aggie put in. "His niece is coming to visit campus soon."

A shrug moved the man's narrow shoulders. "Why didn't he care about that before?"

"Maybe her wanting to attend college here influenced him. It could've been a recent decision," Doro added.

"Maybe. And maybe she'll change her mind," he said.

"That seems likely now," Doro admitted.

"And it seems just as likely that women will be banned when Winwood can manage it. If Pierce and Kitty are somehow involved, he'll make her the reason, and you can bet it'll be sooner rather than later." Stanley got to his feet. "I have no other information, and I'm planning to head into Toledo yet today. Even though it's early to find a position for next year, I'm meeting with several high school principals."

"You should try for another college professorship," Aggie said.

A snort left Stanley. "And have some other egomaniac make my life miserable before destroying my dreams? Ever since I went to college as a freshman, I yearned to be a professor. Getting a bachelor's degree was tough enough. Earning my master's degree was harder. But men like Hemet Corlon, men who went to elite schools because their parents were rich...men like that look down on people like me. Just like they look down at women and athletes. Corlon's dead, but the other three are still here, and they aren't going to let a murder stop them from getting rid of the riff-raff."

"Riff-raff," Doro echoed. "Surely, no one used that word."

"Corlon used it to describe me," Stanley shot back. "My folks worked hard at their general store, but they didn't finish high school. To Corlon, they're worthless. And I'm not a valuable faculty member, due to that. I'm riff-raff that shouldn't be on this campus in any but the most menial role." Anger echoed in his tone while a red flush stained his handsome face.

"You never said he used that word about you." Aggie, her eyes wide with some emotion, stared at the man. "That's awful."

"He was awful," Stanley said. "He deserved to die. I wish the rest of them would."

The assertions alarmed Doro, who got up. "Since you need to get on the road, we should go."

Aggie followed suit.

After bidding the man farewell, they headed to the front sidewalk. "He's bitter and angry," Doro observed. But was he dangerous?

"He is," Aggie agreed. "I was stunned at how bitter."

The pallor in her friend's face telegraphed anxiety, but Doro wasn't sure how to alleviate the situation. "I was, too, but he was probably blowing off steam." Was that all the tirade had been? Doro hoped so, but Stanley had moved toward the top of her suspect list after his outburst.

"I hope that's all it was. He could always be dramatic, and I saw him lose his temper with Corlon. But this was worse."

Doro couldn't disagree. As she fell into step beside Aggie, Doro returned the conversation to other aspects of the case.

"What did you think about what Stanley had to say regarding Pierce?"

"I was surprised to hear he planned to meet Pierce. It isn't good that the boy didn't show up. Not good at all."

Her friend's reaction didn't surprise Doro, since she felt the same way. "Same with Pierce and Kitty missing class. I sure wish we knew where they were, and why he left that note."

"I do, too. It's puzzling."

Or worse, but Doro withheld the comment. Instead, she said, "Let's go to Flanders Hall and talk to Kitty's roommate. Maybe she knows something."

"If she's still here. A lot of students left campus, since classes are canceled indefinitely," Aggie pointed out.

"At least, let's try."

The friends found a few girls in the dormitory. Kitty's roommate was not among them, and no one else knew when or why she had left. A quick conversation with the cook revealed the girl had not appeared for her job in the cafeteria Tuesday morning and had not been in her room when another worker went looking for her.

"Has Kitty ever missed a shift before?" Doro asked.

Mrs. Fields, her plump face flushed from the heat of the oven, shook her head. "Never. I figured she must be ailing. But no. Not in her room, and no one has seen her. Her folks is in Toledo, so maybe she went home. I hope so. Hate to think she might be hurt, especially with a killer on the loose."

Although Doro hesitated to reveal details, she sought to allay the cook's fears. "I'm sure she's fine, and you're probably right about her heading into the city while school is closed." But the girl and her sweetheart had disappeared before then. Since her parents were not home, Kitty going there made no sense. A troubling fact.

"Plenty of the girls have gone home. Almost half. I still need to cook meals, but not for so many. Excuse me, I need to check the chickens." Mrs. Fields turned back to the stove. "These birds is done, and I got rolls almost ready. More than enough for the few still here. Why don't you two stay and eat? Got mashed potatoes and snap beans."

The wonderful aromas filling the area made Doro realize how hungry she was. "I wish we could, but we're meeting someone shortly."

"Take enough for her, too. I'll fix a basket. You can return it any time," the cook said.

Both Doro and Aggie were profuse in their thanks, but neither mentioned who they were meeting, which was apt to evoke questions. Ten minutes later, they left with two baskets. One with a whole chicken and potatoes, and another with rolls and a jar of beans. Mrs. Fields waved them off with a smile. Then, she returned to cooking.

When they were out of the dormitory, Doro took another appreciative whiff of the food. "Let's save some chicken for the pup that's been hanging around Wheaton Hall. Maybe we can entice the little furball to come inside. With the weather turning colder, it needs shelter."

"Good idea," Aggie agreed with a smile.

Chapter Seven

Instead of going to one of their apartments, the friends settled at a table in the reception area of Wheaton Hall after retrieving dishes and cutlery from the kitchen at the back of the first floor. They laid out plates and cutlery for three.

Once they began eating, Doro focused on the food but took covert glances at her watch. Mallow had promised to meet them at six o'clock. "Our new security officer is probably off on his own. I doubt if he shows up. Maybe he never planned to come. That wouldn't surprise me."

"He's only a half-hour late. He most likely got delayed some place, or he stopped to eat. Let's give him more time. Sharing information is the best way to solve the case quickly, and Officer Mallow wants that as much as we do."

"I suppose," Doro murmured, but she doubted if the man offered many revelations. "Just don't blurt out everything we know before he divulges some details."

Aggie pursed her lips. "Why do you have such a low impression of him? You said you understood why you were initially a suspect. Surely, you don't blame him for interrogating you."

"Of course not," Doro replied. "But I can't shake the feeling that Mallow will bend to Winwood's will, and I think our college president simply wants the murder solved in short order. Catching the real killer may not matter much."

"Winwood is overbearing, but I can't believe he'd be satisfied unless the actual killer is apprehended," Aggie said.

With a sigh, Doro leaned back in her chair. "He was quick to point the finger at me and several others."

Aggie drummed her fingers on the chair arms. "He'd undoubtedly like the culprit to be someone who has objected to his policies. As faculty advisor to YWV, you've crossed swords with him on more than a few occasions. And you grew up on campus, so people know and respect you. In Winwood's eyes, you must be a threat to his authority."

For several moments, Doro mulled over the idea. "Maybe so. I don't know many men on the Board of Trustees now." Sadness filled her as she considered the changes on campus and in Michaw. Many were wonderful. Some made her ache for the past.

Whatever else Doro might have revealed was cut off by Officer Mallow rushing into the room. "Sorry to be late. My boss at the bureau tracked me down, and I had to call him back right off. That turned into a long conversation." He shrugged out of his coat before collapsing into a chair.

Despite her misgivings about the man, Doro felt a surge of sympathy. "Does he want you to work again tonight?"

Mallow abruptly sat up straight. "I can't reveal information like that."

The edge in his voice made Doro regret her momentary softening. She lifted her chin. "Aggie and I aren't in league with bootleggers. We don't know any speakeasy owners or their customers, so we wouldn't be passing information on. Not that being aware of your work schedule with the Prohibition Bureau would give us details to share, since we have no idea of where you're going."

Dull color climbed into Mallow's lean cheeks as he briefly bowed his head. When he looked up, a rueful smile was on his lips. "Sorry. I wasn't insinuating either of you were involved in the illicit alcohol business. Or that you'd tell anyone I'm going on another raid." He leaned back in the chair and stuck his long legs out in front of him. "It's just that I was the youngest agent in my office for most of the past few years, so there's been a lot of scrutiny on me. As a result, I've been very cautious about telling anyone about my work hours. Back before my sister married, and we shared a place, she didn't even know."

"Wasn't she worried if you didn't come home at night?" Aggie asked.

"I worked a lot of different hours," Mallow replied. "But, yep. She fretted over me."

"Understandable," Doro put in.

"She married two years ago, so it was a short period when the two of us lived together. She was glad I took this job as a campus security officer."

Maybe that was part of Mallow's reason for being so serious and solemn. He didn't want to lose the job before his official start date. "We should go over what we've learned, so you can share everything with Constable Lammers in the morning," Doro said.

A harsh breath rumbled out of Mallow. "We won't be meeting in the morning. His mother took a turn for the worse, so she's been hospitalized in Toledo, and he's staying there overnight."

Both young women expressed their dismay.

"What about the children?" Aggie asked after a moment. "Mrs. Islington, Wade's aunt, doesn't have any available rooms, and caring for Davey with his broken arm would add a lot of work. She's much younger than the constable's mother, but one person can only do so much."

"The boy is still with Doc and Mrs. Silton," Mallow replied. "The older two were picked up by Mrs. Islington's oldest daughter. They'll stay with her and her family on the farm for a few days."

"Good," Doro put in. "Did you speak with Wade?"

Mallow shook his head. "I stopped at the constable's office. The clerk was there, and she passed the information along. Wade was worried about leaving me to investigate alone, but I asked her to tell him not to concern himself with the case when he calls again. His mother's health is more important."

Mallow's compassion touched Doro. Although her own mother's health had improved, Doro remembered the times when losing her had been a daily concern. Consumption was too often fatal. Heart disease was at least as serious. "You'll have your hands full, especially if you get called to work every night." Perhaps, Doro could leverage the unfortunate turn of events to become more involved in the case. "I know you want to solve the murder quickly."

"I need to figure it out as soon as possible," Mallow muttered, almost under his breath. "I can put in a couple more hours before I need to leave for the city, and I'll have all day tomorrow. With some luck, I won't have to work tomorrow night." Weariness roughened his voice.

Doro hesitated to voice her observation, so she put a place setting in front of him. "Mrs. Fields, the cook at the girls' dormitory, sent supper with us. There's enough for three, if you haven't eaten."

"I haven't, and it smells wonderful." He gave an audible sniff. "I was going to ask if you had extra."

"We definitely do. Help yourself." Aggie pointed to the platters and bowls of chicken, potatoes, beans, and rolls.

Mallow dug in. Between bites, he said, "This is delicious."

"Mrs. Fields is a fine cook. I miss her meals," Doro said with a sigh.

Mallow glanced at her. "You lived in the dormitory when you were in school?"

"I did. In fact, Aggie and I shared a room for three years."

"I miss those dormitory meals, too. Having my own little apartment is lovely, but our kitchenettes don't allow for real cooking." Aggie took another bite of chicken and smiled.

Doro nodded. "Not with a two-burner apartment stove and a tiny icebox. But it's lovely to have peace at the end of the day."

"Unless I visit," Aggie said with a grin.

"I enjoy your visits, and I come to your place as often as you come to mine," Doro observed.

"Visiting back-and-forth sounds nice," Mallow said between bites. "I'm not much of a cook, so the hot plate in my new apartment will suffice."

"Where will you be living?" Aggie asked.

"There's a loft over the garage at the president's house," he replied.

Dismay filled Doro. "It's been a storage area ever since I can remember."

"I was told that when I took the job," Mallow said. "It's been cleaned out and fixed up a bit. I've got a bed, a desk and chair, and a loveseat, along with a kitchenette of sorts."

"If you only have a hot plate, it's not much of a kitchen," Doro said.

He chuckled. "There are some shelves to store canned goods and such, but I can take my meals in the boys' dormitory. I hope the cook there is as good as Mrs. Fields."

"Almost as good, from what I hear," Aggie said.

After another swallow of potatoes, Mallow stifled a yawn. "Sorry. It's been a long day."

Once again, concern hit Doro. Not wanting to appear overly solicitous, she replied with care. "You have to rest sometime."

A rueful smile tugged at the corner of his mouth. "I don't think President Winwood agrees with that sentiment."

"Does he know about Mrs. Lammers being hospitalized?" Doro asked.

Mallow nodded. "I spoke with him on my way over, which is another reason I'm late. He wants the killer in jail as soon as possible. Evidently, he's gotten telephone calls from some trustees and a few parents. The pressure is on to ensure the campus is safe."

"On you," Doro suggested.

"Yep." He rubbed the back of his neck. "Constable Lammers will be back as soon as he can, which will help, and I appreciate the two of you sharing what you know."

"And we're glad you're willing to tell us what you've discovered," Doro said.

Mallow's fingers tightened on the fork. "Miss Banyon..."

Before he could say more, Aggie stepped in. "We should go over everything, so you can have a break before you need to leave." She turned to Doro. "Why don't you share what Mrs.

Gardner told us? Then, Officer Mallow can share what he's learned."

Doro repressed a smile at her friend's diplomatic, but significant, wording. She turned to the officer, who looked ambivalent. After several moments, he broke the silence.

"Sounds fine." Mallow pulled out his pad and pencil. "What did the operator say?"

"You made notes after we left, Doro, so why don't you give the details?" Aggie suggested.

While Doro had jotted everything down, she didn't need notes to go over the scant information. Even so, she pulled out her own pad and provided a summary. Mallow's reaction was a grimace. "Did you expect us to learn more?" she asked.

"I hoped you would. The operator could've told me that much, but she wouldn't." He pushed his plate away, clasped his hands together, and laid them on the table. Mallow looked from Aggie to Doro. "We haven't learned much new, either, but one detail needs to be confirmed. A couple of people saw Pierce and Kitty talking around seven o'clock yesterday morning. They were coming out of the back door of the library. When I asked President Winwood, he thought it didn't lock from the inside, so people could leave but not come in through it."

Anxiety knotted Doro's insides. "That's right. The witnesses are sure it was Pierce and Kitty?"

"Very sure," he replied.

After she and Aggie exchanged a long glance, Doro reluctantly shared what they had learned from Stanley and Mrs. Fields before summing up. "It's all circumstantial."

"Circumstantial?" Mallow echoed with a chuckle. "You have read a lot of mysteries,"

Doro was not sure if he was being snide or making an observation. "But it isn't solid proof."

"Maybe not, but you must know that circumstantial evidence often leads to arrest, prosecution, and conviction," Mallow replied.

A sigh escaped Doro. "I do."

"Neither of them has a key to the library," Aggie pointed out. "How would they have gotten inside?"

Mallow turned back to Doro. "You said Kitty and Pierce are in Professor Gibling's ten o'clock class. Could they also have been in Corlon's earlier class?"

"Neither one is taking a course from him this term," Doro replied.

"But it's not impossible for them to find out from someone else that his seminar was to meet in the library," Mallow suggested.

"No, it isn't. However, who would know he'd be there so early? I didn't expect him until eight o'clock," Doro pointed out.

With one hand, Mallow picked up his notepad, skimmed a couple of pages, and looked back at the two women. "Neither was where they should've been. When I spoke with Professor

Gibling yesterday, he said Pierce was supposed to meet him at the diner. That, Kitty not showing up for her job, their antipathy toward Corlon, and the two of them being seen at the library makes them suspects."

Although not happy to hear Kitty and Pierce were under intense scrutiny, Doro was glad Mallow had given up specific information. "Unless they followed Professor Corlon into the library, how would they have gained access?" As she spoke, another question occurred to her. Why had Winwood been in College Hall twenty minutes before she had seen him in front of the library? "When we talked to Professor Gibling, he mentioned seeing President Winwood yesterday morning shortly after seven." Mallow averted his gaze. For endless moments, Doro wondered if he would respond.

Finally, he looked directly at her. "The professor told me, as well. I asked the president about why he left College Hall and went back a short time later." Mallow cleared his throat. "When he got to his office, his pocket watch was missing, so he went to look for it."

The explanation matched what Mrs. Jones had revealed, so Doro let the point slide to the back of her mind. "Did he mention seeing Kitty and Pierce? The pair following Corlon seems far-fetched."

"Agreed," Mallow said, "but possible. From my travels around campus, I noted the library only has two doors: the one facing the front lawn and the other on the opposite side. Or did I miss something? Is there another way in?"

His observation had Doro reviewing the layout of the building. As she did, a memory asserted itself. "Not really. The library has a back door with access through an old tunnel from the lowest level of College Hall to a staircase leading to Founders Library. It's dank and dark, and use is discouraged by signs at both ends saying *No Admittance*. Kitty and Pierce may know about it, though. It's not a secret."

Mallow sat up straight. "Are both ends usually locked?"

"The doors don't have locks. At least, they didn't in the past. I haven't been to the basement level in years." Doro glanced at her friend. "Do you know?"

Aggie shook her head with animation. "No, I don't. I went down there and looked into the tunnel once when I started teaching here. That was enough."

"It is creepy," Doro agreed.

"If people are dissuaded from using it, why is it there?" Mallow asked.

"From what I know, the tunnel was built along with the library. It was supposed to be extended to what's now the male faculty residence building, so professors didn't have to walk in rain and snow," Doro said. "They could go from their rooms to their offices, and to classrooms and the library."

"But it wasn't extended?" Mallow asked.

"No. Most of the trustees thought the money would be better spent on erecting a men's dormitory and a residence for the president." Aggie added the information. "Doro knows more about the school, since she's been here all her life."

"But not from when the college was founded," Doro said with a trace of asperity. "The tunnel went in at the very beginning."

"You've heard all the stories, though," Aggie pointed out, "and you've shared many with me."

"I'd like to know more, and I definitely want to see the tunnel before I leave this evening," Mallow put in. "I can get into College Hall, since I have keys to all the buildings, but how do I get to the tunnel entrance?"

"I can show you," Doro offered. The likelihood of Kitty and Pierce using the tunnel seemed slim, but someone might have. Stanley Gibling, perhaps. Or President Winwood? Even Coach Ayers. Multiple possibilities existed.

For a moment, Mallow looked like he might object. "I'd appreciate that."

"You two go ahead." Aggie shivered and frowned. "From what I saw with my only glimpse, half the lights are out. The musty smell hit my nose right off, and the floor was filthy. There could be creepy, crawly things, too."

The image conjured by her friend's words had Doro cringing, but she was tagging along with Mallow, no matter what. "All right. Stay here where it's cozy, dry, and well-lit."

Aggie grinned. "I plan to snuggle in a chair by my fireplace. I'll wait there to hear what you discover."

"If anything," Doro remarked as she rose from her chair.

Mallow did the same, but he paused for a moment. "Do you think anyone will be in the building?"

"Most of the administrators don't stay this late even when classes are going," Aggie said. "No professors will be around because we've all been told to stay home."

"And the janitors were given time off, too," Doro added."

"Let's head over there," Mallow replied.

～☙～

On their way to College Hall, Mallow made a stop at his vehicle, a shiny Willys-Knight roadster. He reached into the glove box and pulled out a flashlight. "Since Miss Darwine said the tunnel isn't well-lit, this should help."

"I went with Aggie that time, and I didn't go into the tunnel, either. In fact, I've only been inside once when I was a little girl, and my dad showed it to me. There were sconces every twenty feet or so, but he took a flashlight, too. And I remember it being eerie then. I imagined monsters living there."

A low laugh left him. "How old were you?"

Doro smiled in return. "Eight. I'd pestered Dad to show me the place from the time I heard about the tunnel," she said as she led the way to the building. "Once was enough, though. The last time, Aggie and I only peeked inside."

When they reached the building's main door, he slid a key in and pushed it open. "Here you go." After Doro stepped inside, Mallow spoke again. "You don't actually have to head into the tunnel with me. You can point me in the right direction and stay up here while I poke around."

The suggestion held appeal, but what kind of sleuth didn't go digging for evidence? Not that she was a sleuth. Not exactly. "I'm not eight, so I can manage."

He studied her face. "If you're certain."

"I am." With that, Doro headed down the long corridor to the far end. They passed several offices, including the president's domain. As they did, Doro wondered if the security officer would report their findings to Winwood later. She also wondered how the president would feel about this foray. When they reached a large, metal door, she looked over her shoulder at Mallow. "The passage is at the foot of this staircase." At the entrance, Mallow swung the door open and let Doro continue to lead the way. When they reached the bottom, she stopped in the archway in the area between the steps and the tunnel.

"This is a cellar," Mallow commented as he halted beside her.

"It's only under part of the building. The custodians have a supply room, and some old items are stored in another room. The boiler is down here, along with a coal room." Doro gestured to the doors on both sides of the large space in the middle. "Here's the tunnel entrance."

"Let me get it." Mallow stepped ahead of her. As he swung the iron door open, the hinges creaked loudly. "Evidently, not many people come through here."

"Probably no one besides the janitors."

Mallow turned on the flashlight and focused the beam along the passageway. "Few of the sconces are lit. Your friend said half were, but it looks like more burned out since the two of you were here."

"It does," Doro agreed. "It's good you brought your flashlight." Although she had insisted the tunnel would not bother her, Doro gave an involuntary shudder. She wasn't eight, but she could imagine vermin in every nook. As they went forward, she focused on Officer Mallow's tall, lean figure. If something—or someone—jumped out at them, he would handle it. Almost immediately, Doro inwardly chastised herself for her fanciful meanderings. Nothing out of the ordinary would happen. Nothing at all.

After they got thirty feet down the passage, Mallow stopped and swung the flashlight from wall to wall. "There's another opening. Do you know where it goes?"

Doro peered into the shadows. Cobwebs, littering the ceiling, came as no surprise, but the break in the concrete did. "I don't recall seeing it."

"It's not very noticeable." Mallow turned sideways in order to enter the narrow egress.

"No, but you saw it."

"Coppers have to take special note of their surroundings."

"Good ones do, I'm sure." The words were a concession, albeit a small one.

"We all try our best," he replied, while keeping his attention on the passage.

After only a brief acquaintance, Doro was willing to admit Mallow was competent and diligent. At some future point, she might voice the opinion. For now, she stuck to their task. "It's hardly spacious," Doro said as she squeezed through the entrance behind him. Again, she followed the beam of light to see what was beyond. A wooden panel, which was set about fifteen feet down the constricted side corridor, came into view. "I wonder where that goes."

"Let's find out." Mallow moved forward as he spoke.

With her curiosity outweighing her trepidation, Doro followed him. The musty, moldy stench got worse as they approached the door. She struggled to keep from gagging. Aggie had been smart not to come along.

"You okay?" Mallow glanced over his shoulder at her.

"Sure." But she wasn't. Doro could hardly wait to get out of this cramped, smelly niche.

"Stand back. I'm going to open the door, and it swings this way."

She took two steps away from him as he yanked on the rusty handle. Once the door was ajar, Doro peered around Mallow. "Can you see where it goes?"

"There's a set of wooden steps just inside." He moved far enough for her to see.

"How strange," Doro murmured. "I've never heard anything about another set of steps. There's one under the library, but I thought it and the one we came down were the only ways between this level and the first floor."

"Evidently not." Mallow shone the light beam up the spiral staircase. "There's a narrow door. You're familiar with this building. What would be up there?"

For a moment, Doro considered the layout of College Hall. Surprise rippled through her as realization hit. "The President's office."

Mallow swiveled to face her. "I don't recall seeing an extra interior door there. Only the one from the outer office and a connecting door between the president's and provost's offices."

"Neither do I," Doro said. "I've only been in there once since Winwood took over. Prior to then, I was in the office several times every academic year. I would've noticed another door." In her mind's eye, Doro saw an image of the office. "One wall is all bookcases. Could one of them hide a secret passage?" When he didn't immediately reply, she hurried on. "I'm aware you don't have high regard for armchair sleuths, and I'll admit I've only heard of hidden hallways and such in books, but it is possible."

"Most definitely," he agreed.

His acquiescence was a welcome surprise. "Should we go up and see if we're right?"

A pause preceded his response. "Winwood should be gone."

The comment caught Doro off-guard, since they had already discussed the improbability of anyone being around now. "Even when things are normal, he wouldn't be in his office this late. We didn't see signs of anyone at all when we came in."

"All right. Let's look. I'd usually say *ladies first*, but I'd like to go ahead." He cleared his throat. "Just in case something creepy or crawly is around."

His voice held a lilt of humor, which made Doro chuckle. "Good idea."

Mallow's answer was to head up the creaky staircase.

Doro trailed after him until they reached a small landing at the top. Once again, she was glad he had a flashlight because it was the sole source of illumination.

"There's another door," Mallow muttered as he opened it. "And another small passageway." He went inside and held the door for Doro, who slipped into the space beside him.

"This hall is short at least," Doro said. Ten feet was between them and access to what had to be the president's office. Her pulse pounded at the thought. Could Winwood have used this route the previous morning? If so, why? This wasn't a propitious time to discuss the possibility, but she would bring it up when they got back to Wheaton Hall.

The officer pointed the flashlight down the little corridor. "We're getting closer."

He moved on, and so did Doro. "Is there a knob on this side?"

"There is." After opening the door, Mallow stepped back. "And a lever." With that, he pushed on the handle. Loud creaking ensued, but a large panel swung out to reveal President Winwood's office.

Since the sun had set, only faint twilight permeated the spacious room. The beam of the flashlight once again proved crucial.

Doro looked around, but saw nothing else unusual. Not that a mobile bookcase wasn't odd enough. "Let's push the panel shut and see if we notice any signs now that we know there's a secret passage."

Mallow swung the shelves back until a click sounded. Then, he moved to stand by Doro. "It's perfectly flush. If I didn't know the entire section opened, I'd never guess."

For a long moment, Doro studied the set of shelves. "I wouldn't, either. They look to be permanently attached to the wall, not a moving part. It's amazing."

"Like a priest hole from centuries ago in England."

The observation had Doro turning to face Mallow. "You know about priest holes?"

A grin curved his mouth. "I went to school, Miss Banyon."

"I did, too, but I didn't learn about priest holes in school. I learned about them in novels."

"Which is where I got my knowledge," he replied, his smile still in place. "I know how to read, and I love to do it. I only wish I had more time."

Learning he was a fellow book lover further eroded her antipathy, which had been constantly dwindling. "What books do you prefer?"

Several heartbeats passed before Mallow responded. "There's nothing like a good whodunit."

Doro stared at him in disbelief. "You enjoy playing armchair detective?" She didn't even try to keep the amusement from her voice.

A chuckle escaped the officer. "I do. When I was growing up, I devoured the Sherlock Holmes stories. It's part of why I became a copper. I love figuring out puzzles. Of course, real life detective work isn't quite the same."

"I wouldn't think so," Doro replied. "What about being a Prohibition agent? Does that involve much sleuthing?"

All amusement left his gaze, and his lips flattened. "Not for me. I mostly go where I'm sent after others figure out the locations of speakeasies, blind pigs, manufacturing places, or distribution points."

"Then, you raid them."

He nodded. "Yep."

"Which is what you did last night and what you'll do tonight."

He nodded again. "With that in mind, we need to move on. I've only got an hour before I have to leave for the city."

Anxiety clutched at Doro. Anxiety for him, she realized. He had a dangerous job, one that would end soon, but his life would be on the line again tonight. Briefly, she scanned his face. Not even the semi-darkness hid his exhaustion. He should have taken a nap. Since Doro doubted that he'd appreciate the admonition, and she had no right to offer it, she responded casually, "Of course. Maybe we should close the inside door and push the panel back before leaving from here. I'm afraid it won't shut completely from the other end." As soon as the words were out, Doro realized what they revealed—her lack of trust in Winwood. Hurriedly, she offered an excuse. "I wasn't planning to tell the president or others about what we found. I'll let Aggie know, but it might be best to not share the news more widely. At least for now."

"I agree."

Doro stared at him in what she felt sure was obvious shock. "You aren't telling anyone else?"

"No one except Lammers." Mallow's gaze narrowed on her. "You look stunned, Miss Banyon. Did you think I'd run right to Winwood?"

She shrugged. "He's your boss."

"He is, but he's not my conscience."

The words echoed endlessly in her mind as Doro grappled with their import. Aggie had been right about Mallow, while Doro had harbored skepticism. "I see," she said at last.

"I'm not sure you do, because you've obviously worried all along that I might hurry to solve the case in order to please Winwood." Mallow ran his free hand over his face. "As I've said, he has put pressure on me, and I'd want to wrap up quickly, even without that. Everyone, in town and on campus, is concerned about a killer being on the loose. Lammers and I agree the murder was probably personal, so most people aren't in danger. But they feel uneasy, and neither of us wants that. Still, folks won't be one bit safer if the wrong person is arrested. I want the killer behind bars. No one else."

His sincerity was obvious. "That's why you don't plan to tell President Winwood what we found." While Mallow's comments relieved her mind, they didn't explain why he'd keep knowledge of the secret passage from the college's top administrator.

"It's part of the reason," he replied.

"What's the other part?"

"You saw Winwood on your way to work yesterday morning."

"I did," she agreed. Had her suspicions somehow telegraphed themselves to the officer? Or did he have reasons for doubts of his own?

"You must have thought about whether or not Winwood had been in the library, especially since Professor Gibling saw him in College Hall only twenty minutes or so before you ran into him. And he made the excuse about losing his watch. All that creates uncertainty about him. Then, there's Corlon easing his stance on female students. With his niece scheduled to come for a visit, he wasn't apt to go back to supporting an all-male campus, but Winwood is set on the idea. He's mentioned it a couple of times."

The officer was revealing additional details, but Doro wondered about his perspective. What was his opinion? "Do you agree with him?"

"Not at all," was his fast and firm reply. "My sister has a college degree. I supported her in getting it. I've worked with female agents, and they do a great job. I'm not a man who thinks women need to stay home and raise a family. Since the Great War, times have changed. Women have the vote, as they should. Many have careers. More will in the future."

"Did you mention any of that to President Winwood?"

"No, but he didn't ask for my opinion. He and the others didn't reveal their plan to remove women from campus until I got here a couple of days ago. I promised my sister I'd leave the Bureau before the end of the year, so I'm careful about what I say. I figured on looking for something else, if big changes occur at this college. I don't want to work with people determined to turn back the clock."

His revelations eased Doro's mind enough for her to make a more direct comment. "It still seems unlikely Winwood or Pottiger killed Corlon, and Jerritt went out of town on Sunday."

"Jerritt has never been under scrutiny for that reason." Mallow took a breath before hurrying on. "Another concern is Winwood pushing Kitty and Pierce as suspects. Innocent people may have important information, but he's been eager to scrutinize others. As for the young couple, there are other details putting them in a bad light."

Doro shoved her hands into her pockets. "I can't disagree, but I know them, and it's hard to believe they'd kill anyone."

"Remember, the card catalogue drawer is a weapon of opportunity."

"It's a weird weapon," Doro murmured.

"True. Not only that, whoever wielded it had to use a fair amount of force. That points to lashing out, maybe without forethought."

"So, maybe the killer wanted to injure or scare Professor Corlon."

"Possibly." Mallow studied her face for a moment. "When I interviewed you, you mentioned that President Winwood was in a hurry. The bad weather could've been why. But did he seem upset in any way? Flustered, unnerved?"

For a moment, Doro considered what she had witnessed the previous morning. "He's always somewhat abrupt with me. And critical. I mostly focused on defending myself." As always.

"I see."

His thoughtful expression made Doro wonder what he saw. "The case is more complicated than I figured at first."

A rueful smile moved his lips. "At first, you thought it was an accident."

"I hoped it was. Professor Corlon was short, not much taller than Aggie. If he pulled the drawer out too fast, it could've hit him in the head. Maybe not with enough force to kill him, but murder didn't come immediately to mind."

"Even though you teach a course on murder mysteries?" His question held a note of amusement.

"Most of the books involve homicides, but a few don't," Doro said. "Besides, actually finding a body is disturbing. At first, I didn't want to believe he was dead."

"That's understandable," Mallow replied in a soft, sympathetic tone. "Let's get this area restored to normal and move on."

While she helped him put the door and bookcase back in place before leading the way out of the office suite, Doro made an observation. "Sounds like you have several suspects."

Mallow's gaze narrowed on her. "Are you asking who they are?"

"I could guess."

"You could."

"Would you tell me if I'm right?" she asked.

He shifted from one foot to the other. "You aren't a law officer."

Doro rolled her eyes. "I know that. I'm an armchair detective, and you'd prefer I stay in my chair."

Laughter rumbled out of him, and his silver eyes shone with humor. "You don't seem like the type to stay next to the fire and ruminate or read."

Doro put her hands on her hips. "Is that a compliment?"

"It is."

Optimism made Doro grin at him. "So, who's on your list?"

He waved one hand in the air. "Sorry, I need to keep that confidential."

Her optimism deflated like a pierced balloon, and her smile flattened like a bad tire.

"I've shared a lot of information, which I probably shouldn't have done," Mallow hurried to say, "but you and Miss Darwine have been helpful, and I appreciate it."

The admission went a little way in muting her annoyance. "All right. I understand. Where to now?"

"I still want to see where the tunnel leads."

"Let's go." Maybe he would not reveal his suspect out right, but Mallow was sharing tidbits. And he might let even more slip.

Chapter Eight

In short order, they were back in the passageway. "Before we go, let me make sure the door on this side is the way it was."

"Good idea," Doro replied. While Mallow climbed the steps, she waited at the bottom.

Before heading to the main tunnel, he paused. "I'd sure like to know how many people realize there's a little passage from the president's office to the tunnel."

"Me, too," Doro said. "I never heard anything about it. Winwood must know. Pottiger, too. The janitors come to the basement regularly, so they might."

"And they might've told others." Mallow released a long, low breath. "Mrs. Jones could be aware it's here."

Doro's stomach clenched. "She wouldn't kill anyone. Besides, she has an alibi witness because her neighbor dropped her at work shortly after seven o'clock."

"I know. I spoke with the man, and he confirms those facts," Mallow replied. "But I wasn't fingering her as a suspect. I'm wondering if she has some idea of who else knows about the secret panel and has access to the president's office."

The explanation relieved Doro's mind. "The janitors would, but they wouldn't be around early in the morning. They come to work at noon and leave around nine in the evening. Besides, what motive would either one have?"

"None that Wade or I could find, and we checked to make sure they had alibis, which they do. I just want to cover all the bases. Maybe you could ask Mrs. Jones about anyone else who might have access. I'd do it if I wasn't working my other job tonight."

"I'll be happy to ask her," Doro replied.

"Great. Now, let's get going."

Ten minutes later, Doro and Mallow were inside the library. Getting out of the cramped, clammy tunnel made her breath more easily. Since only one light was left on overnight, the area laid in shadows. But it was a familiar area. "The back door is here." Doro pointed to the right.

Mallow, who had gotten the flashlight from her in the tunnel, focused the beam in the same direction before surveying the entire space, which was narrow. "Do students and faculty enter this way?"

"No, it's used for deliveries, mostly. Sometimes, boxes get put here. Like now." Doro gestured toward three crates sitting against a wall. "The card catalogues are through that door."

"I'd like to take another look."

Doro led the way and pointed toward the catalogues. "Someone who came this way would've been close to where I found the body."

"True." The officer took a few steps before stopping again.

"If Professor Corlon was checking the catalogue, his back would've been to the tunnel door and to the circulation desk. He might not have even heard his attacker." She turned toward Mallow. "Do you think the killer came in this back way?"

"It's a possibility. Since there were puddles near the front door and back here, we know some person came in, or out, or both through the two places." Mallow made a 360-degree turn. "Corlon could've come in the front. His attacker might've followed him and left out the back. Or the killer entered on this side and left on the other. It's hard to know for sure without more witnesses or evidence. I want to speak with Coach Ayers in the morning. He might reveal something important."

"As a witness or as a suspect?" Doro asked.

Mallow shrugged. "Not sure which yet."

His answer provided food for thought. "I hadn't considered the killer coming in the back and going out the front. Kitty and Pierce wouldn't be able to do that. At least, not easily, since neither has a key. The same with Coach Ayers."

"True, but any of them could have a lock pick."

The statement surprised Doro. "I've read mysteries where one was used. Is that common in real life?"

Mallow shook his head. "Not common, but it happens. Ayers has locked himself out of the locker room on multiple occasions, so he may have one. Evidently, he's lost his keys, and Winwood doesn't want him to get another set."

"Interesting," Doro murmured. And troubling on two counts. For one, she liked the coach, but he was well-known for his hot temper, especially where his players' eligibility was involved. For another, the president refusing to give Ayers another set of keys indicated hostility. Could he be trying to provoke the coach? If so, to what end?

"It's definitely something to keep in mind. But so is the likelihood that Corlon and his killer argued. Like I said, clues point to the murder not being planned, so a lockpick being used isn't at the top of my list of possibilities."

Since Mallow had shared so much, Doro pursued a deeper examination of the evidence. The officer might balk, but he might open up even more. "You know Aggie and I talked to Stanley Gibling, and what he told us about seeing President Winwood. You didn't comment much on that." With the heel of one hand, he rubbed his temple. Doro wondered if he was fighting a headache, fatigue, or both.

Mallow took a deep breath before responding. "As you know, he said the same to Lammers and me, but I'm not sure I believe him on the time element. In any case, Winwood has claimed a reason for retracing his steps. He said his watch chain broke a few days ago and, when he pulled it out to check the time, he didn't get the timepiece back in his pocket. With a loose chain, it fell to the ground."

"And he found it."

"He did," Mallow said. "I've seen the watch and the chain, which is broken."

"So, Winwood isn't a suspect." Doro couldn't keep the disappointment from her voice.

"I wouldn't go that far. After all, he could've broken the chain at any point and never lost his watch at all. Before I'd move him to the top of my list, I need more evidence. On the other hand, he isn't in the clear, which is why I don't want to turn lights on. He might be able to see that from his residence."

Doro had thought the same thing, so she hadn't balked at using only the flashlight.

"The hidden door and tunnel may be important, or not." Mallow paused a heartbeat before saying, "It won't come as a surprise to you that Professor Gibling is a top suspect."

A sigh escaped Doro. "No, it's not a surprise." Should she reveal Stanley's outburst and anger? Not yet. Surely, he wasn't the killer. Doro posed another question designed to take a different direction. "What about your talk with Mrs. Jones? Did she mention Winwood unlocking the doors for her very early? Long before I saw him."

He nodded. "She did, and so did he—even before I asked."

"When I saw President Winwood at seven-thirty, he was on his way to his office. After I found Professor Corlon and called,

Winwood was furious about me interfering with his planning for a meeting."

"I've noted that." Mallow moved toward the library's back door. "I want to look around here a little more. Hold on to the flashlight while I move the crates."

"They were in the same place yesterday morning," Doro said, as she took the lamp.

"Even so, it won't hurt to check things out."

While Mallow shoved the crates away from the wall, Doro kept the beam on the area. When something shiny reflected back, she murmured, "I wonder what that could be."

"Let's find out." Mallow crouched down and picked the item up. When he rose, the officer extended his hand.

Doro studied the object in his palm. "It's a cufflink."

"I don't suppose it looks familiar to you."

Uneasiness plagued Doro as she reached for the sterling silver jewelry. "There are initials on it."

Mallow bent his head. "There are. In a very fancy script, which makes it hard to discern the letters."

Doro stared at the inscription. "SPG. Stanley Palmer Gibling."

"He's the only one on campus with that monogram?" Mallow asked.

"Maybe not, but Aggie gave those to him last Christmas, when she figured he was going to propose. He never did, but at the time, I went into the city with her to pick them up."

His sharp intake of breath echoed in the room. "You're sure this is one of them?"

"Very sure," Doro said, but she wished she wasn't. For several moments, she struggled to regain her composure. Now, she had to reveal all of what Stanley had said a few hours earlier. After she finished, Doro ended with, "I should've told you, but despite his anger, I couldn't believe Stanley would kill Corlon. Or anyone."

A moment preceded Mallow's response. "Understandable. He's a colleague and your friend's former beau."

"Maybe so, but it's important to the case, just like this cufflink is." She chewed on her lip.

"I'm surprised the janitors didn't find it when they cleaned Monday night," Mallow put in.

"They were focusing on the public part of the library. This back area got spruced up before the semester started. It's impossible to keep neat during the term." She handed the cufflink back to Mallow.

"Does Professor Gibling have a key to the library?" he asked.

"No, he doesn't."

Mallow glanced around the small space again. "Does he ever come back here?"

The question made Doro pause. "He was here before classes started, because we ordered some books for him. Stanley had the janitors haul most of them to his office, but he took a couple of copies himself."

"The term began about six weeks ago, didn't it?"

"Yes," she replied.

"Is it possible the cufflink wouldn't be discovered in all that time?"

Doro stared into the corner. "These crates weren't here then, but others were. Those were hauled off. Considering how far in the corner it was, I'm not surprised it wasn't noticed."

Mallow swung the flashlight around. "Gibling could've followed Corlon in the front door and left this way. If the two struggled, the clasp could've gotten caught on something and fallen off as Gibling ran out."

Although Doro hated to consider that scenario, she had to be honest. "If Stanley was here, that seems most likely."

"I'll talk with him again, but it'll have to be tomorrow." After checking his wristwatch, Mallow went on. "I don't have a lot of extra time. I'll walk you back to your residence before I get on the road."

"You don't need to do that."

His expression grew solemn. "There's a killer on the loose. It's dark, and many people know you're digging into the case. Ease my mind by letting me escort you home."

The reasoning left little room for complaint, so Doro led the way out of the library with the officer at her side. Normally, she enjoyed walking around the campus at any time of the day or night. The post lights, spaced at twenty-foot intervals, gave a warm glow, but shadows were on each side of the path. Deep shadows where a killer could hide. A shiver rippled through Doro.

"Are you cold?" Mallow asked.

Because she didn't want to admit her anxiety, Doro hurried to agree. "A little, but we're almost there." When they reached Wheaton Hall, she turned to Mallow. "Before you leave, why don't I try to call my friend, the one who lives near the Tensengs' store? The connection shouldn't take longer than thirty minutes."

Mallow glanced at his watch again. "All right. I can wait that long."

Doro went to the wall phone, lifted the earpiece, and waited for the operator to come on the line. After explaining her task, Doro hung up and glanced at Mallow. "She says to wait nearby for a few minutes. She may get through quickly. A couple of earlier calls to the city did."

"All right," he replied.

"Let's sit on the bench." Doro suggested that primarily because the officer looked ready to drop. How he could drive to town, take part in a raid, make arrests, and come back by morning, Doro didn't know.

He nodded and crossed the wide hall to where an upholstered bench sat. A sigh left Mallow as he settled back and thrust his long legs out in front of him.

Before joining him, Doro made another recommendation. "There are usually cookies or cupcakes in the kitchen. During the day, they're in the main reception room, but whatever's left gets put away. Some milk is often in the icebox, too."

"Sounds good," he replied, "but don't go to any trouble. I had a wonderful dinner, thanks to you and Miss Darwine. And Mrs. Fields."

"It's no trouble." Doro hurried off and returned within moments. "Here you go." She handed him a plate of cookies and a tall tumbler of milk. "I'm afraid it's not as cool as it could be, because most of the ice has melted, so one of us will have to fetch some from the icehouse tomorrow. We were supposed to get electric refrigerators last year, but President Winwood nixed the idea."

After expressing his thanks, the officer bit into a cookie and followed it with a slug of milk. "Very good," he said with a smile. "There's an electric refrigerator in the president's house. I was there when he showed me the garage apartment. I had the impression the faculty residence buildings have them, too."

Another wave of annoyance swept through Doro. "Madden Hall, where male faculty live, got electric appliances, as planned. Updates to the women's areas are on hold."

"I suppose I shouldn't be surprised. But wouldn't men move in here if all women leave campus?"

"I'm sure they would," Doro replied, "and I'm equally sure Winwood would immediately do modernization." The ringing of the telephone interrupted, so she hopped up.

Mallow, another cookie and the glass in his hands, trailed after her. Doro breathed a sigh of relief when her friend came on the line. While she posed her questions and listened, Doro noted the officer watching her intently. As soon as she hung up, she would share additional details with him. Maybe important details. After saying goodbye, Doro turned to Mallow. "Alice says the Tenseng grocery is closed for several days, because Mrs. Tenseng's mother died. She lives on a farm near here. As far as Kitty, Alice thinks she might've gone straight to her grandmother's home. Unfortunately, she doesn't know Mrs. Tenseng's maiden name, but the homestead is outside Richfield Center."

"We could place a call to the operator there. It's a little village, isn't it?"

Doro nodded. "Yes, so the operator is apt to know Mrs. Tenseng. Let me put in a call now."

"Great."

While Doro spoke with the local operator, Mallow went back to get another cookie from the plate he'd left on the bench. After hanging up, she joined him. "This connection is apt to take longer. While we're waiting, why don't I run upstairs and make coffee? I have a flask you can borrow, if you want to take some with you."

For a moment, she thought he'd turn the offer down, but he nodded. "That sounds good."

"I'll be right back."

When she returned, Doro had a mug and a flask. "Here you go."

A bright smile lit his face. "I really appreciate this. I planned to stop for coffee on my way to work. This will give me a little more time, and I'd like to hear if Kitty and Pierce can be located.

It won't eliminate them as suspects, but at least we'll know they didn't run off to parts unknown."

Doro would be relieved to have that possibility removed, too. Their sudden, unexplained disappearance made them look guilty. While they waited, she and Mallow chatted about casual matters. When the telephone rang twenty minutes later, Doro jumped up to answer. Mallow kept his attention on her, especially when she hung up.

"Well?" he asked.

"Kitty and Pierce arrived in Richfield Center yesterday around noon. The operator actually saw the pair getting out of his vehicle. They stopped at the general store for a few items, which is where the switchboard is. She also said the funeral is tomorrow morning at eleven. The kids will head back in the afternoon. Like most little villages, everyone knows a lot about everyone else."

"Not a bad thing. I want to talk with them, but I'll be here before they are." He laid his empty mug on the tray and picked up the flask. "I appreciate this."

"Of course," she murmured. Doro cleared her throat. "I'll discuss everything with Aggie tonight and get her opinion, and I'll talk with Mrs. Jones tomorrow morning."

His gaze lingered on her. "That's fine, but be careful asking questions or even being out alone, especially after dark. If the killer knows you two are digging into the case, he might get nervous." He shoved his hands into his jacket pockets and rocked back on his heels. "Even worse, you've been seen with me. I should've considered that earlier."

The look of contrition on his face convinced Doro to offer reassurances. "Neither Aggie nor I will go out until tomorrow morning. After you leave, I'll lock the front door behind you. The other women have keys, and the back door is already secured. I checked when I was in the kitchen."

Mallow nodded. "Just to be safe, could you and Miss Darwine spend the night together? You said some of the women left campus, since classes are canceled. Being alone in an apartment with fewer people around...well, it might not be a good idea."

Although Doro thought he was worrying needlessly, she agreed to his suggestion. "Aggie's floor is still filled. I'd be the only one on mine tonight, so I'll grab some things and head to her place."

Relief took some of the tension from his face. "Great. When I get back to campus tomorrow, I'll check with you and let you know if Constable Lammers will be on the case. We still don't know how Miss Tenseng and young Dudley got word of her grandmother's death. It's bothersome she wasn't at work, and he didn't meet Gibling."

Although those points nagged at the back of her mind, Doro aimed for a positive response. "They'll undoubtedly explain when we talk with them."

"I suppose so." He slipped his cap on. "Have a good night, Miss Banyon."

"You, too, Officer Mallow, and be careful."

His expression was unreadable, but he nodded. "I will."

After the door closed behind him, Doro slid the bolt into place but did not immediately turn around. Instead, she laid her palm against the smooth wood and murmured, "I hope you are, Officer Mallow, because I think you're going to make a better campus security man than I figured at first."

Chapter Nine

The next morning, Doro woke early, mostly because sleeping on Aggie's loveseat had not led to solid rest. As she swung her feet to the floor and stretched out, she groaned. Staying with her friend might have been a strong safety measure, but Doro wasn't sure she'd do it again. Not that discomfort had been the only impediment. Going over and over clues had kept her mind churning. And, if she was honest, so had fretting about Officer Mallow. Going after bootleggers was fraught with hazards, and Doro didn't enjoy thinking about him being in harm's way.

Aggie appeared just as Doro finished stacking the bedding on the footstool. Her friend frowned. "You look tired. Did you sleep at all?"

"A little."

"You should've taken the bed, and I could've slept out here. I'm shorter than you, and I wouldn't need to scrunch up as much."

"It wasn't only that. I kept thinking about the murder." The previous night, Doro had shared what she and Mallow discovered, along with their plans to investigate further. "After we dress and eat, we could call Mrs. Jones. I'd like to talk with her about the secret passage, Winwood's meetings, and such."

"We already decided she must not know about the hidden door, or she would've mentioned it."

Doro perched on the edge of the loveseat. "I'm sure that's right, but I told Officer Mallow I'd check."

A grin lifted Aggie's lips. "You two work well together."

Warmth rose in Doro's face, but she kept her voice cool. "Since Wade is busy with his mother, Mallow needs help. He appreciates you and me pitching in."

Aggie's smile stayed in place. "All right, but shouldn't we wait for Officer Mallow? He's probably back from his other job."

A knot formed in Doro's stomach. Was he? She had no way to find out, and he wasn't apt to report his return to her. But he had promised to talk this morning. Exactly when, she did not know. "We may hear from him by the time we're ready to leave." Her voice sounded normal, didn't it? Too bad she felt so uneasy. All too often, gangsters engaged in violent confrontations with each other and with coppers. Little wonder Mallow's sister wanted him in a safer occupation. Doro barely knew him, and she did, too.

The pair took turns in the apartment lavatory before having toast and coffee. Doro kept listening for a knock at the door, but none came, which increased her apprehension. Where was Mallow? The previous morning, he had been back before now. Aggie's voice broke into her errant thoughts.

"You look far away. Are you thinking about Corlon's murder?" Her friend paused for a heartbeat. "Or Mallow?"

Heat again climbed into Doro's cheeks. "The case, of course."

A low chuckle left Aggie.

"I am," Doro said too quickly and too defensively. "I hope Mallow lets us know when he's back. With Constable Lammers out of commission most of yesterday, Mallow needs our assistance."

Aggie's expression grew solemn. "I hope Mrs. Lammers improves soon. She's had several bouts with her heart."

Doro laid one hand on Aggie's arm. Her friend's mother died a while after rheumatic fever had damaged her heart. Mrs. Lammers' issues were different, but the outcome might be the same. "Her doctor has told her not to overdo, but she does. Running a boardinghouse and helping with her grandchildren keep her busy. Some rest will help, I'm sure. She and the constable may both be back soon."

"Probably so." Aggie finished her coffee and stood up. "I'll wash up the dishes, and we can go."

Normally, Doro would have insisted on helping, but her friend might need a few minutes alone to regroup. Although Doro only saw her mother and father during summer vacations, she still had them. Besides, her grandmother was nearby in Sylvania, and Aggie was as close as any sister could be. She hoped her friend's spirits were buoyed by their connection. Being alone would be a sore trial.

Within minutes, Aggie was back in the parlor with a smile on her face. "Let's go down and call Mrs. Jones."

Both young women grabbed their coats and headed to the staircase. Doro stopped abruptly when they reached the entry, and she heard a noise at the front door. Was it a knock? Or someone trying to pick a lock? Or both? "Wait," she whispered to Aggie. Doro took several long, deep breaths. Probably another resident had gone out early and was returning, because the sound of a key in the lock became clear. Even so, Doro stood stock-still as the door opened. Relief spread through her when Officer Mallow stepped inside.

"I knocked. When no one came to the door, I used my key," he said.

"Come in." Doro stepped back. As she looked more closely, alarm hit her. Mallow, leaning heavily on a cane, limped inside. "What happened to you?"

A rueful grin pulled up the corners of his mouth. "I impeded a bullet. It's a flesh wound, but the doctors suggested using the cane today."

His reassuring, light-hearted words were at odds with his drawn features, heavily shadowed eyes, and dark stubble. Yesterday morning, he'd looked weary. Now, he appeared to be fighting exhaustion and pain. His hand gripped the walking stick so tightly, his knuckles showed white. Not to mention his slow progress, which indicated the cane was a necessity, not merely a recommendation. "I see," Doro replied.

"Why don't we sit down while we talk?" Aggie asked. "You can rest your leg for a bit. Have you eaten breakfast?"

He nodded. "I grabbed something at the hospital. Since Mrs. Lammers is a patient there, I talked with Wade while we both ate."

"Then, you can update us on her condition, too." Aggie led the way into the reception room and took a seat in the closest group of chairs.

Mallow followed. As did Doro. When he levered himself into a seat, the officer briefly caught his lower lip between his teeth. Doro bit back a query about the exact nature of his wound. They were on friendlier footing than two days ago, but too much concern would be unseemly and, most likely, unwanted.

"Mrs. Lammers had another heart attack, and she's not out of danger yet. Wade plans to stay today and tonight. He'll keep his aunt and sister updated as much as he can. They'll let me know when he'll be back at work." While he spoke, Mallow rubbed his leg.

"So, you're on your own as far as the investigation." Aggie made the observation.

Mallow let his hand rest on his thigh. "It appears so."

"Does President Winwood know about Constable Lammers not being able to help you?" Doro asked.

"Not yet, but he wasn't enthusiastic about involving the local lawman. I had to explain to him that, as a campus security officer, I won't overrule the town constable, even when a crime occurs at the college." His brow furrowed, as if the idea troubled him. "Constable Lammers is a good man, and he's fine with me having status as a deputy of sorts. As for now, I'm still authorized as a federal agent, which gives me extra leeway. I'd rather not make an arrest without Lammers, but I could."

Doro blinked in surprise and confusion. "Have you narrowed your number of suspects down?" Not that she knew the exact length of his list.

"I'm afraid not, and that's my biggest problem," Mallow replied. "I stopped to speak with Stanley Gibling again on my way here. His landlady agrees about the time he left, which doesn't clear him. More information is necessary, and I may need to enlist help to get it."

Mallow's observations sounded casual. Was it? Who would he enlist? Dare she ask? Aggie's next words kept Doro from giving the questions more consideration.

"Who's going to assist you, Officer?"

His gaze moved from Aggie to Doro, while he cleared his throat. "You two have already asked questions of people and gotten solid information."

When he did not continue, Doro took a sidelong look at Aggie, who appeared to be fighting a smirk. Since she did the same thing, Doro kept her face averted as she spoke. "Is that a question, a statement, or a suggestion?"

Mallow let his head fall back against the wall. "All three, I suppose. I'm in a pickle, and we all know it." He gripped the head of his cane. "Walking everywhere isn't doable and repeatedly shoving in the clutch is a bit of a problem, too."

The admission came haltingly. Mallow would permit their involvement because, as he said, he was *in a pickle*. With effort, Doro repressed a triumphant smile. "We'll be happy to help you."

"We will," Aggie agreed.

Amusement sparkled in his eyes. "I thought you might."

When his reserve flagged, the man was quite appealing. Doro quickly pushed that errant thought aside. "So, what you do you want us to do? Besides chat with Mrs. Jones."

"I want to talk with Coach Ayers," Mallow replied, "and having one of you drive me to his house would be great. I know it's south of the football field, and that's a jaunt."

"I could drive you over," Doro said. "Are you calling first or surprising him?" Privately, she thought catching the man off-guard would be better.

When Mallow replied, he revealed the same strategy. "I plan to just show up. Of course, he may not be there. He wasn't yesterday. No one was, so maybe he and his family went away."

"His children are in grade school, so I doubt they all took off," Aggie put in. "It's possible he drove his wife and mother-in-law into Sylvania on some errands."

"With luck, he'll be home today." Mallow shifted to face Aggie. "Do the residents here come downstairs much? To socialize in the reception area or use the kitchen?"

"Most of us keep some items in the big icebox," Aggie replied, "so people come before preparing meals. Yesterday, I heard a group ate lunch together down here, and several came after you two went to College Hall. I'd already eaten, so I didn't stay."

"Could you join them today, if anyone comes down?" Mallow asked. "You might hear something useful."

"Sure," Aggie agreed.

"What other plans do you have?" Doro asked Mallow. Would he talk with President Winwood and the others again? Interrogating them would be tricky, but a few questions were in order. Pointed questions.

"Talking with Pierce and Kitty is important, but they won't be back until this afternoon. I don't have a telephone in my apartment, so I'll have to check in at his boardinghouse and her dormitory," Mallow said.

Doro shifted toward Aggie. "Would you mind if Officer Mallow asked Pierce's landlady and the housemother at Larson Hall to call here when the pair return?"

"Not at all. I can stay downstairs all day," Aggie said. "I'll run up and get my writing materials, along with a couple of books. Since it's chilly, I can start a fire and relax in the reception room."

"Let me get the blaze going," Mallow offered. "It's the least I can do, since you're willing to stay down here instead of in your own place."

"That's very kind of you," Aggie said.

Doro agreed. Mallow was definitely showing his best side. Maybe it was his true nature shining through. Time would tell. "Anything else we should go over?" Doro asked.

"Not right now," he replied. "We can check back here around lunchtime."

The two friends concurred. After Aggie retrieved her things from upstairs, she settled by the reception area's hearth, where a cheerful fire flickered. "This is perfect. I'll be cozy and comfy."

For a moment, Doro envied her friend. Snuggling by the fireplace seemed like a lovely way to spend a chilly fall day. But such a luxury would not solve Corlon's murder.

※

A cold gust of air hit Doro as soon as she stepped outside. With one hand, she tugged her coat collar closer around her neck while the other clutched her pocketbook.

"I assume you know how to drive," Mallow remarked as they headed toward his Willys.

"I do, and I have my vehicle parked right over there." She pointed to an Essex Roadster.

"Very sporty," Mallow said with a trace of awe in his voice.

Pride swelled Doro's heart. "She is a splendid vehicle. My pride and joy."

"She?" His dark brows lifted a fraction.

Doro shrugged. "That's how I think of her. It. My parents bought her for me when I went to Ann Arbor to get my master's degree."

A thoughtful expression blanketed his face. "Does the head librarian have a graduate degree?"

"In English, yes. In library science, no. It's not a common advanced program yet." As she watched his reaction, Doro wondered what he was thinking. His next words provided a clue.

"Winwood and his group want to eliminate more qualified women and keep less qualified men?"

"My boss does a good job," she hurried to say. "Mr. Quartine is fair-minded and well-versed in library operations. He's fought hard against the proposed changes."

"Which doesn't address my point."

"The Fearsome Foursome doesn't care about credentials. They think women belong at home."

"Fearsome Foursome?" he echoed.

Heat scorched Doro's cheeks as she realized the derogatory nickname had slipped out. "Sorry. It's what some of us call Winwood, Corlon, Pottiger, and Jerritt."

For a long moment, he gazed at her. Finally, his lips twitched. "An interesting moniker, but we've learned Corlon might've changed his mind. Another point to be further explored. Now, we better get on the road. Lead the way to your vehicle. She looks ready to roll."

The undercurrent of amusement in his voice had Doro grinning. "I'm sure she is."

Within a few minutes, Doro pulled to a stop in front of a rambling white frame two-story home. "Here we are."

As the pair got out, Mallow gestured to the side of the house, where a black sedan was parked. "Does that automobile belong to the coach?"

"It does. The Ayers family only has one vehicle, so they must be home," Doro said as she went to stand beside him. "Or Coach walked to his office, but that seems unlikely since we were told to take time off."

"Would he do as he was told?"

Doro shrugged. "Maybe not, especially since the order came from President Winwood. As you know, Coach Ayers had run-ins with him and Professor Corlon."

A nod was Mallow's response. "Let's see if he's here." Mallow let Doro precede him on the porch steps, but he reached around her to rap on the door. Within a moment, two voices—one male, one female—could be heard, although the words could not.

When the exchange ended, footsteps sounded, and the door swung open to reveal a tall man in his forties. His gaze went from Doro to Mallow. "What do you two want?"

The question reverberated with annoyance and matched his harsh expression. Doro, who had known the man for several years, knew this was his typical attitude toward uninvited guests. "Coach Ayers, I don't know if you've met Mr. Mallow yet, but he's the new campus security officer."

"Heard you were looking for me." Ayers folded his arms over his broad chest as he addressed Mallow.

"I have been," the officer replied. "I'd like to talk with you. It shouldn't take long."

The coach's attention went to Doro. "Why are you here?"

"I gave Officer Mallow a ride," Doro replied.

Ayers glanced at the cane in Mallow's hand. "Get hurt?"

"A minor injury," the officer replied. "Like I said, I have a few questions for you."

For a moment, Doro thought Ayers would refuse. Then, he stepped back and led the way to a small office off the front hall. The coach settled behind the paper-strewn desk, leaned back in his chair, and propped his feet up. "Fire away."

Since two Windsor chairs faced Ayers, Doro and Mallow sat down, despite not being invited to do so. The officer stuck his wounded leg out in front of him before retrieving his notepad and pencil from his pocket. "It's my understanding you and Professor Corlon argued on multiple occasions."

A snort left Ayers. "Anyone on campus could tell you that." His attention went to Doro. "They could also tell you about Miss Banyon and her dislike of Corlon. In fact, most every female on campus had it in for him. Not that I blame the girls. He, Winwood, Pottiger, and Jerritt were set on getting rid of them. At least that's been the campus gossip. I don't know where else so many females could work. As for the coeds, they could find other schools easier. It wouldn't surprise me if one of the lady professors or librarians acted before any policy change was made."

The thinly veiled accusation sent anger hurtling through Doro. How dare the man turn the tables and put her, and the other women on campus, in the hot seat? And she was the only female librarian, which raised her hackles. Doro was about to fling a sharp retort when Mallow spoke.

"I deal with facts, Coach Ayers, and the facts point away from Miss Banyon and most other women who work on campus. However, they don't eliminate you."

The bold assertion made Doro want to smile, and it made Ayers squirm. Good. He deserved to feel the heat.

"I didn't kill the man," Ayers said in a far less cocky tone.

"Then, answer my questions, so I can eliminate you as a suspect." Mallow spoke with authority and insistence.

The coach's jaw tightened and his eyes narrowed. After a moment, he gave a curt nod. "Like I said, fire away."

"I've heard your usual routine involves a long walk around campus. Often, you're out-and-about by six-thirty. Were you on Tuesday morning?" the officer asked.

"It was cold and rainy," Ayers replied.

"I know, but that doesn't answer my question." Mallow stared steadily at the other man.

Ayers's shifted until his feet were on the floor and his hands were on the desk's edge. "I walked my usual route, which takes me past the library. I got that far around quarter to seven. Didn't see a soul, although a light was on in the back. That's not unusual, though, so I kept going. I cut through College Hall, since the rain got heavier. Since I was wet, despite wearing a slicker, I came home instead of going to the office like I usually do. Got here a little after seven. My wife can confirm that."

Mallow scratched a few words on the pad. "Did you see anyone when you cut through College Hall?"

The coach stroked his chin. "Nope. I passed by the administrative office, but I didn't dawdle. Frankly, I didn't want to run into Winwood. As you know, he and I don't hit it off. My feeling is he'll get rid of sports after he bars women from the school."

"I've never heard any of them mention that possibility," Doro murmured, but the coach's comment set her to thinking. "Professor Corlon has been accused of assigning low marks to papers from athletes."

A humorless guffaw escaped Ayers. "I don't need to tell you that grading compositions is subjective, which makes it nearly impossible for the boys to challenge him. I've lost two outstanding players. Last season, we couldn't defend our league championship. This season, we'll be without my best forward, Pierce Dudley. The football team is down several athletes, because the kids went elsewhere to school, schools that offered scholarships and have professors who treat them fairly. Losing teams aren't popular. Neither are losing coaches." He released a long breath. "Another reason for me to be a suspect. The possibility of getting fired is a powerful motive."

Mallow nodded. "I won't deny that fact. But I've also heard Winwood, Corlon, Pottiger, and Jerritt weren't sports fans."

"They aren't. Jerritt only teaches one section of advanced algebra. I keep my boys out of it." Ayers glanced at Doro. "Winwood and his crew spout nonsense about making Michaw College a stellar academic institution. In their minds, that means no women, no sports, and only scholarly courses. That targets you in two ways, Miss Banyon."

Once again, Doro felt her ire rise. While she and the coach were not close friends, Doro had liked him. Until now. Hadn't the officer already said she wasn't a suspect? This time, she rose to her own defense before Mallow could reply. "President Adams thought my class on mystery books was scholarly. Many others do, as well."

"We're getting off-track," Mallow said, his attention on Ayers. "You also had a narrow window of opportunity, but you're not at the top of my list."

Ayers shrugged. "That's something, I suppose." He leaned back in the chair. "Any other questions for me?"

"No, but I want to talk with your wife," Mallow replied.

"I'll get her." With that, the coach left the room.

As soon as he was gone, Doro spoke. "He isn't high on your suspect list?"

"Not if his wife confirms his timetable. She could lie, but I'll weigh how she acts as much as what she says. Do you feel differently?"

Because he asked with genuine interest, Doro responded candidly. "Even though Coach Ayers had means, motive, and a bit of opportunity, I agree with you. Unless he saw Professor

Corlon go into the library, Coach wouldn't have any way to know the man was there. Also, all their past run-ins have been in front of others. I chalk that up to Ayers wanting people to hear his accusations. Sports have always been popular at Michaw College, and the teams have won a lot of championships. If he can get alumni and donors on his side, he might win."

"The popularity of athletics could result from successful teams. It's usually that way," Mallow said.

"I suppose so, but it hadn't occurred to me that hindering the teams could be a stepping stone to scrubbing athletics. Most colleges have sports teams."

"Now, but when Winwood was an undergraduate, they didn't. His cronies are about his age, so the same is likely true for them. Maybe they really believe in schools with purely academic pursuits."

"They're all rigid and old-fashioned, but I can't see the Board of Trustees going along with such a sweeping change. Unless the teams really go downhill, and attendance at games plummets." Doro folded her hands in her lap. "It all seems illogical and extreme."

"Some leaders want to shape an institution in their own mold. Winwood couldn't do that at a large school. Too many people to object."

For a moment, Doro considered the point. "That oddly makes sense. Winwood is dictatorial. The entire Fearsome Foursome is. Was," she corrected herself. "Only three are left."

Coach Ayers returned with his wife, which ended the exchange. The woman confirmed her husband's story, and seemed forthright, so Doro and Mallow headed back to her vehicle. Once inside, she asked, "You don't think she's lying for him?"

"I can't be sure, so I'll keep checking with others about possibly seeing him. But I'm inclined to accept her story. Mrs. Jones didn't mention Ayers, but I'd like to talk with her again. Sometimes, folks have clearer recollections later. A murder is shocking, and she was clearly shaken. She might be more comfortable if you're along, since you've known her for years."

"Very well," Doro agreed as she pulled away from the Ayers' house. She tempered her enthusiasm, as best she could. "I'd like to know if she heard or saw something significant, that she might remember now. Sometimes, witnesses have information deep in their minds and don't recall it right after a crime. That happens..." She let her voice trail off, before making a possibly foolish admission.

"That sounds like an unfinished sentence."

When Mallow shifted toward her, Doro felt a wave of discomfort. Amusement once again sparkled in his gaze. He knew what she'd been about to say, so Doro went ahead. "It happens in books. As an armchair detective, I've gotten most of my expertise from them. Not that I'm an expert. Far from it, as I'm sure you'll agree." As the words poured out, she chastised herself for babbling. As a chuckle left him, Doro found mirth spreading across his features. "What's so funny?" she asked, looking back at the road.

"Your explanation. You're well-informed and insightful with a manner that puts people at ease," he said. "Mrs. Islington wouldn't have been so open with only me. That's often the way when folks are questioned by lawmen. She might've felt more at ease with Wade, since he's her nephew, but me...not really. And the town operator wouldn't tell me a thing."

The observations piqued Doro's curiosity. "Have you interrogated a lot of people in your work? You said you mostly go on raids with the Bureau, but you must question suspects and witnesses, too."

"Sometimes. I did more of that when I was a policeman. Now, I hit the places with other agents, arrest folks, and take them to jail. Others handle most of the questioning, which is just as well. I don't have a knack for making people relax." He laughed again. "You surely agree, since you didn't seem at all eager to answer my queries on Tuesday morning."

Doro could not repress a smile. "It was the situation more than your manner that made me prickly."

"Maybe, but putting folks at ease usually leads to gleaning more information."

As she drove past the main part of campus, Doro caught sight of President Winwood and Provost Pottiger as they emerged from the side entrance to College Hall. Tension engulfed her when she considered what they were discussing. A quick glance at Mallow revealed he had seen them, too. "I'm glad you went back and secured the door from the secret passage side, too."

"As am I." He turned his attention to her. "They'll undoubtedly see us. I don't suppose there are other roadsters like this one in town."

"I'm afraid not." Since the road passed within twenty yards of the building, the pair of men was sure to notice the vehicle and identify it as hers.

"It might look suspicious, if we whiz by. Slow down, and we'll wave at least."

"Suspicious?" she echoed. "In what way?"

"We're pretty sure we didn't leave any sign of being in Winwood's office and, as far as we know, we weren't seen. Even so, that pair may find you driving me as odd."

The phrases *pretty sure* and *as far as we know* set alarm bells clanging in Doro's head, but she didn't have time to mull them over because the two administrators turned to stare at the automobile. When Mallow threw his hand in the air in a casual acknowledgement, she did, as well. Winwood's response was to wave them over. Her heart hit her heels. What did the man want? Nothing good, she was sure. "I suppose we have to stop."

"Yep," the officer said. "Let me do most of the talking, okay?"

Doro didn't want to exchange words with either Winwood or Pottiger, so she agreed. "Fine." After she pulled to a stop, the two administrators approached the vehicle.

Winwood's attention flitted from Doro to Mallow. "Officer, shouldn't you be investigating Professor Corlon's murder, instead of jaunting about town with a young woman?"

THE CATALOGUED CORPSE

Holding back a stinging retort was difficult, but Doro managed. A look at Mallow revealed he found himself with the same dilemma.

"I haven't stopped investigating, and I won't. Miss Banyon is driving me due to my leg injury." Mallow lifted his cane as he spoke.

"Leg injury? What did you do?" Pottiger's round face appeared in the driver's side window. Despite the cool temperature, sweat beaded his brow.

Doro shifted away from the man. As usual, his breath smelled of tobacco and Limburger cheese, his favorite snack. Combined with the odor of perspiration and some noxious cologne, it made Doro wonder how he stood himself.

Before Mallow could reply, Winwood spoke. "You need to tell your former boss about our murder case. That should come first. At least it should if you really want this job."

He came closer, but didn't bother to bend over, so seeing the president's expression was no longer possible. His imperious tone didn't surprise Doro. Nor did his threat to Mallow. President Winwood expected everyone to dance to his tune.

"Until Sunday at midnight, I'm employed by the Bureau, sir. Technically, my first day of work here isn't until Monday." Officer Mallow kept his voice calm and courteous, but tension laced his lean body.

Winwood moved back far enough to see into the vehicle. "I expect the murder to be solved shortly, Officer."

"That's what Constable Lammers and I want, too." Mallow cleared his throat. "We're making progress. I've spoken with several people who were at odds with Professor Corlon. In fact, I just interviewed Coach Ayers."

Pottiger jumped back into the discussion. "Good. Ayers is a typical sports guy. He thinks athletes should get special breaks. He and his ilk don't understand that a college is an academic institution. Sports detract from a serious, scholarly atmosphere." Pottiger jerked a thumb at Winwood. "We both come from top-notch schools where coursework was rigorous. Michaw could be an elite institution in the future."

Winwood cut him off. "I knew sports were important at Michaw when I took the job, and I certainly don't plan to make drastic changes. Some people have spread false rumors about my intentions." He stared directly at Doro as he spoke.

Since that was an out-and-out lie, Doro bristled, but she had no chance to comment.

"We're still looking into a few people, sir," Mallow replied.

Winwood and Pottiger both nodded. "Just see that you keep on the ones who have caused the most trouble for Hemet," the president said.

"I'll definitely remember that," Mallow said. "Now, if you two will excuse us, I don't want to take up all Miss Banyon's time, but I need to delve into several leads. Yours included."

A look of satisfaction blanketed Winwood's features. "Wonderful." He put two fingers to his bowler hat. "Good day."

Chapter Ten

After Pottiger and Mallow said their farewells, Doro put the vehicle into gear and headed away from the curb. How she wished some puddles from Tuesday's rain remained. Splashing the two administrators appealed to her far more than was sensible.

They hadn't gone a block when Mallow's voice intruded on her thoughts. "You look rather miffed. Any particular reason?"

In order to quell her annoyance. Doro inhaled deeply. "I thought you believed Coach Ayers' alibi, which seems adequate to me."

"I do, which is why I didn't ask him to be fingerprinted. As far as what I said to Winwood, that was to pacify him."

The response satisfied Doro, so she asked for clarification of his suspect list. "What fingerprints do you want?"

"Professor Gibling's, and I'll get prints from Pierce and Kitty this afternoon." He paused for a heartbeat. "I need them from Winwood and Pottiger. The pair seem very close, which makes me wonder if one wouldn't cover up for the other. If other evidence points toward Ayers, we can circle back to him."

"You can ask Pierce and Kitty outright, because they'll feel pressured to cooperate," Doro said.

"I will, but I'm not so sure about Stanley Gibling. Finding his cufflink bothers me," Mallow observed.

The clue deeply troubled Doro, who hadn't shared the news with Aggie. Her best friend seemed upset by her former suitor's possible involvement in the crime. If he was the killer, Aggie would have to face it. They both would. "Me, too. What about Winwood and Pottiger? They won't want to provide prints."

"True. Mrs. Jones has been cooperative. Maybe she can identify places in the office that Winwood regularly touches. Same with Pottiger."

"I'm sure she'll be happy to help again."

"We'll need some luck, because the prints need to be clear for a solid match to be made. Not all the ones from the drawer are as full and precise as I'd like, but an expert should be able to do something with them." Mallow folded his arms across his chest.

Relief flooded Doro. Along with it came embarrassment, since she had not given Mallow nearly enough credit. "You can tell something from the fingerprints, can't you?"

"Wade and I will look at them, but we aren't experts."

"Where are you storing the prints you already took?" Doro asked.

"There's a lockbox at the constable's office, so they're safe and secure."

Before Doro formed another comment, the Jones home came into view and she pulled to the curb. "Here we are."

"Let's take care in how we ask more questions," Mallow said. "I don't want to taint her recollections or evoke any bias. Besides, if she stops to really think back, she could have a breakthrough. That happens during investigations." One corner of his mouth lifted in a half-smile. "And not only in books."

"Nice to know." Doro climbed out of the driver's side and met him at the front gate, which he held open. She murmured her thanks before leading the way to the front porch.

Mrs. Jones, an apron over her housedress, answered almost immediately after Doro's knock. A smile curved her full mouth. "What a lovely surprise. Come in, come in."

"I hope we're not interrupting," Mallow said. "You look busy."

"Cooking and baking while I have extra time. I'm used to being at work every day, so not being busy is an oddity. I thought I'd make a few meals for Mrs. Lammers' boarders. With her laid up in the hospital, they're fending for themselves. Poor boys. Her younger sister has enough to do already, although she's helping as she can." Mrs. Jones gestured to the back of the house. "If you don't mind sitting in the kitchen, I could watch the stove."

"Of course not," Doro assured her. Mallow readily agreed and, within moments, the pair was seated at a battered oak table in the center of a large, bright kitchen. "You made your wonderful cinnamon rolls." Doro sniffed appreciatively.

"They were always your favorite, as a little girl. And an older girl." Their hostess put several on a platter, which she laid in the middle of the table. "How about coffee to go with them? I just made a fresh pot."

"Please don't go to any trouble," Mallow said.

"No trouble," the woman said. After pouring three cups and taking a seat at the table herself, Mrs. Jones glanced at the cane leaning against the table. "You didn't have that yesterday, Officer."

As Doro studied his face, she wondered if he would be honest. Clearly, he disliked people fretting over him.

"No, ma'am, I didn't. I got called into my other job last night, and we ran into some trouble." He offered a rueful smile. "Some folks don't want to get arrested."

She clucked her tongue. "I won't ask exactly what happened, but I hope Doro is making sure you take care of yourself."

When both Mrs. Jones and Officer Mallow looked at her, Doro felt heat invade her face. She quickly focused on her cinnamon roll and popped a chunk into her mouth. "Delicious." The older woman's gaze narrowed, which only increased Doro's discomfort.

Finally, Mallow responded. "Miss Banyon and Miss Darwine are being kind and helpful."

Some deeper emotion replaced embarrassment. Surely, she was not disappointed at his inclusion of her best friend. Doro shook off the odd thought.

Mrs. Jones nodded. "They're both lovely girls. I've known Doro since she was born. Her mother and I were dear friends. Still are, and we keep in touch with regular correspondence. It's not like sitting down and chatting, though."

Doro's hand went to the locket beneath her blouse. "I know what you mean."

With one hand, Mrs. Jones patted Doro's arm. "It's good of you to stay in the area. Otherwise, your grandmother would have no relatives nearby and moving away at her age would be difficult."

"I don't mind," Doro replied. "I love my job at the college." Would Corlon's demise mean she could keep it? While suspicion fell on Winwood and Pottiger, it also lingered on others. Not wanting to sound callous, she did not voice the idea. Besides, so much was left to unravel.

Sadness filled Mrs. Jones' gaze. "I'm so sorry you found Professor Corlon's body. It had to be a terrible shock." She looked at Mallow. "It's not a nice way for you to start your new job, and you weren't supposed to begin until Monday, but we're all glad you're here. Wade can't be in two places at once, and his mother needs him."

"I'm happy to handle things while he's at the hospital." Mallow cleared his throat. "I'd like to ask you a few questions."

"Of course," she replied.

After another swallow of coffee, he reached into his jacket for pad and paper. "You usually arrive for work early. Is that right?"

"I'm in my office by eight," Mrs. Jones replied. "Sometimes, a little before then, which was the case on Tuesday. Why do you ask?"

The secretary was sharp. Clearly, she knew something was up. Mallow had been loath to reveal much to witnesses, so Doro doubted he'd tell all to Mrs. Jones, and he proved her right with the next words.

"You and I spoke already, but sometimes people remember more later. After the original shock of a crime wears off. I wondered if that happened with you," Mallow said in a low, easy tone.

"I'll admit I've tried not to think about the killing since my interview. Such a dreadful crime." Mrs. Jones' forehead furrowed, as if she was searching her memory.

Moments of quiet passed during which Doro felt the urge to pepper the woman with more questions. But she followed Mallow's lead. He remained silent and consumed more of the snack. So did Doro. Finally, Mrs. Jones offered a detail.

"President Winwood unlocked the back door for me, because he wanted me to help him prepare for a Board of Trustees meeting on Wednesday. Of course, that was canceled after the murder."

Mallow scribbled something on his notepad. "Did you notice anything unusual? See anyone else? I asked before, but maybe a memory has surfaced since then."

Again, she paused for a moment. "Only one thing was different. The doors to both inner offices, the president's and the provost's, were ajar. I don't have keys to either door, but they're almost always locked when I arrive at work. President Winwood might've been in ahead of me and done so. Typically, when he opens the door early for me, he goes on his daily walk. So, perhaps Provost Pottiger was, although he's not an early bird."

"Do they have keys to each other's offices?" Mallow asked.

"They do," the secretary replied.

He made more notes before tapping the pencil against the pad. "Is it possible one came in, unlocked their doors, and left—maybe for coffee or to go to someone else's office?"

"Very few people come in so early," Mrs. Jones said. "It's not impossible that the President or Provost could go to the main floor snack bar for coffee, although no one would have been there to make any at that hour. They'd need to do it themselves, something else they rarely take on."

"I see. Can they go between their offices without coming to your area?" he asked.

Doro wondered why he asked. After all, they had seen and used the connecting door the previous evening, so Mallow knew that was possible.

"They can. When President Adams was here, the provost's office served as a conference room," Mrs. Jones said.

Mallow nodded. "Do only the two of them use that inside door?"

"Oh, yes. I'm not to go into either office when they're out. No one else is, either," she replied.

"What about the janitors?" Mallow leaned forward as if in anticipation of her reply.

"They come twice a week to do light cleaning. Tuesday and Thursday evenings. Thorough cleanings are done at the end of each term." Mrs. Jones rose to stir the stew. Once finished, she returned to her chair. "I won't ask who the suspects are, or the reason for all the new questions. I'll only say I hope you find the guilty party soon."

"Thank you, ma'am. For your help and for the snack." Mallow rose to his feet. "Now, we'll let you get back to work."

"I hope I helped a little," the woman replied.

Doro expressed her gratitude to Mrs. Jones before leading the way to her vehicle. When they got inside, she glanced at Mallow. "Do you think the knobs on the door between the offices are the best place to get fingerprints?"

He grinned. "I do. If they match ones from the card catalogue, we're a step closer."

"Only one step? I honestly don't believe Pierce and Kitty were involved at all."

Mallow's good humor faded. "He missed a meeting, and she didn't show up for work. Then, they both left town. Admittedly, for a reason. But I'll need to talk with them. We still have no idea how they got the message about her grandmother dying."

"You'll interview them, even if the fingerprints in the administrative inner offices match ones on the card catalogue?"

He nodded. "I have to cover all the bases. To that end, we need prints from Gibling, Winwood, Pottiger, Pierce, and Kitty in order to make an arrest. Or arrests. I'm pretty sure the killer is in that group. If not, I'll talk with Ayers again." Mallow sighed.

"Of course," Doro said with a nod, but disappointment encompassed her. Realization followed. "A good detective doesn't get emotionally invested in cases. He needs to keep an open mind."

"She does."

For a moment, she stared at him. He had given her detective status. The thought lifted her spirits. "Both he and she do," Doro agreed. "Where to next?"

Because the noon hour had passed, Mallow suggested going by the Islington boardinghouse to see if Pierce and Kitty were back. Doro concurred.

Within a few minutes, they were on the porch. Several knocks on the door went unanswered.

"I wonder if the landlady is out," the officer said.

"Possibly, since we know she runs to her sister's place to help. The front door is usually unlocked, so we could go in and see if Pierce and Kitty have returned."

"I suppose that's all right."

"Mrs. Islington won't mind. She's always had an open-door policy." When Doro opened the door, she heard voices coming from the second floor—one male, one female. As she started forward, Mallow clasped her forearm.

"Wait," he whispered. "Do all the boarders stay upstairs?"

"Yes. There are several rooms on the next level and two on the third story." Doro glanced up the steps. Although the voices carried, the words were not clear. "Only male students live here, and no women are allowed beyond the first floor."

"Where do the boarders park?" Mallow asked.

"On the side of the house toward the back. You can see from the dining room."

"Please show me."

Doro led the way to a large window overlooking the yard, where she pointed toward two vehicles sitting at the back of the lot. "Over there."

"Do you know if either belongs to Pierce?"

"The black Packard roadster is his," she replied.

"All right. Let's go back to the front hall. I'll call up and see if they'll come down. Even if they do, I'd like you to stand over to the side. The voices might not belong to Kitty and Pierce, but if it's them, they may not want to be found. Especially by a lawman."

His serious tone and expression gave Doro pause, so she nodded before following him to the front of the house. She stood by as he called up the steps.

"Pierce. Kitty. If the two of you are up there, come down now. It's Everett Mallow, the new campus security officer. We need to talk."

The voices stopped immediately, but no acknowledgement followed. Neither did footsteps. Mallow glanced at Doro. "It has to be them up there. I'd rather not go after them, but I will if they refuse to come down. You need to stay here, no matter what. All right?"

She nodded, but without enthusiasm. The likelihood of Pierce or Kitty becoming violent seemed slim—to Doro, at least. But she knew the young couple. Mallow didn't. Not only that, he had experience dealing with fierce criminals, which had to shape his perspective. For now, she would give him the benefit of the doubt.

His response was to ascend the staircase using both the handrail and his cane. When he got to the landing, Mallow paused and called out again. "Pierce and Kitty, you need to come out."

After a few moments, Doro heard a door open before the floor above her head creaked. A male voice, probably Pierce, echoed down the steps. "What do you want?"

"Just to talk," Mallow replied. "Come on downstairs."

Another hesitation followed. Despite her faith in Pierce and Kitty, Doro experienced a wave of apprehension. What if the pair panicked and went after Officer Mallow? The question echoed through her head. Could they have seen Corlon, argued with the man, and ended up killing him in an outburst? Almost immediately, she chastised herself for the wild fancy. Reading mysteries had clearly amplified her imagination. Or maybe writing one had. Still, she held her breath until Kitty spoke.

"Let's talk with him, Pierce," the girl said.

"All right," he replied after a brief hesitation.

Within moments, Mallow came back downstairs with the young couple following in his wake. He turned to Doro. "Do you think Mrs. Islington would mind if we use her parlor?"

"Not at all," Doro assured him.

When the group assembled in the front room, Kitty and Pierce took the loveseat while Doro and Mallow sat in chairs across from them. The officer leaned his cane against his leg before taking out his pad and pencil. "Thank you for agreeing to talk."

Kitty nodded as she looked at Doro. "What are you doing here, Miss Banyon?"

A snort left Pierce. "That's what I'd like to know. I'd like to know why the security man wants to talk with us, too. We've been gone, but it's none of your business. We didn't do anything immoral. Not that you'd need to know, if we had."

Color swept into Kitty's pale face. "Pierce, don't say such things."

He took her hand and laced their fingers. "I'm sorry. I don't like being hounded."

"I'm not hounding you," Mallow put in. "I have a few questions, and I want honest answers from both of you. Maybe I should separate you for questioning."

"That's not necessary," Kitty replied, clutching Pierce's hand harder. "We won't lie."

"No, we won't." Pierce laid his free hand over both of theirs. For a moment, silence filled the homey room. When he spoke again, his voice was rough and ragged. "I hope you can forgive me for not telling you everything about Tuesday morning."

The little color left in the girl's face drained away. "What happened?" she asked in a broken whisper.

Kitty's anguished expression tore at Doro's heart. Had the boy killed Corlon? She waited with growing dread.

"Perhaps, you ought to tell all of us what happened," Mallow suggested.

Pierce released Kitty's fingers, braced his elbows on his knees and put his head in his hands. "I was supposed to meet Professor Gibling at the diner. He felt bad about me losing my scholarship, due to Corlon. Last week after class, I told him I might not finish school."

"You only have the rest of this year left," Kitty said. "You told me you could make it through to graduation." Her eyes filled with moisture.

He glanced at her before again bowing his head. "I can finish this term, but there's not enough money for next semester. Gibling wanted to discuss a couple of ideas with me."

"But you didn't meet him," Doro put in.

Pierce lifted his head and met her gaze. "No. I was on my way there, when I saw Corlon. Of course, he had something nasty to say."

"Exactly what?" Mallow asked.

The boy exhaled sharply. "*Why are you still here? You oughta be back on the farm behind a plow.*"

Kitty laid her hand on his shoulder. "You didn't tell me. I thought we shared everything."

When Pierce didn't respond, Doro spoke. "Those were mean comments."

After a moment, Pierce sat back on the loveseat. As he moved, he again took Kitty's hand. "He is mean. Was mean, but you know that, Miss Banyon. He's been terrible to the women on campus."

"He was," Kitty said. "But lately, that changed. I hoped he'd modify his feelings about sports, too."

A snort left Pierce. "He hasn't. Corlon, Winwood, Pottiger, and Jerritt think colleges should focus strictly on academics. High-brow academics for scholarly young men. Farm boys like me don't belong in their world."

"How did you respond to his remarks?" Mallow asked.

"I said he ought to shut his mouth, or I'd shut it for him," the boy replied.

"Oh, Pierce." Kitty's voice was a plaintive murmur.

"I didn't mean it." Pierce's voice softened as he addressed her. "I just wanted to scare him, but he threatened me, said he'd see I got kicked out of school right away, and he could do it. I knew that, and so did he. Then, he stalked away. I followed him to the library, but I only wanted to talk."

"Really?" Skepticism was clear in Mallow's one-word question.

"I wanted to make sure he didn't follow-through on his threat. Money is a big problem, but if I got expelled, I'd have no chance of coming back to finish. I plan to be a lawyer eventually, and I couldn't let him stop me," Pierce replied. "Anyhow, while I considered what to do, he took off. He moved fast for an old guy, so I didn't catch up until he was unlocking the library's back door."

"The back door?" Doro echoed. "You went in that way?"

"Both of us did."

"What happened then?" Mallow asked.

Pierce let his head fall forward. "He told me to go away and leave him alone. I tried to be civil. I pleaded with him not to have me expelled."

"He wouldn't listen?" Doro posed the question.

"Not really. He was meeting someone before his class came. He claimed we could talk later. I finally agreed, because he wouldn't listen," Pierce said in a defeated tone.

Doro surveyed the boy as he spoke. Did his frustration indicate anxiety about not being believed? Or did it signal a guilty conscience? She wondered how Mallow assessed the responses.

Mallow made more notes. "Where did you head from the library?"

"I went back toward town. By then, the rain had started. Before I got a block, I was soaked. I came back here to call the diner, but Professor Gibling had left. Then, Kitty showed up with the bad news about her grandmother."

"Back up a bit," Doro said. "Did you go out the back door of the library?"

Pierce shook his head. "No. Professor Corlon went to the reserve shelf near the circulation desk, and I went along because I was still trying to talk with him. That's when he told me about meeting someone, and he insisted I leave. Since he promised to talk with me later, I did. Arguing more wouldn't have helped my case."

"Probably not," Doro agreed. "So, you went to the main door in front and left from there?"

"Yep," the boy replied.

Out of the corner of her eye, Doro saw Mallow turn toward her. Since he seemed to wait for her to continue, she did. "Didn't you have to turn the inside lock to get out?"

Pierce nodded. "Sure."

"Do you know if Corlon locked it behind you?" The boy wasn't being completely honest, which troubled Doro. Was Pierce covering up for Kitty? The girl had been seen with him at the back of the library. Doro studied Kitty, who was pale and shaky.

"I doubt it, since he didn't walk that far with me," Pierce responded.

"Where did you go then?" Mallow asked.

"To my boardinghouse," Pierce said. "Like I said."

Mallow posed another question. "Somehow, the two of you connected because you both went to the funeral in Richfield Center. But how did you find out about your grandmother?"

Kitty sighed. "The telephone at the dormitory front desk was ringing and ringing when I was on my way to the cafeteria. That doesn't happen often, but somehow a call got through from the Richfield Center operator." With the back of one hand, she wiped at her eyes. "I never thought it would be for me. But it was..." Her voice broke. When Pierce slid his arm around her slender shoulders, Kitty rested her head on his chest.

"What time was that?" Mallow asked.

"After five-thirty," Kitty replied. "I slept poorly, so I planned to have coffee before I started work at six."

Mallow and Doro exchanged a long look before he made more notes. Mrs. Gardner had mentioned new lines making calls to dormitories possible. Doro hoped Wheaton Hall would soon have the same availability. But did this information absolve the young couple? Doro wasn't sure. "You found out your grandmother died." Doro spoke in a hushed murmur.

"Yes. It was my mother calling. She was distraught and wanted me to come right away, since she was already at the farm. I ran to my room, packed a bag, and headed to town. I didn't want to telephone the boardinghouse so early," the girl said. "I should've let someone know I was leaving, but my gramma and I were close, and I just wanted to get there."

"And Pierce agreed to take you," Mallow suggested.

"I did. No one was up at my boardinghouse, so I scribbled a note, packed a bag, and we left." Pierce patted Kitty's back.

"Why did you two stop at the library?" Mallow's query had the young couple looking at each other, but neither hurried to reply. "We know you did, because you were seen there."

213

Doro held her breath as the bold statement pierced the air. The couple huddled closer together, as if warding off the pending accusations.

After what seemed like an interminable silence, Kitty nodded. "When Pierce told me about his run-in with Professor Corlon, I suggested we stop briefly so I could talk with him. He'd softened his attitude about a coeducational campus, and I wondered if he might be less hostile about sports. Or at least, about not having Pierce expelled."

The slow drip of information pointed to the pair killing Corlon, which filled Doro with horror. Both young people had been in her class, and she liked them immeasurably. Unable to form a question or comment, she waited for Mallow to go ahead.

"How did he react to seeing the two of you?" the officer asked.

The two both looked uneasy. "He didn't see us," Kitty said.

"Why not?" Mallow kept his voice well-modulated, but tension filtered into it.

A long moment passed before Pierce murmured, "He was on the floor by the card catalogue. I bent to see if we could help him. It was too late."

Kitty's free hand went to her mouth. "It was awful. We were both shocked."

Torn between doubt and sympathy, Doro used the latter to shape her comment. "I'm sure it was terrible." If the two were lying, they would be caught soon enough. If they were innocent, Doro empathized. Finding a dead body was an awful experience.

Mallow did not follow suit. Instead, he got down to brass tacks. "What time was that?"

"Probably around seven," Pierce said.

Kitty nodded. "That sounds right. By the time, I packed and got to the boardinghouse, it was after six. We didn't get away from there and to the library for another forty minutes. It took me a while to convince Pierce to let me try talking with the professor."

"It did," he agreed. "Now, I wish we had gone straight to Richfield Center."

"I do, too," Kitty said in a broken whisper.

Her sweetheart hugged her closer. "You wanted to help me. Neither of us could've guessed what happened."

Doro watched with mixed feelings. Was the pair acting? Or sincere? A glance at Mallow revealed little of his perspective, so she again waited for him to proceed.

"You realized he was dead," Mallow said.

Doro listened for one of the pair to confirm the statement. When neither did, she turned it into a question. "Did you know?"

A harsh sigh left Pierce. "We did."

"But you didn't report the death," Mallow put in. "Instead, you went out-of-town, stayed away two days, and hid upstairs when I came to talk with you."

His words held unvarnished skepticism, bordering on accusation. Doro could not find fault with either sentiment.

"We weren't hiding," Pierce shot back.

"Then, what were you doing?" Doro asked. "Mrs. Islington doesn't allow women upstairs."

Once again, color surged into Kitty's cheeks. "We weren't doing anything wrong."

"Maybe. Maybe not, but your behavior since Tuesday morning makes both of you look guilty," Doro told the girl. "Your story is weak, at best. You were in a hurry to get to Ridgefield Center due to the death of your grandmother, but we're to believe you stopped at the library to chat with Corlon, who has given both of you no end of trouble. He's also trying to disband YWV, a group you head, Kitty. You were very upset about that when we last spoke."

The girl shifted restlessly on the loveseat. "Since then, I heard he had proposed keeping the college open to women. His niece is interested in coming here."

Since they had heard as much already, Doro didn't argue the last point. "What about not going straight to Richfield Center?"

"I told her how upset I was, Miss Banyon, so that's my doing," Pierce said. "When Kitty suggested talking to Professor Corlon, I finally gave in because it might've worked, and I was desperate."

"I wanted to help," Kitty added. "We plan to get betrothed after graduation. We'll both teach for a year or two, so we can save money for a house and a family. If Pierce doesn't graduate, he'll have a harder time finding a job in the city, and we both want to live there. And you know he wants to go to law school as soon as he has enough money."

The story made sense, but a glance at Mallow told Doro that he wasn't completely convinced. She waited for him to continue the interview, since she had already interceded at points. Maybe he could glean more.

"I agree with Miss Banyon that your tale is suspect," the officer said.

"You aren't going to arrest us, are you?" Kitty sounded distraught and afraid. "We did nothing wrong."

"I don't have enough evidence to take you in," Mallow assured the girl. "But I have evidence. More than enough to keep you near the top of my suspect list. To exclude you two, I'd like you to come to the constable's office, so I can get your fingerprints."

Kitty and Pierce exchanged a long look, before he spoke. "We were in the library, so our prints are there, along with hundreds of others."

"There aren't many on the card catalogue and drawer," Mallow began. "The janitors did a thorough cleaning Monday night, so the only prints are from Tuesday morning."

Doro wondered why Mallow didn't mention three sets of prints, but she waited to hear how the young couple would respond.

Pierce again hung his head. "The drawer was against the professor's head. I moved it away," the boy said.

"He just wanted to check the wound. At first, we didn't realize that the man was dead. We were trying to help," Kitty said. "Really."

Mallow paused in his notetaking to look at the pair. "You both touched it?"

"Only me," Pierce replied.

"I'll still want prints from both of you." The undercurrent of anger in Mallow's voice was palpable.

"We didn't do it," Kitty said in an urgent, pleading tone. "We wouldn't do such a thing. Not either of us. Someone else had to be in the library."

Pierce's head jerked up as he turned to Kitty. "Someone else was. Remember, we thought we heard a door close even before we got to his body?"

Kitty's eyes widened as she nodded. "I do. The sound was from the back of the library."

"That would be convenient," Mallow observed in a flat tone.

Despite his statement, Doro figured he must be thinking about President Winwood. While Kitty and Pierce hearing noise wasn't solid corroboration, it was a tidbit to pursue. "Maybe someone else saw a person near the back door at that time."

When Mallow turned his head toward her, a slight smile played across his lips. "Maybe so. We'll have to go on investigating."

Doro bit her lip to keep from grinning in response. They were on the same page. With luck, that page was close to the end of this whodunit.

Mallow snapped his notebook shut. "Sooner would be better than later in terms of getting fingerprints. Miss Tenseng, you can ride with Miss Banyon. I'll go with your beau."

෴

Kitty remained silent on the way to the constable's station, and so did Doro—at least she did until she pulled into a parking place and killed the engine. "I hope you haven't told any lies about this situation. You were wrong not to report the death right away, although I understand why you didn't." The girl's stricken expression was hard to bear.

"We made a terrible mistake by not staying and getting help. Not that anyone could've helped him. But Mr. Quartine probably found him shortly after we left," Kitty observed.

Doro shook her head. "No, he didn't. I did, and it wasn't a pleasant experience."

Kitty's hand flew to her mouth. "I'm sorry."

"You should be," Doro told her. "Officer Mallow and Constable Lammers could've saved time and energy with extra information from the start. They probably interviewed more people than necessary because you didn't report what you found. I'm disappointed in you."

A shuddering sigh left the girl. "I'm disappointed in myself. I know better, but I was worried about Pierce. He was really upset and afraid of being blamed. I was, too. He'd had a few run-ins with Professor Corlon. Run-ins witnessed by other people."

"You and the professor had a shaky history, as well."

A soft sigh left the girl. "He wasn't a nice man, but I think he was sincere about keeping the college coed. Maybe only because of his niece. Even so, other girls can study here, too."

"He wasn't the only one against admitting and hiring women, so that could still be an issue," Doro said. Solving the crime might not influence that.

Chapter Eleven

An hour later, Doro and Mallow were alone in the constable's office. "Now, you have sets from two suspects, and a way to get prints from Winwood and Pottiger. But what about Stanley? Are you going to ask him to come in, or are you planning a covert foray into his office?"

Mallow shook his head, but amusement danced in his gaze. "You'd probably vote for a *covert foray*."

A chuckle escaped Doro. "All the sleuths in books are surreptitious." The jangling of the telephone interrupted. "I'll run and get it." Doro didn't wait for him to agree, since he'd been furtively massaging his leg off-and-on. And no wonder. He had been on it all day and, most likely, a good part of the previous night. Despite that, he got up, grabbed his cane, and limped over to the front desk behind her. Doro spoke with the operator, who relayed the caller's name. After thanking Mrs. Gardner, she handed the candlestick base and earpiece to Mallow. "It's Constable Lammers."

"Thanks." Mallow braced himself against the counter.

Doro listened intently to Mallow's side of the conversation. When he hung up, she made an observation. "His mother is better, so he can return to work." Disappointment fell over her like a shroud. Her help would not be needed much longer.

"Pretty much. He'll be back tonight. Before then, we need to get prints from Gibling, Winwood, and Pottiger. Then, Wade can take all the fingerprints to the sheriff's department for comparison. With some luck, we may have evidence to arrest the killer tomorrow."

"That would be wonderful." Doro wholeheartedly hoped that would happen, but who did Mallow mean by *we*? Not wanting to assume, she strove for clarification. "You're going to get the prints without Wade's help?"

A frown furrowed his brow. "I need them when he arrives. He'll have to turn around and go back to the city, but Wade is taking his aunt to stay near the hospital, in case another emergency arises. His mother is better but not out of the woods." Mallow shifted his cane from one hand to the other and back. "You and I discussed returning to the administrative offices already."

Relief filled Doro. She wasn't done sleuthing yet. "Of course. I thought you'd work with Wade instead."

His puzzlement disappeared. "I want him in on the arrest. As for collecting evidence, you've been doing that already. You and Miss Darwine have done a lot of good work."

The praise lifted her spirits. "When do you want to go to College Hall?"

"More toward evening," he replied. "I definitely don't want to cross paths with Winwood or Pottiger, since they can't be ruled out."

"Agreed. What about Stanley?"

"I'll call and see if he'll come here."

For a moment, Doro considered that avenue. "What if he won't cooperate?"

"I plan to start by asking about his interactions with Pierce. At the end, I'll bring up fingerprinting."

"Will you suggest it might clear him?" Doro asked.

"My exact plan."

"Are you going to mention the cufflink?"

Mallow narrowed his gaze. "Would you?"

She shook her head. "No, I'd whisk it out after he gets here and assess his reaction."

"Smart thinking."

The two words pleased Doro beyond measure.

Within thirty minutes, a flushed Stanley Gibling stepped into the constable's office. His narrowed gaze went from Doro to

Mallow. "I could've answered extra questions on the telephone. Not that I know more than I told you before."

"Thank you for coming," the officer said. "I'd rather not conduct business over the phone lines, which is why I wanted you to come in. As for our previous discussion, I know more than I did then, so I have more questions."

Stanley stiffened. "I have no idea what you've heard, but I didn't kill that man."

"Officer Mallow didn't say you did," Doro put in, mostly to keep Stanley from stalking out, which seemed all too likely. He appeared as unsettled as when she had last seen him.

"Why are you here? Don't you have other things to do, Doro?" Stanley asked in a cutting tone.

"Miss Banyon is assisting me," Mallow said, "since Constable Lammers is handling a family emergency."

Stanley looked around the front office. "Where's the clerk?"

"She only works part-time," Doro replied.

"Seems like she ought to be here more, everything considered." Stanley laid his arms across his chest. "What do you want to know?"

"Let's sit at the constable's desk." Mallow gestured toward the far corner.

Doro watched as the two men settled on the opposite side of the space. For the first time, Doro was glad the office was one large room. Bigger departments had sequestered areas, but Michaw, with a small population and few crimes, needed nothing more. She hoped it never did. At the moment, she primarily hoped to overhear the exchange between Mallow and Stanley.

That proved to be no problem. Mallow's voice carried well, and Stanley spoke as if he was in a large classroom. Since the professor's back was to her, Doro didn't pretend to be doing something else. Instead, she listened intently as Mallow provided selected details from their conversation with Pierce and Kitty. She noted how careful he was to only focus on matters directly related to the planned meeting between student and professor.

"What I'm wondering is if you saw the young couple later. Maybe driving out of town," Mallow suggested. "I can understand why you wouldn't want to make them look guilty, even to clear your own name."

Doro wished she could see Stanley's face. Mallow's amiable tone and casual words combined to make it seem like he no longer suspected the professor. In her mind, the man was not completely exonerated, but Stanley's reaction might be revealing.

"I shouldn't have to clear my name, because I've done nothing wrong. As for seeing Pierce and his sweetheart, I didn't." Stanley cleared his throat. "I'm sorry she lost her grandmother, and I understand the boy driving her to Richfield Center."

Since Mallow had not mentioned the young couple stopping at the library, Stanley's assumption that Pierce had missed their meeting due to Kitty's family emergency made sense to Doro. But didn't Stanley know anything of note? Or was he guilty? That possibility seemed strong.

"I didn't want Pierce, or anyone else, to suffer because of that insufferable snob and his cronies. You may not realize it, Officer, but Michaw College was a progressive school under President Adams. Not only were women admitted and employed over the past decade, the scholarship program grew by leaps-and-bounds. Few average folks can afford to send their children to a private college. Adams ensured that bright students from every socioeconomic class could come here. I admired that. I wanted to be part of it. Then, Winwood, Pottiger, Corlon, and Jerritt arrived and started ruining the place. Someone needs to stop them, but knocking off one won't solve the problem. I know that much."

Mallow leaned back in his chair. For a fleeting moment, he glanced over Stanley's shoulder at Doro. Then, he continued. "Pierce was furious with Corlon, and he says you sympathized, which I understand. After all, you had issues with the man yourself."

"Issues?" Stanley echoed. "That's putting it mildly, Officer Mallow. He planned to keep me from getting tenure. After six years here, after working on various projects to help the school, after dedicating myself to my students...after everything I did, he wanted to get rid of me. Do you have any idea how hard it would be to find a comparable position elsewhere? Even if I do, I'll have to start all over and work hard for another six years to be eligible for tenure. Chances are good I won't get it, because being denied here is something I won't be able to hide."

As Doro listened to the exchange, she knew Stanley was right. Killing one of the Fearsome Foursome wouldn't change the path of the remaining three. For a moment, she reviewed the clues and suspect. She was still considering all angles, when Mallow said what had come to her mind.

"Whoever killed Corlon acted on the spur of the moment, so I doubt he thought about the others. He may not have thought about changes at the college. He may have simply lashed out in anger," Mallow said.

Stanley clasped the chair arms until his knuckles went white. "But that person was not me."

A wedge of silence opened. As it did, Doro saw Stanley's shoulders stiffen. After a moment, Mallow reached into his jacket pocket and pulled something out. Undoubtedly, the cufflink. Her heart raced while she waited for Mallow's next move.

The officer thrust his hand across the desk and opened his palm. "Is this yours, Professor?"

Gibling leaned forward. "Where did you find that?" he asked.

"Does it belong to you?" Mallow asked.

"It does," Gibling replied. "I lost it before classes started."

When the professor reached for the cufflink, Mallow closed his fingers around it and sat back in his chair. "Where did it go missing?"

"I have no idea. I looked all over my apartment and my office. And in College Hall." Gibling shot a glance over his shoulder at Doro. "It was a gift from a friend."

The paltry explanation annoyed Doro. Aggie and Stanley had been more than friends. With difficulty, she withheld comment.

"It's an expensive piece of jewelry, so it must've been from a good friend," Mallow said.

Gibling shrugged. "In any case, I'd like it back."

"I need to keep it for now." Mallow put the item in his pocket again. "It's evidence."

"Evidence," Gibling echoed. "That's ridiculous."

A few moments passed before the officer responded. "We found it near the back door of the library."

"What?" Gibling turned toward Doro. "It couldn't have been there all this time, so you must've found it and kept it. Now, you want to frame me because I didn't propose to Aggie."

Shock momentarily held Doro mute. The man was a cad, but was he a killer? Although Doro wanted to hurl an accusation at him, she resisted. Instead, she stuck to the case. "No one planted the cufflink, Stanley. It was in the corner behind some crates. We saw it because Officer Mallow had a flashlight. The sterling silver shone brightly in the beam."

Gibling turned back toward Mallow without responding to Doro. "I picked up books before classes began. I probably lost it then but didn't notice because I was busy. It's not solid evidence of me killing Corlon." His terse tone revealed little.

"You can prove you didn't touch the drawer by providing your fingerprints," Mallow said.

From her vantage point, Doro saw Stanley's shoulders stiffen. Would he cooperate? Resistance would be a red flag.

"Where do I have to go?" Gibling asked.

"I've got a kit here." Mallow reached into the desk and pulled it out. "I have prints from the drawer, and the county sheriff will have someone compare yours, along with a few others, with those."

"So, I'm not the only suspect left," Gibling said.

"Nope," Mallow replied. "One of several."

The professor agreed to the process and, after the prints were taken and stored away, he spoke again. "Can I leave now?"

Mallow shook his head. "I'd like to ask a few more questions."

"I answered a lot on Tuesday, and I told you. I don't know more," Gibling shot back.

"And I told you," Mallow said, "I know more than I did then."

The professor rubbed his neck and sighed. "Go ahead."

Stanley's tone indicated resignation, but at least he had provided prints. Doro wasn't at all sure he would say anything useful, since he was apt to point a finger at others.

"What about meeting Pierce Dudley?" Mallow began in a calm voice.

"What about it? He didn't show up," Gibling said. "Does he deny it?"

"Not at all, but the boy was out and about early on Tuesday. Did you see him?" Mallow asked.

"I already said he didn't come to the diner," Gibling replied in a curt voice.

"And you saw no sign of him anyplace else?" Mallow continued.

Doro saw the professor sit up straighter. Clearly, the question had hit home with him. With her pulse pounding in her ears, she waited for a response.

"No sign," Gibling said. "Was he seen around the library? He'd have come from the same direction as Corlon. Maybe Pierce trailed after him. The boy has been upset for a while. He lost his scholarship due to Corlon, who also picked on Kitty Tenseng, which made matters worse."

Mallow nodded. "Being threatened with expulsion had to upset Pierce more."

Since they knew that to be true, Doro silently credited Mallow with clever interrogation. Despite his insistence that he was no detective, the officer was skilled in revealing only dribs and drabs—just enough to get a suspect to talk.

Stanley ran one hand over his dark hair. "He was distraught. Pierce doesn't want to go back to the farm. He wants to teach in the city, save money, and go to law school. Following a plow, slinging hay, and tending critters won't further that dream."

"The boy shared a lot with you," Mallow said.

"He has," Stanley agreed. "His parents allowed him to attend school due to the scholarship, but they've always wanted him to come home after graduation, teach in their local school, and help on the farm. Since he has to pay his own way, they think he should leave now. My ma and pa were much the same, so I understand his dilemma. And he has an additional one. He and

Kitty want to get married, and she's averse to living on a farm. She's a city girl."

The new details reinforced what Doro already knew about Kitty and Pierce. Although she had not experienced it herself, young love created powerful responses and, sometimes, reckless actions. A reading of "Romeo and Juliet" had convinced her of that, not to mention her grandmother's tales of *"foolish young folks who let their hearts overrule their heads."* Did the couple fall into that category?

"She was pressuring him?" the officer suggested.

A half-shrug lifted one of Stanley's narrow shoulders. "Pierce felt pressured. He was in a bad situation, and I wanted to help him. Finishing school here would be ideal. If that's not possible, I was looking into him transferring to another college. He's a good athlete, so snagging a scholarship elsewhere could happen. I have a friend at my alma mater, who works with the coaches, and he's looking into options for the boy." Stanley's voice had lost most of its edge. Now, he sounded sincerely concerned.

"That's kind of you," Mallow observed.

"He's a fine young man, one who deserves a break. If you're thinking Pierce killed Corlon, and I suppose you are, think again," Stanley said.

At least Gibling wasn't trying to save his own neck by pinning the blame on Pierce. Doro gave him credit for that.

Mallow looked down at his notepad before responding. "I'm gathering information. We need to find the killer, or classes may be suspended indefinitely. No one wants that. And no one wants the campus and town communities living in fear."

"Is that what Winwood said?" the professor asked.

"No, he didn't. I made an assumption, since no restart date was announced," Mallow replied. "Constable Lammers and I want to solve the case quickly. Some students and employees were nervous enough to leave campus. Townsfolk are on edge, too, but few of them have the option of going elsewhere until the killer is behind bars. Although I work for the school, I want everyone to feel safe."

For a long moment, silence filled the room. Finally, Stanley nodded. "It's a nice town with good people. They deserve peace and security."

"If you have information that might help, I'd appreciate hearing it," Mallow said.

Would his earnestness move Stanley to reveal more? As Doro waited to find out, she held her breath.

"You must already know Corlon and his cronies raised plenty of hackles around here. I'm not the only professor who clashed with them. I'm just the only one coming up for tenure this year," the man replied. "Several others will be next year. All women. My guess is they'll be turned down, and men will be hired in their places. Men who think females belong at home, not in classrooms."

As she listened, Doro felt her insides knot. What Stanley said was true. Too true for comfort. Maybe the Fearsome Foursome had planned to change tactics and weed out troublemakers with denial of tenure. Since almost all women faculty members had been labeled as such, they could be gone within a few years. When they were, would any girls want to come to Michaw College? Would any be admitted? Doubtful. Very doubtful. But what about Corlon's evident change of heart? Was it genuine? If so, had it been a factor in his death? That question kept resurfacing in her mind.

Mallow again glanced beyond Stanley to look directly at Doro. Unless she was mistaken, his silver eyes held a silent query—*do you think he's right?* Unsure, she shrugged. The officer returned his attention to the professor.

"I'm aware a lot of people had reason to dislike Corlon and the others. But who among that group would kill him? That's what I have to discover," Mallow said.

"Good luck to you," Stanley said.

"We could use luck," Mallow replied. "Thanks for coming in. I'll let you know about the fingerprint results when we hear, probably tomorrow."

Chapter Twelve

When they were alone in the office, Mallow crossed to Doro. "Now, we need the Troublesome Trio's prints, and we're all set."

"Troublesome Trio?" The phrase amused her.

A grin curved his lips. "The three remaining administrators. I figured you needed a new moniker for them. Of course, one isn't in town, so maybe the Terrible Twosome."

Laughter escaped her. "Very clever."

As he leaned against the front counter, his expression became serious. "What did you think of Stanley's idea about weeding women out as they come up for tenure? Does that affect you as a librarian?"

"Librarians are faculty members, but I've only been here for a couple of years, so I won't be up for tenure soon. I hadn't considered that as a way to eliminate female faculty. It's certainly less confrontational than outright banning women as students and employees." She grimaced. Would she be allowed to stay until she could be denied? The question struck at the heart of Doro's dreams. "I imagine they'd continue to employ the cooks, since they were here when the school was all-male."

"Interesting."

What a ubiquitous word, and one he had used in the past. Doro never knew quite how to interpret it. "Maybe to someone who isn't directly involved."

"Michaw has been well known as a progressive school. My sister wanted to come here, but we couldn't afford the tuition."

The revelation surprised Doro. "You didn't mention that before."

He shrugged. "It's got nothing to do with the murder. What we need to do is get those other fingerprints."

His abrupt uneasiness kept Doro from inquiring about his sister or his past. Neither was any of her business. "Before we go to College Hall, let's stop and see if Aggie has any news. While we're there, I can get my heavy coat. It felt colder on our way back here. With dusk coming, the temperature will fall farther."

"All right. Let's head out," Mallow agreed.

Within a few minutes, they were back at the women's faculty residence, where Aggie remained sitting near the fireplace with a pad of paper. She looked up as soon as Doro and Mallow approached.

After studying the pile of papers and books on the table next to her friend, Doro grinned. "Looks like you kept busy."

"I did." Aggie set aside the notebook in her lap. "But I also learned a couple of things."

"Do tell." Doro perched on the chair next to her friend, while Mallow sat opposite the pair.

"Several people came down and asked about the case. A lot of conjecture about who killed Professor Corlon, but none based on facts. I didn't share anything. Just listened," Aggie replied.

"What was the bulk of the supposition?" Mallow made the query.

"Two people think Stanley is guilty, since they witnessed the blow-up last week in the English department. One person mentioned Coach Ayers, and another wouldn't be surprised if the crime involved Pierce, who evidently told more than one of his professors about Corlon mistreating him," Aggie said. "I was careful not to react in any way. After all, those three are among the suspects. At least, they were. Did anything you learned change that?"

"No." Mallow glanced toward the arch at the far end of the room. Even though no one was there, he lowered his voice when he went on. "Fingerprints need to be compared. We have sets from Gibling, Kitty, and Pierce."

"Now, you need Winwood's." Aggie finished for him.

"We do," Doro agreed. "And Provost Pottiger's, as well. Officer Mallow asked the others outright, but that isn't likely to work with those two."

Aggie rolled her eyes. "I'm sure it won't, so what's your plan?"

Mallow provided a summary before looking at his watch. "We'll want to leave in short order."

Doro noticed the concern on her friend's face. "You don't think President Winwood or Provost Pottiger will be in their offices this late, do you, Aggie? The Fearsome Four-some usually had dinner at one of their homes on Thursday evening."

"I doubt if they'll change that," Aggie said. "Of course, there's only two of them with Corlon's death and Jerritt being out of town for the week."

Relief spread through Doro. "Officer Mallow and I will be on our way. We'll go back to the constable's office with the prints before returning to campus. Wade Lammers will pick them up later this evening."

"I don't know about the two of you, but I'm eager to discover whose prints are on the card catalogue drawer," Aggie observed.

"Me, too," Doro added. When she looked at Mallow, he seemed oddly unaffected.

"We may know tomorrow." Mallow used his cane to get up, nodded to Aggie, and limped toward the door.

Doro stood, as well. "You might as well go back to your apartment, Aggie. I'll stop when we're done and get you up to date."

"Good, but be careful." Anxiety crept into Aggie's voice. "Pottiger and Winwood won't be around, but you don't want anyone else seeing you and blabbing."

"No, we certainly don't," Doro agreed before turning to Mallow. "I'll run up to get my heavy coat before joining you in the front hall."

⁎

Within a few minutes, she and Mallow headed out again. The pair crossed the Commons and entered College Hall through the nearest door. Mallow's keys made getting into the building and administrative offices simple.

"Like Miss Darwine said, we don't want to be noticed, so let's keep the lights off," Mallow remarked, as he turned on his flashlight.

"No, we don't want anyone to see us," Doro agreed. Especially not the killer.

They went down the dark corridor in silence. When they reached the main office, Mallow said, "Let's go in from Pottiger's side. I'd like to take a look around."

Doro followed him into the provost's area. When Mallow focused the beam on various parts of the room, she studied each one carefully. Before the Fearsome Foursome had come to Michaw, she had been inside the office many times, because the previous president had welcomed faculty members—female and male—to meetings. Those gatherings had stopped when Winwood took over. Since then, only a few men had been invited to meetings. Her perusal turned up nothing important, but Mallow was looking back over the entire interior. Finally,

Doro's curiosity got the better of her. "Are you searching for something in particular?"

"Not really. Just want to make sure I don't miss something." He trained the flashlight on the door between the two offices. "If you hold this," he said, handing her the lantern, "I'll get the prints."

Doro carefully focused the beam and watched as Mallow took tools out of the kit and put them to use. He brushed a dark dusty substance on and around the knob before pulling out adhesive tape and carefully applying pieces to several areas. "I read a recent book, where fingerprints were taken like you're doing it. Amazing."

He glanced over his shoulder at her. "Tape like this is readily available now. The dusting substance is pretty new, but used often by lawmen. Both are great tools." Mallow pressed the tape against a clean sheet of paper, also from his kit.

Doro leaned over to study the imprints. "They look clear and sharp," she said.

"We're lucky, because they are. Now, let's get some from the other side and be on our way."

Within five minutes, Mallow had the samples and equipment back in the kit. Then, he and Doro were on their way out of the building. The pair was within forty feet of the main door when the sound of a key turning in the massive lock reached them. The officer snapped off the light and pulled Doro behind him. She froze in place. Very few people had keys. Mallow was one of them, of course. Besides him, only the top administrators and the department chairmen did. Men's voices floated to her. What they said was not clear. All Doro knew for sure was that they were moving closer, too close for comfort. She stared into the shadows and struggled to orient herself. They could hide some place, but where would they be safe from notice? Suddenly, the perfect hideout came to her. "There's a ladies' lavatory just a few feet up on the right side of the hall," she whispered. "We can go in there."

Mallow hesitated for a second before murmuring, "Lead the way."

Doro stepped in front of him and covered the distance in record time. When the door closed behind them, she breathed a sigh of relief. Next to her, Mallow exhaled sharply. For long moments, she strained to listen. As footsteps joined the voices in the hallway, she caught enough words to know who was there. Winwood and Pottiger. But what were they doing at this time of night when the school was closed? Although their presence didn't mean either was guilty, what did it signify? She heard a few words as they passed by.

"We need to go over those papers," Winwood said.

"I don't see why we couldn't do it in the morning," Pottiger replied. "I'll have to dig in my file cabinet to find them. That'll take time."

"Not a problem. I want to check the door between our offices. The latch hasn't been working right," the president put in.

As they moved away, their voices faded. Doro couldn't wait to get out of the building and hear what Mallow thought. Several moments after the sounds died away, he shifted toward her.

"Do the windows in here open?" he asked in a quiet voice. "I don't want to take a chance on going back into the corridor."

"They do. It may be a tight squeeze, but we can get out. What about your leg? Are you sure you can manage without doing it more harm?"

His response failed to ease her mind. "Climbing through the window will create less damage than getting caught sneaking out of the building would. I don't know if the president or the provost had anything to do with Corlon's death, but I'm sure I'd be off the case if we're discovered skulking around here. And you might get fired before you come up for tenure."

Unable to argue either point, Doro led the way to the windows, undid the swing lock, and pulled the glass panel open. Since it came inward, she pushed it down as far as possible. "Do you want to go first?"

Mallow stuck his head through the opening. "No, you go ahead. Luckily, the window is only a few feet off the ground, so you can drop down safely. I'll hand you the kit and my cane before joining you."

His explanation made the action sound simple. For Doro, who was several inches shorter and some pounds lighter, making an escape wasn't easy, but she managed. After taking the kit and cane from him, she stepped aside. Although Mallow was lean, he was bigger overall and hampered by a leg wound. He moved carefully and, when he groaned, she asked, "Are you all right?"

"Fine."

The ragged quality to his voice said differently, but Doro didn't press him. "I can carry the kit," she offered. When he readily agreed, Doro wondered if he had done more damage to his leg. As he started hobbling away, she knew he had because he was leaning much more heavily on the cane and edging over the uneven ground with great care. Doro felt a stab of relief when they got to the sidewalk. "My vehicle is in the lot next to Wheaton Hall."

His response was more of a grunt than anything coherent. She didn't waste more time talking. Instead, she proceeded to the roadster. Doro hurried to stow the kit in the back and when Mallow half fell into the passenger seat, she got the automobile moving. After they reached the constable's office, Doro said, "The lights are on, so Wade must be here."

"Good."

Again, he sounded breathless, so Doro made no further comments. She killed the engine, got out, and headed to the station's front door. Mallow followed much more slowly. When she entered and saw the constable's familiar, kindly face, Doro smiled. Wade rose from his desk and crossed to meet them.

"Glad you two are here," the constable said. His attention went to Mallow, who hobbled across the room. "You should've listened to the doctors and stayed off that leg for a few days."

The comment had Doro turning toward the officer, who was avoiding her gaze. "You said you only need to use the cane today and never mentioned taking time off." She tried to keep any hint of accusation from her tone.

A snort of laughter left Constable Lammers, but he didn't speak before Mallow intervened.

"I feel fine," the officer objected.

Wade frowned. "You're limping pretty badly."

Mallow's jaw tightened. "We almost got caught leaving College Hall, so we climbed out of a lavatory window. It was a tight squeeze, and I banged my leg."

Although Doro wanted to chastise him for not saying so immediately, she simply asked a straightforward question. "Is the wound bleeding again?"

Mallow shook his head. "No. It just hurts a little."

The comment was probably a gross understatement, but Doro let it pass. She handed the fingerprinting kit to Wade. "We have prints from all the suspects now."

The constable smiled. "That's great, but why were you in College Hall, and how did you almost get caught? I thought you were getting people to come here for prints."

"It wasn't possible to get all of them that way," Mallow replied before explaining what else they had learned and why they'd beat a hasty escape.

"Interesting," Lammers observed after Mallow finished the tale. "Hearing Winwood and Pottiger was helpful. Did you buy their excuse for going back to the offices?"

"It could be a valid reason. Or not," Mallow replied. "But I didn't notice the latch on the door between their offices being faulty."

"Neither did I," Doro agreed.

The constable frowned. "If Winwood wanted a reason to tinker around the door, he might've wiped the knob clean."

"My thoughts, too," Mallow said. "I'm glad we've got the fingerprints."

"As am I. Could both of them be involved in Corlon's death?" Lammers asked.

"Possibly," Mallow said. "But Winwood wanting papers from Pottiger's file cabinet this evening strikes me as odd, especially when the provost thought they could wait."

Doro and Lammers expressed their agreement.

"A lot is riding on the fingerprints. Neither of us is an expert at examining them, Wade, but let's compare the ones from the catalogue drawer with those Miss Banyon and I just got," the security officer said.

Excitement spiraled through Doro as she looked from Mallow to Wade. "You still have the original prints here, right?"

The constable nodded. "Yep. I'll get them out."

After he disappeared into the adjacent storeroom, Doro turned to Mallow. "Do you think you'll be able to tell if there's a match?"

He shrugged. "I'll still want confirmation from an expert, but we should be able to narrow the suspects down."

"I hope so," Doro said.

Within moments, Wade Lammers was back. He carefully arranged the original prints on the desk, while Mallow did the same with the most recent ones. The trio studied the evidence in silence. As they did, Doro focused on each set separately before repeating the process over and over.

"I wish every print from the drawer was complete." Mallow pointed toward the partial one. "Part of one from Winwood's doorknob looks similar."

As Mallow spoke, Doro scrutinized both sets. "I think so, too."

"I agree," Lammers added, "but the guy at the sheriff's department should be able to make a confirmation. He's got a lot of experience."

Mallow rubbed his leg. "We need that validation before we make an arrest."

Lammers leaned back in his chair. "I'm going to pick up my aunt before heading back to the city yet tonight. She'll stay with a cousin, who lives close to the hospital. That way, she can be with Ma all day, and I can get back to work. After I drop her off, I'll get these fingerprints to the sheriff's office."

Doro turned her attention to the constable. "Your mother is doing better?"

"Much better. They'll probably keep her in the hospital for another week. My aunt can't remain in town that long, because her youngest in high school. On top of that, she has a houseful of boarders. Their cousin will fill in, when needed," Wade replied.

"After we catch the killer, you can take time off," Mallow said. "I'll handle whatever happens in town while you look after your mother and your boy."

Relief spread across the constable's face. "That'd be wonderful, and I bet the mayor and town council would be fine with the idea. I'll certainly support you continuing with special deputy status."

Doro listened to the conversation with interest and acceptance. "I agree."

Mallow's features softened. "Good to know."

She ignored the note of amusement in his voice and asked a question. "We're assuming the fingerprints from Winwood's side of the connecting door belong to him. Right?"

"We are," Mallow agreed.

"It's a logical assumption," Wade added.

"But is it enough to arrest him?" Doro made the query.

"It should be, along with other clues related to his movements on Tuesday morning," Mallow replied. "We'll take another set of prints then, to tie up loose ends. But him being around the library after he unlocked the door to College Hall, his lost watch story, his words tonight, the fingerprints, and Corlon's change of heart are powerful circumstantial evidence. I'm not willing to pin it on him yet, but I'm very close. What about you, Wade?"

The constable nodded. "I feel the same way. Winwood is in the top spot, but Gibling hasn't dropped off my list."

"Will Pierce's prints on the drawer be a problem?" Doro asked.

The two men exchanged a long glance before Mallow replied. "He's admitted to being in the library, and I believe his story. President Winwood's prints appear to match the partial print from the drawer. So far, he hasn't mentioned being there, just passing by."

"I agree," Lammers said. "Of course, a confession would be nice."

All three chuckled.

"Are you planning to speak with President Winwood again?" Doro asked.

"He wants a report tomorrow morning," Mallow replied. "Since Wade has his hands full, I'll be in the office. Winwood can come here."

"Thanks," Wade put in. "That will give me some breathing room, but I'll be in as soon as I can."

After putting the fingerprints into the kit and locking it away, Wade offered to drive Mallow back to his quarters, which left Doro out of any further conversation. Both bid her a good night before leaving the office, while the security officer once again recommended Doro stay with Aggie. The constable seconded the idea, so she agreed.

The two men also insisted on following her back to campus and waiting while she went into Wheaton Hall. After closing and locking the door behind her, Doro looked out the small window. The tail lights of Wade's Model T were already disappearing into the darkness. A sigh escaped her as she went upstairs. What would the two lawmen discuss? She would love to know.

Doro spoke with Aggie before the pair went to bed. Although exhausted, she found sleep elusive. Had an argument between Corlon and Winwood about coeducation turned into a physical altercation? Or had the college president snuck up on his friend and killed him? The latter seemed worse than the former, but both were troubling. Extremely troubling.

Chapter Thirteen

E arly Friday morning, Doro awoke with gritty eyes. A poor night's sleep, filled with nightmares about Winwood stalking the campus to kill again, sapped her usual energy.

After washing and dressing, she and Aggie had a light breakfast. Afterward, Doro helped clean up. When the task was done, she said, "Surely, the county sheriff's department will confirm information about the fingerprints soon. Officer Mallow will be in the constable's office, so I'm going to head over there."

Aggie nodded. "I'll go downstairs. Call if you learn anything new."

"I hope I do," Dora replied, but how long would it take to get results? What if the sheriff had more pressing matters? What if they couldn't make a determination about the partial print? With a sigh, she donned her coat and headed out.

While she made her way to the middle of town, Doro reviewed the evidence and the suspects. Pierce's prints were on the drawer, which put him in a bad light. What if the killer had used gloves? That could put them back at square one. Anxiety filled her, and she reminded herself of her mother's frequent recommendation: *"Stop ruminating so much."* Guilty as charged, Doro thought, with a combination of amusement and wistfulness. She missed her parents and their wise words.

When she entered the office, Doro saw Officer Mallow behind the counter. "Good morning."

He offered a smile. "Good morning."

The ringing of the telephone cut off further conversation. Mallow hobbled to the front desk and answered. Since Doro heard one side, she knew someone was calling from the sheriff's department. Exactly what was being conveyed was unclear. For what seemed like an eternity, but could only have been a few minutes, she waited. Finally, Mallow returned to his chair and gestured for her to sit across from him.

After she was settled, Doro said, "They got the fingerprint tests back."

Her pulse raced. "What did they show?"

"The prints from Winwood's interior door knob match one set from the card catalogue. It's a clear, solid match despite being a partial print on the drawer."

For a long moment, the statement hung heavily in the air. As it did, Doro slowly absorbed the information. "How many different prints are on the drawer? You and Wade thought three were."

"The test confirmed we were right about three sets."

When he didn't continue, Doro's curiosity grew. "So, the prints on the drawer belong to Corlon, Pierce, and Winwood."

"That's right."

Doro's pulse raced. "When is President Winwood coming for your interview?"

"At eleven o'clock," Mallow replied. "Wade will be here then, so we can make an arrest."

Excitement continued to escalate inside Doro. "I'll be happy to see the man get his comeuppance."

A frown pulled at the corners of Mallow's mouth. "I don't want you to be present for the arrest. Winwood probably isn't armed, but let's not take a chance."

Disappointment fell over Doro like a dark, dense cloud. Logically, she understood his concern. Emotionally, she yearned to witness Winwood's reaction. "All right."

"I'm sorry," he said. "You've been a big help in solving the case."

The compliment did little to mute her discontent, but she nodded. "Will you try to make him confess?"

Humor flared in Mallow's eyes. "We won't be using physical force on him."

Amusement sapped some of Doro's melancholy. "I didn't think you would."

"A confession would be ideal," Mallow replied. "I tried to call Provost Pottiger earlier, because I'd like to question him about being in College Hall with Winwood. No answer, but I'll keep trying."

"I could do that periodically. It's not nine o'clock yet, so President Winwood won't be here soon."

For a moment, Mallow looked like he would disagree. Then, he nodded. "That's a good idea. I've been considering how to approach him. I don't want to start with accusations."

Doro leaned against the counter. "Maybe you could begin with the basic facts and our suppositions. We know Professor Corlon was meeting someone, and we guess he and the other person argued."

He ran one hand over his face. "I can start with those facts, and include Corlon's apparent change of heart about keeping the college coed. If Winwood met with the professor, they probably argued, and it could've gotten heated."

Doro drummed her fingers on the countertop. "You said right off that the killing was most likely done on the spur of the moment and set into motion by anger, probably a dispute."

"That's a highly likely scenario, and it fits Winwood meeting with Corlon."

"It does," Doro said. "Especially when Professor Corlon's niece was coming to visit soon. Maybe Winwood was encouraging him to send the girl elsewhere. Maybe they were meeting to discuss it. President Winwood and Mrs. Jones both mentioned him preparing for a meeting with the trustees on Wednesday.

What if Winwood and Pottiger planned to discuss the possible change to an all-male campus with the board?"

Several seconds of silence elapsed as Mallow appeared to mull over the idea. "That seems possible. Jerritt is gone this week, so he wouldn't have been at the meeting to support Winwood. If Corlon changed his mind, that would've given Winwood only one ally. Pottiger has few social graces and wouldn't impress trustees, in my opinion."

A low laugh left Doro. "That's a diplomatic way of saying he's a clod. A smelly clod." She couldn't help but wrinkle her nose.

"Count yourself lucky that you didn't have to meet with the man while he gnawed on his favorite snack."

Doro put one hand to her face. "When was that?"

"The day I came for my first interview, I spoke with him before the rest of the committee. He was nibbling while we talked."

"On Limburger cheese."

Mallow grimaced. "Limburger on an onion roll. I have a strong stomach, but that tested it."

Queasiness hit Doro. "I can only imagine. Not that I want to think about it. The man is malodorous, even when he's not eating his favorite cheese."

"I know, and it's a big reason why I don't think he was there when Corlon died. You would've noticed a lingering stench, don't you imagine?"

As Doro thought back over previous encounters with the provost, she realized Mallow was right. "My sleuthing skills could use some fine-tuning, because I've been considering him as the killer or, more likely, an accomplice."

"Accomplice after the fact is conceivable. Maybe he wasn't in the library to kill Corlon but, if Winwood did it, Pottiger helping cover up is likely."

"Like helping clean the doorknobs last night?"

"Maybe, although Winwood having him look for papers points away from that," Mallow said. "Haven't they been friends since their college days?"

"They have, and they worked together at a couple of schools recently." Doro paused before continuing her thoughts. "I've always thought Pottiger waddled along in Winwood's wake, like a duckling following its parent."

What could only be called a guffaw burst from Mallow. "That's quite an image."

Warmth suffused Doro's cheeks as she realized her lack of restraint. "I shouldn't have said that. It was inappropriate."

Mallow shrugged. "Maybe, but not inaccurate. Pottiger seems like a devotee to me, too. It's definitely something to consider. You're very astute, which is an important quality for a sleuth."

Pleasure over the compliment surpassed embarrassment about her remark. "Thank you."

"It's true, although I was skeptical at first."

Doro figured that was an understatement, but she didn't press for more. "I wonder how Dr. Jerritt figures in all this. I don't know him as well as the others, since mathematics classes don't come to the library for research."

"Jerritt didn't sound as outspoken about removing women from campus when I met him."

"He's made comments about mathematics being too hard for girls," Doro replied.

Mallow shook his head. "My mother was a whiz at sums and such. My dad, not at all. As for my sister, she's followed in our mother's footsteps. Better at math than me."

His admissions about his mother and sister raised his stock a notch in Doro's opinion. "Dr. Jerritt isn't as vocal, but I can't see him going against Winwood."

"Who is the kingpin, like the top gangster. Barks orders and his minions jump or else."

The comparison amused Doro, who could not withhold a chuckle. "I hadn't thought of it that way, but I agree with your assessment."

The ringing of the bell over the front door was followed by Mallow scowling, so Doro turned to see who was coming in. President Winwood stared back at her with contempt clearly etched on his features.

"Once again, I see you're entertaining a lady and not even in your own office," Winwood said, as he crossed the room to stand over Doro. "You work for the college, Mallow, which I've explained to you more than once. I'm glad I came early for our meeting, since I presume you would've gotten her out of here before eleven o'clock."

Doro heard the security officer suck in a long breath and knew he was fighting for control. Would he get fired on the spot? If so, would he need to assert his special deputy status and arrest the college president here and now? Anxiety rattled through her. What if Winwood wasn't the killer? False arrest would end Mallow's time at the college.

Mallow rose from the chair and stood to his full height, which had him looking down at the shorter man. "I explained to you that Constable Lammers has a family emergency. Since I've gotten permission from the town council and mayor to serve in a special capacity, and I'm still a federal agent, I can man this office myself."

When Mallow slanted a glance at her, Doro wondered if it was a signal for her to depart. But she wasn't leaving him alone with a killer. Besides, Wade would come soon. The sooner, the better.

"I didn't give you permission to take on another job, Mallow, and I don't approve of it." Winwood jerked a thumb at Doro. "Nor do I approve of this young woman trailing after you. It's unseemly."

Anger flared inside Doro, who no longer tried to restrain herself. "I'm not trailing after anyone, sir. You know Officer Mallow was shot and needs a driver. That's my role." Actually, her role was considerably more, but Winwood need not know.

"That's right," Mallow agreed. "Miss Banyon is doing me a favor by playing chauffeur."

The look on Winwood's face said he was skeptical. "It's still unseemly, but that's hardly unusual for Miss Banyon."

His criticism did not surprise Doro. Winwood had never liked her and never would, not that she cared. Doro kept her attention on Mallow, who looked every inch the federal agent at the moment. His broad shoulders were squared, while his back was rigid, and his jaw was set. As she studied him, Doro wondered what he planned to do next. And what Winwood intended.

"Let's sit down and discuss the case, President Winwood." Mallow gestured toward an empty chair next to Doro.

A wedge of silence sliced into the discussion. In the interim, Winwood pulled out his pocket watch, studied it, and tucked it away. "Let's get started."

Amazement assailed Doro. From what she had seen, the watch's chain was in pristine condition. Had the president gotten it fixed so quickly? Possible but not probable. Her attention moved to Mallow, who was still looking in Winwood's direction. At his watch pocket, perhaps?

"Fine," the officer replied.

"I could take notes," Doro offered before Mallow could send her away.

"Miss Banyon needs to take her leave," Winwood sputtered.

Doro, not caring if she seemed desperate, turned to the officer. "Having a written record is important, isn't it?"

Conflicting emotions crossed his face. "It is," he said in a grudging tone. "You can sit behind the desk."

Doro figured he wanted her away from Winwood, but she wasn't worried. Surely, the president wouldn't attack either of them.

Winwood, his face flushed with anger, finally agreed. "Let us proceed, so I can be on my way."

Chapter Fourteen

After Doro took a seat behind the desk, Winwood and Mallow sat across from her. She took the notepad offered by the security officer before extracting a pencil from her pocketbook. Managing her excitement was challenging. After reading dozens of mysteries and teaching a course on them, she was capping a first-hand sleuthing experience by being present for an arrest. Finding the lost exam had been fulfilling, but the end had not been so dramatic.

"You haven't kept me abreast of the investigation, Mallow. Bring me up to date now," Winwood said.

The president seemed calmer, which gave Doro pause. Perhaps, Pierce and Kitty had lied. Maybe Stanley had, too. All of them had seemed upset and anxious, while Winwood did not. As she thought back over the dozens of mysteries she'd read, Doro considered the killers. Some were cool and collected.

Others were frantic. But they were all fictional characters, not real people. Her status as an armchair detective didn't quite meet with Mallow's position as a real-world lawman. Those facts kept her from blurting out the questions rising in her mind like bread dough in a bowl. That and knowing it wasn't her place to question the president.

"I told you about the fingerprinting," Mallow said.

"Did you get prints from all the suspects? Or did some refuse to give them?" Winwood asked.

Mallow leaned back in his chair. "Everyone cooperated, but prints can be lifted from hard surfaces, so it isn't necessary to have all suspects come in."

Winwood's gaze widened. "What? Those prints couldn't be used in court, because you'd have no idea whose prints they were."

"Not true, sir," Mallow replied. "Some surfaces are touched by only one or two people. For example, there are places in your office that you primarily handle. Isn't that the case?"

For a long moment, Winwood sat still and silent. "Maybe, but going into a private office to collect fingerprints wouldn't be right."

"It's completely legal." Mallow maintained his schooled expression.

Again, the room echoed with silence. As it did, Doro sensed a battle of wills between the two men. Winwood's reactions indicated uneasiness, which could relate to guilt.

Winwood appeared to regain his composure before he said, "You already told me about being in Professor Gibling's office. He's a likely killer, since Hemet was about to deny him tenure."

Mallow neither confirmed nor denied going to Stanley's office, which had not happened. "The professor voluntarily provided his fingerprints."

Again, the president looked taken aback. "Is he the murderer? Or did the Dudley boy do it? Both have ample reason."

"Actually, neither of them is guilty." Mallow let the statement hang in the air long enough to have Winwood shifting in his chair.

"Then, who is? Although a number of people clashed with Hemet, you said only a few were near the library Tuesday morning." Winwood's voice grew tauter with each word.

"Several people were in the area. Professor Gibling, Pierce Dudley, Kitty Tenseng, Miss Banyon, and you," Mallow replied.

"Me?" Winwood barked. "I saw Miss Banyon on my way back to my office. I explained why I needed to retrace my steps. Since she discovered the body only moments later, Hemet was already dead when we crossed paths. That eliminates me, not that I had any reason to kill a friend and colleague."

"I'm afraid it doesn't eliminate you, sir," Mallow said. "You lost your watch because the chain was broken, but it looks fine now."

While the officer did not make any accusation, his words rang with challenge. Doro focused on Winwood, who inhaled and exhaled sharply.

"Chains can be replaced," the president said.

"There isn't a jeweler in Michaw," Mallow said, "and I'm not aware of you leaving town over the past few days."

"I don't report to you, young man, so my comings and goings aren't your concern," Winwood said in a rough tone that did nothing to cloak his obvious anger.

"You wanted me to run a thorough investigation, and I have." Mallow left the statement hang heavily in the air. "May I see your watch and chain?"

For several moments, Winwood sat stock-still. Finally, he reached into his pocket, removed the items, and handed them to the officer.

As Mallow scrutinized the jewelry, Doro watched carefully. To her eyes, the chain looked pristine, but not brand-new.

"I noticed your watch and chain when I came for my first interview, because both looked expensive and had the patina of vintage gold. New links wouldn't match so well," Mallow said.

"Are you a jeweler, young man?" Winwood asked in a clipped tone.

"He isn't, and you know it," Doro, unable to remain quiet, put in. "Anyone can see the chain hasn't been repaired. And it isn't new. Besides, we also know Professor Corlon planned to meet someone in the library. The two of you have had a few meetings lately, sometimes with raised voices. More than a few people are saying the professor was softening his attitude about returning the school to men-only. Was that the source of your conflict with him?"

The president's hands clutched the chair arms until his knuckles turned white. "I'm not answering your questions. You have no right to ask any. When I took this job, I heard about you being a spoiled girl, who was hired due to her daddy's influence. Instead of finding you a job, he should've gotten you a husband. Then, you wouldn't have time to poke into matters that don't concern you."

Although his opinion didn't matter, Doro felt like she was on the defensive. Should she respond? If so, how? Doro was still considering her options when Mallow returned to the conversation.

"You didn't argue with Corlon over no longer admitting women or firing female faculty members?" Mallow asked.

Winwood's beady eyes narrowed to slits. "Why are you listening to gossip from this girl? She and her ilk want to cause trouble." The words shot out with speed and force, while his voice shook with apparent rage.

"A few people mentioned Corlon's change in attitude," the younger man said, "and we also heard his niece wants to attend Michaw, which seems like a solid reason for him to stop supporting that agenda."

Winwood's face went beet red. "We all agreed when we came here that Michaw could become an elite academic institution. That can't happen with women as students and faculty."

"By all, you mean Corlon, Jerritt, Pottiger, and yourself," Mallow said.

"Of course," Winwood replied.

As Doro listened, she figured Mallow's strategy was to push Winwood until the man lost control. If the security officer wanted her to chime in and continue pressuring Winwood, she would. Filleting and grilling the administrator like a fish would be her pleasure.

The officer did not let up when he continued. "And Corlon was backing off the proposed policy, so you were meeting with him again. After all, his niece was coming to visit soon, and dissuading the young woman after that would be harder. This is a pleasant town, and the campus is lovely. Most anyone would want to attend school here."

Mallow's observations reminded Doro that his sister had wanted to attend Michaw. How many students, like her, had not because of finances? After this case was closed, Doro planned to see about more scholarships being offered. President Adams would have continued growing the funds. Winwood had cut them.

"College is not for everyone. Some have no need of an education," Winwood said.

"You haven't answered my question about meeting with Corlon on Tuesday morning," Mallow said.

"You can ask Mrs. Jones about my schedule. She keeps track of it," the older man said.

"But she wouldn't know about you meeting with him before regular office hours," Mallow observed. "Did you go to the library for a discussion?"

Winwood's lips flattened. "He could've scheduled a meeting with anyone."

The words revealed the president was probably aware of a meeting. Doro once again noted Mallow's skill at drawing facts from suspects.

"Not all of them were angry with him," Mallow stated in a firm, fixed tone.

"How dare you continue to suggest I killed my friend? We've known one another since our undergraduate days. I'm the one who convinced him to come here and who put him in charge of the English department. It's ridiculous to think I'd harm Hemet." He turned an icy gaze on Mallow. "You're allowing yourself to be influenced by a pretty face. She's used her wiles to sway you, and to protect Miss Tenseng and her beau. It's obvious they're behind Hemet's murder. That girl hated him because he was against her group...Young Ladies Who Vote, or some such."

"Young Women Voters for Equality and Justice," Doro corrected in a stony tone. Wiles? She had none. None at all.

"Of course," he shot back, a sneer on his face. "The group, students and faculty members, would like to run this campus like you're running Officer Mallow. But I should say, former Officer Mallow." Winwood turned to Mallow. "You're fired. Pack up and leave."

Mallow lifted his chin. "You can fire me, but it won't change the fact that you're going to be arrested as soon as Constable

Lammers arrives. I have the authority to do it myself, but he'll be here in short order."

The assertion filled Doro with relief. Winwood was about to get his comeuppance, and she would witness it.

"Your so-called proof is laughable," Winwood insisted.

"In addition to everything else," Mallow said, "You had to be the one Professor Corlon expected to meet. That had to be you, sir. Constable Lammers agrees."

The older man's face went beet-red. "He doesn't know how to investigate a homicide, which has become abundantly clear. Wandering through town and glad-handing the locals is about all he's good for. Neither of you is fit to serve as a lawman."

"Is that so?" Wade Lammers asked as he entered the office and moved to stand by Officer Mallow's chair. His attention riveted on Winwood.

The color in Winwood's face deepened, but he jumped to his feet and faced the constable. "Neither of you is unbiased or competent," Winwood said, but his tone had lost some of its bluster. "We need real lawmen to handle serious crimes. I'm calling the county sheriff for his assistance."

"I talked to him the first day," Mallow put in. "About finger-printing. In fact, Constable Lammers took the card catalogue drawer to him, along with the prints I got. The sheriff's people have the right equipment and expertise. Getting the tests done and results back took a little time, is all."

"It did," Lammers agreed, "but they checked the ones you gathered against those on the drawer, as you know." He removed a sheaf of papers from inside his jacket. "The report confirms who touched the drawer."

Doro listened with interest as Wade and Mallow worked in tandem. Giving bits of information, instead of blurting everything out, seemed wise.

"I'm not giving you my fingerprints," Winwood put in.

"You don't need to," Mallow said. "We already have them." He continued by revealing how the president's prints had been extracted.

"Why, you..." Winwood sputtered to a stop before regrouping. "It means nothing if my prints are on the drawer. Nothing at all. Lots of us go to the library to do research."

"But you've never been back by the card catalogues," Doro pointed out, although that didn't figure in the evidence. She wanted to make him squirm even more.

When Winwood turned on her, his face was a frozen mask. "You are not in the library every hour of every day, Miss Banyon."

"No, but not a single person has seen you back there. I spoke with my boss and others. No one ever noticed you around the card catalogue."

His voice sliced through hers. "Just a bunch of unrelated details that you've trumped up. I've always known you have a wild imagination, especially where crime is involved. You fancy yourself as an amateur sleuth, because you're an avid mystery reader. Adams was a fool to let you teach a course on such drivel. Students need rigor in their academics. Consider this fair warning, Miss Banyon, you won't be instructing in the future. Not your mystery class or any other course."

How did he have the utter gall to bully her when he was on the verge of being put in handcuffs? Doro had always thought Winwood was overbearing, but his current audacity was stunning.

"Miss Banyon will be here long after you're gone, Mr. Winwood," Mallow said.

"President Winwood," the older man corrected. "And you'll be gone, along with her. I'll make sure of that. And I'll make sure any future employer knows you tried to railroad me."

Constable Lammers concurred with Mallow when he spoke again. "You won't have that chance, and Ev—Officer Mallow—won't need to worry about future work because I'm sure both he and Doro will still be in Michaw when the prison doors clang shut behind you."

"You've let the girl convince you, as well. Ridiculous," Winwood snapped. "Your penny-ante clues won't stand up in court...if it gets that far, which I doubt."

"We have plenty of evidence," Lammers said, in a calm, composed tone, "including your fingerprints."

Winwood threw his hands in the air. "I am dealing with idiots. Complete idiots. I'm sure there were many, many prints on that drawer."

"Actually, there weren't. Sit down, and we'll tell you the details." Mallow turned to Doro. "Do you want to explain why?"

The opening made her smile, but she let several seconds elapse before addressing Winwood. "If you had let Officer Mallow or me finish, instead of berating us, we could have already explained why the fingerprints are so significant." Again, Doro allowed an interlude of quiet to develop.

"Well, what's the significance?" Winwood asked. "Or are you simply wasting more time? If so, I have important duties to perform." Anger blazed in his eyes.

With no real reason for further delay, Doro met the man's furious gaze. "As you may know, the janitors clean the library once a week. Once a semester, they do a thorough sprucing up. Usually, before classes start. This term, they got behind because you had many extra tasks for them. Finally, they got to the major work Monday evening."

"What does that have to do with anything?" Winwood asked. "You are still wasting my time, Miss Banyon. All of you are."

"Then, I'll get to the key aspect." Doro's tone became clipped. "The card catalogues were cleaned, dusted, and waxed Monday night. That process removed all fingerprints, smudges, and marks. So, only the prints of Professor Corlon and his killer were there." She didn't mention Pierce, since the boy was in the clear as far as she was concerned. The lawmen had agreed. With luck, so would the county prosecutor.

Winwood's gaze went wide and his jaw dropped, but he made no verbal response.

"Nothing to say, Winwood?" Mallow asked.

Doro repressed a smile when the older man failed to correct the officer. Of course, he would not be president much longer. Even sooner, he would be behind bars. Where he belonged.

"I want to contact my attorney," Winwood replied.

"Sir, it would be better for you if you tell the truth first." Mallow spoke in well-measured tones. "We're fairly certain you didn't go to the library planning to kill Professor Corlon, since the catalogue drawer is a weapon of opportunity."

"That's true," Lammers agreed, "and maybe his death was an accident. Maybe you swung the drawer at him out of anger, but didn't mean to kill him."

Doro watched as Winwood's face contorted with an odd array of emotions. Anger, remorse, resignation. Would he explain what had happened? As moments ticked away, she became less and less optimistic about a confession.

"A murder charge would mean the electric chair," Mallow put in. "Manslaughter would only merit prison time."

As she listened, Doro was torn between getting the details and seeing Winwood booked on the highest charge. More long moments passed before the man finally responded.

"Hemet and I were meeting to discuss ending co-education," the president said in a voice lacking his usual command. "He'd changed his mind, due to his niece. I couldn't understand it. Until recently, we both agreed that a serious academic atmosphere can only be achieved on an all-male campus." He bent forward to brace his elbows on his knees and put his head in his hands. "When I got to the library, he was fussing with mislaid books and such. I got more and more upset because he wouldn't discuss the change. He kept talking about how smart his niece is. I had to follow him around the place. Such disrespect."

"What made you hit him?" Mallow asked.

Winwood sat back in the chair. "Hemet went to the card catalogue, where a drawer was sticking out. He fussed over that instead of responding to me. I finally got disgusted and grabbed the drawer from him. He laughed, like ignoring me amused him. That was the final straw, and I reacted without thinking. I slammed it against his head, and he collapsed. When I saw the blood, didn't know what to do. I tried to rouse him, but I couldn't. Panic hit me. If only he had taken the time to listen to me. I didn't want to kill him..." His voice trailed off.

"So, you used the tunnel to go to your office," Mallow suggested.

"I did," the president admitted. "Then, I remembered I was supposed to unlock the side door for Mrs. Jones. I hurried down there and went around to the back of the library. I wanted to be seen heading to my office. Coach Ayers is usually on his constitutional, so I went out and acted like I was going to College Hall."

"Which is when you saw me," Doro said.

He shot her a glance. "That was a surprise, but it worked for my purposes," Winwood admitted.

Recalling the man's accusation angered Doro, but she focused on another aspect of his tales. "As did your story about the lost watch."

"It gave me a reason to be around that part of campus, just in case someone saw me when I first went to meet Hemet," Winwood said.

Doro couldn't deny that the man had been clever, but she wasn't going to tell him so. Lashing out in anger might not be as bad as planning a murder, but a man was still dead. "You pointed the finger at others to keep suspicion from yourself," she said. Winwood nodded but did not look her way or speak again.

"What about last night?" Mallow asked. "Why did you go to College Hall? Were you worried about me getting fingerprints from your office?"

Winwood clasped his hands together and stared down at them. "You said I'd probably be charged with manslaughter instead of murder, but extra crimes could be added."

A quick look at Mallow revealed he didn't like what the president had said. "Crimes like destroying evidence?" the officer asked.

A shrug moved Winwood's narrow shoulders. "I don't have anything more to say."

Mallow glanced at her. "You got everything down, Miss Banyon."

"I most certainly did," she replied. With luck, his reason for skulking around College Hall the previous night would come out at trial. But it was a minor point.

"Good." The officer looked from Doro to the college president. "Unless you want to share additional details, Winwood, you can call your lawyer."

"You can do that from our telephone," Lammers said.

The president's answer was to walk to where the candlestick telephone rested on the front counter.

Chapter Fifteen

A n hour later, exhausted but elated, Doro sat in a comfortable armchair next to her own fireplace with her best friend seated on the other side of the hearth. Aggie had made coffee and set out a plate of sandwiches as soon as Doro got back. While they enjoyed the refreshments, the pair discussed the case. When Doro finished a summary of Winwood's arrest, she smiled. "Constable Lammers was grateful you and I helped so much. It took a load off his mind while he was at the hospital with his mother."

The expression on Aggie's face telegraphed her pleasure. "I didn't do nearly as much as you did."

Doro shook her head. "You gathered important details when Officer Mallow and I were out-and-about. And you went with me to talk to several people. Plus, you had great insights."

"I'm glad I could contribute. It was unnerving to know a killer was on campus." A little shiver rippled through Aggie.

"It sure was," Doro agreed. "Even though it looked like an act of passion, not a planned murder, I hated to think about the guilty party attacking someone else out of anger."

Aggie chewed on her lower lip. "Do you think President Winwood would've killed again? He's always been curt and cold, but I never considered him as a violent man."

For a moment, Doro thought back to Lammers and Mallow interrogating Winwood. "He was furious about being accused and insisted his fingerprints on the drawer meant nothing, since he'd been in the library before and after hours many times in the past. That wasn't true, but he lied a lot. He also insisted with so many people using the drawers, it would be impossible to isolate fingerprints."

"He didn't realize the card catalogue had been dusted, cleaned, and waxed the previous night."

"He did not," Doro agreed. "Even after it was all explained to him, Winwood said the janitors surely hadn't taken out and cleaned each drawer, but the prints used were on the front and inside the front, where he gripped it when he hit Corlon. That gave him plenty of leverage. It turned out Pierce's prints were only on the sides."

"Because he picked it up to move it away from the professor and check the wound," Aggie supplied, repeating what they had already discussed.

"Exactly, but we didn't mention Pierce to Winwood, who kept whining and complaining. More than once, he reminded Lammers and Mallow to call him President, not Mister." She rolled her eyes.

"A good reminder for me, too. I'll just call him Winwood, for now. In the future, I won't have to use his name at all." Aggie took a sip of coffee.

"That's a relief," Doro agreed.

Aggie narrowed her gaze on her friend. "I'm surprised he admitted to what happened."

"I was a little, but he only did it to avoid the most serious charge." Doro recalled Winwood's expression as he confessed. "He might've felt somewhat guilty."

"But not enough to stop pointing the finger at innocent people," Aggie said.

"No, not that much."

"I wonder how long it will take the Board of Trustees to fire him."

"I'm guessing they'll call an emergency meeting as soon as they find out he's in jail."

"I hope they don't make Provost Pottiger the interim president. He's almost as bad as Winwood."

"I'm with you," Doro said, "but I don't think the entire board realized what the Fearsome Foursome planned, so they may choose a long-time faculty member to serve until they find a permanent replacement. That'd be best."

The sound of the door buzzer interrupted them. Doro looked at her friend. "When did the bell get fixed?"

"This morning. A couple of the other residents were tired of it not working so, they puttered around themselves."

"It's a good thing Winwood is out. I can't imagine what he'd say if he knew ladies had done repairs."

Aggie frowned. "He'd blather about how we should cook and clean instead."

"Probably so." Doro said. "It has to be Officer Mallow, because he planned to stop by and update us. Let's take a flask of coffee and a couple of sandwiches for him."

Within moments, the two women were in the reception area, where Officer Mallow sat at the far end of the room in front of the brick fireplace. Doro was relieved to find him alone, instead of surrounded by other residents. The news about Winwood would travel fast, but she didn't want to deal with questions right now, and she doubted Mallow wanted to announce details to a crowd.

After the trio exchanged greetings, Mallow glanced at the tray Doro had placed on the table. "Dare I hope that's for me?"

"It is." Doro wanted to ask if he had eaten a meal, but quelled the idea. Fussing over the man would be unpardonably foolish. Besides, she was not the sort of young woman who did such things.

"I wanted to tell you both what else happened." He helped himself to refreshments before glancing back at her. "I assume you told Miss Darwine about the arrest."

"I did," Doro replied. "And the confession."

Mallow released a deep sigh. "I wish he would've admitted to wiping fingerprints off his doorknob, but it won't make much difference."

"You got him to explain why and how he killed Corlon. That's a major accomplishment," Aggie put in.

A shrug lifted one of Mallow's shoulders. "You two were a tremendous help, especially when Wade had to stay at the hospital. I couldn't have done it without you."

When his gaze moved to her, Doro felt warmth rise in her face. "The main thing is that Winwood is behind bars. With luck, he'll stay there."

"It's not likely he'll get out on bail, but we'll see. His lawyer will be here tomorrow. Until then, Winwood isn't going anyplace." Mallow took another slug of coffee before speaking again. "The provost got wind of the arrest and showed up at the constable's office. He's calling the Board of Trustees about taking over as president. At least, that's his aim."

"I hope he misses the mark," Doro said. "With luck, the trustees will realize they made a mistake hiring Winwood and his crew. Now that their plans are out in the open, alumni and donors may be more vocal about not banning women as students and employees."

"And critical of the lack of judgment involved in hiring someone who killed a friend and colleague," Aggie added.

"That should be a factor," Mallow agreed. "Wade and I talked with Pottiger at length. I asked outright why he and Winwood were in College Hall the other night."

"What did he say?" Doro asked.

"First, he wanted to call his lawyer. When Wade pointed out that cooperating might get the provost farther, Pottiger revealed he and Winwood had dinner together, just like you figured," Mallow said. "Winwood asked Pottiger to go with him to the offices. Supposedly, as we overheard, he wanted the provost to get some papers to review. He confirmed that Winwood went into his office alone. Pottiger heard a scraping, creaking noise."

"Like we heard when we opened the bookcase door," Doro put in.

"Yep," he agreed.

"I think Winwood was making sure he closed it correctly and left no trace of using it on Tuesday morning. Maybe he was worried about us looking in there." Doro offered the ideas.

Mallow nodded. "A guilty conscience usually escalates worry."

"Pottiger didn't know about the hidden passage?" Doro voiced the inquiry.

"Evidently not, and I didn't tell him. The provost also saw Winwood tinkering with the connecting door. I asked if Pottiger had trouble with the doorknob, and he hadn't."

"So, Winwood went to wipe off his fingerprints," Doro put in, "just as we figured."

"Seems that way," Mallow agreed. "Winwood knew I took fingerprints from the catalogue drawer as soon as I had the kit."

"Which probably weighed on his mind, even though he figured a lot of prints were on the drawer," Doro said. "But he acted like he was surprised about you getting prints off his doorknob."

"Winwood is a decent actor," Mallow responded.

"He is," Aggie agreed. "He can be charming, if he wants."

A sigh escaped Doro. "True. What about changing college policies? Did Pottiger mention that?"

Mallow shook his head. "He's being cautious in that regard. We asked if he knew Corlon had changed his mind about co-education, and he did. It was definitely a bone of contention between Corlon and Winwood. Pottiger confirmed that the president was furious with the professor."

"So, you were right about them meeting and arguing," Doro said.

"Which Winwood admitted," Mallow agreed. "Like he told us, Winwood felt betrayed by his old friend. Corlon virtually ignoring him on Tuesday morning lit the last match."

"How sad," Doro murmured.

"It is," her friend agreed. "I'm sorry for Professor Corlon and his niece, but I think coeducation will stay. Two of the trustees have daughters in high school, and both have visited campus. One has a son who's an outstanding basketball player. I know Coach Ayers would like him on the Michaw team. Those could be big factors," Aggie suggested.

"I hope Pierce will be back playing, too," Doro said before directly addressing Mallow. "You said you wanted to bring us up to date, and I'm guessing there's more to tell."

He glanced at his notepad before replying. "We spoke with one janitor to get additional confirmation. Since the other is out-of-town today, I need his address. Having him confirm they cleaned the card catalogue thoroughly—among other things in the library—will bolster our case." Mallow glanced from Doro to Aggie and back. "Both of you may be called as witnesses."

"That's fine," Aggie agreed.

"Of course," Doro said. "Before we got the vote, women couldn't testify in court. I'm sure Winwood will be peeved if and when we take the stand."

"I'm sure he will," Aggie agreed. "Do you know when the trial will be?"

Mallow shook his head. "There are some steps to be taken before it's scheduled. Winwood consulting with his attorney is one. The county prosecutor formally charging him is another. Before the latter occurs, Wade and I will need to pull the facts together. Luckily, we have solid evidence, so that won't take long. We'll recheck some odds and ends, just to tie it all up in one package with a neat bow." He finished his coffee, polished off another half-sandwich, and laid the mug aside. "There wasn't much to tell, but I wanted you both to know. Other than what I've said, Winwood will be taken to the county lockup tomorrow—probably shortly after his lawyer gets here."

"That's good news," Aggie said.

"It sure is," Doro agreed. "I suppose classes will resume soon."

"There's no reason they can't," Mallow replied. "Since Winwood canceled them until further notice, who knows? Faculty members, including librarians, are supposed to be back Monday. With that in mind, I'm guessing classes will restart then. I imagine the board will make the final decision about firing him when they meet."

"There's a big event coming up next weekend," Aggie said. "I'm on the planning committee, so I suppose we can go ahead now. We'd put things on hold."

"Sure," Mallow replied. "What kind of event?"

"A Halloween party. Music, food, costumes," Aggie replied.

"It's a lot of fun. Harmless fun," Doro assured him.

"Good to know," Mallow said with a grin.

"Is the library still a crime scene?" Doro asked.

"I'd like to keep people out until the prosecutor has a chance to look at it. He's planning to come first thing tomorrow. I hope that won't inconvenience you," Mallow said.

"No, it'll give me an excuse not to do any work for another day." Doro chuckled.

"You've been working every day," Mallow pointed out. "Solving this case was a big job."

His observation pleased Doro. "Then, I'll enjoy time off. What about you?" She glanced at his cane. "You aren't working your other job tonight, are you?"

"Surely not," Aggie added.

"Nope. I need to use the cane for a couple more days. Then, I probably won't be going on any more raids, unless Pottiger succeeds in getting me fired. He wasn't happy about being questioned." Mallow levered himself to a standing position. "Thanks again. For the food and your help. I'll be in touch when you can go back inside the library, and about when you two might need to testify or provide statements."

After Mallow limped out, Aggie turned to Doro. "Surely, he won't be fired."

"I wouldn't think so, but I'll feel better when a new president is named, and it isn't Provost Pottiger."

Chapter Sixteen

Within three days, news about changes in the administration came, which lifted Doro's spirits and sent waves of relief over the campus. Pottiger and Jerritt, who had been out-of-town interviewing for another job, were both leaving, and Thomas Adams was coming back as the interim president. Classes would not resume until Wednesday, to give all those who had left campus time to return, so Doro spent part of Monday in her library office. When she returned to her apartment, she tried on her costume for the weekend party and studied her reflection in the mirror. She had waited longer than usual to assemble an outfit because last year's event had been canceled at the last minute by Winwood, who stated that such events were not seemly at an academic institution. The awful man had likely enjoyed waiting to make his announcement until costumes were gathered, and the auditorium was decorated.

Doro pushed back thoughts of the previous year's disappointment. Putting this outfit together had been fun, but she was surprised at the overall effect. Gathering elements of flapper attire was one thing; looking like a speakeasy customer was another. Was that the image she wanted to present?

As Doro thought back to the last costume party, she recalled several women of middle years wearing similar dresses. Everyone, including President Adams, had chuckled over the ensembles. Surely, the same would happen this weekend, but Doro wanted a vote of confidence from her best friend.

A quick look at the clock revealed her neighbors might be coming and going to the downstairs kitchen. Not wanting to be seen yet, Doro decided to use the fire escape. Before stepping outside, she scanned the area. Not a soul in sight, so she carefully descended the steps. When she reached the second-floor, she went to pull the key from her little evening bag, but the sound of a puppy yipping distracted her. The bag and key hit the ground near the little dog, who shot off. "Oh, no," she muttered. Not only had she lost her key, the pup had gotten away again. For several moments, Doro stared in the direction it had gone. Even if she descended to the ground, catching it would be impossible.

Abruptly, Officer Mallow's voice called up, "Miss Banyon, is there a problem?"

"Too late," she murmured under her breath.

"I'm sorry. I didn't hear you," he said. "Is there a fire? I can sound the alarm."

She spun to look down at him. "No, there's no fire. Everything's fine. I'm just...well, stuck."

"Stuck," he echoed in confusion. "How do you mean? What can I do?"

Clearly, the man was not about to simply move along without hearing a sensible explanation. "I'm locked out."

The bewilderment in his gaze did not lessen, but he nodded. "I can help you."

Before Doro could reply, Mallow levered himself on to the bottom of the fire escape and climbed to her level. Evidently, his leg was better, because the cane was gone. So was any trace of a limp. "Your bullet wound must be healing." The comment was part curiosity and part cover-up. Focusing on his injury instead of her predicament seemed like a sound strategy.

"Much improved."

As he spoke, Mallow looked from the feather tip of Doro's sequined headband to the toes of her spike-heeled, t-strapped shoes before settling on her face. The scrutiny had her shifting from one foot to the other. Doro cleared her throat, but words failed her.

After a lingering silence, he said, "That's an interesting outfit."

Although his tone was controlled, amusement danced in his gaze. Heat scorched Doro's cheeks as she considered how her attire looked to a former Prohibition agent. "The girls in YWV are sponsoring a costume party."

"So, you and Miss Darwine told me last week." Mallow bit on his lower lip, but the effort didn't quell his burgeoning grin.

Doro held his gaze with difficulty. "I'm going as a flapper."

"That's pretty obvious." Amusement crept into his deep voice as the grin grew.

The comment reminded Doro of his previous job. "I suppose you've seen quite a few. Flappers, that is." Seen them and disapproved of them, she figured.

A half-shrug lifted one of his shoulders. "Some, although a lot of the places we raided weren't fancy, so most ladies weren't dressed as elegantly as you are."

His sincerity had Doro looking down at her frock, which was unlike anything she had ever worn in the past. Or would wear any place other than a masquerade. The sleeveless dress, made of pink satin and trimmed in matching lace, barely touched her knees. Several strings of faux pearls, along with two bangle bracelets, added to the effect. The above-elbow gloves were supposed to be a classy touch. Or so Aggie had advised. But was any aspect of her attire classy? Doro doubted the wisdom of wearing what could be considered a scandalous get-up. Another perusal of Mallow's expression increased her uncertainty. Was that admiration in his gaze? Did she want it to be? She cleared her throat. "I don't know if many people consider flappers to be elegant."

"Some are," he replied. "In general, I know little about women's wear, but I've seen photographs of ladies in the newspapers. Some attire is like yours."

"That's where I got my idea for this outfit," Doro admitted. "It seemed perfect for the party, which is usually well-attended. Of course, this is only the third one. President Winwood banned it last year." A sense of satisfaction filled her, but Doro bit back any comment. The jailed former president wouldn't spoil any parties in the future. When Mallow voiced what she was thinking, she grinned.

"He won't be forbidding anything else." His tone was cryptic but his gaze sparkled.

"No, he won't." Another idea occurred to her. "I don't expect any trouble at the party, so you shouldn't be burdened with keeping order."

He smiled again. "I've been invited as a guest, and I won't be going in uniform. I need to arrange a costume. Are you going someplace else this evening?"

The fire in her face only increased. "I was going to Aggie's apartment to show my outfit to her. She helped with ideas, but she hasn't seen me in it. I took the fire escape, so I wouldn't be on view to others."

His brows drew down as a puzzled expression blanketed his features. "You're in view of anyone who passes by." Mallow gestured to the sidewalk below.

Currently, no one was around, but the route was often taken by both faculty and students. Some were still, or already back, on campus, so she had taken a risk. A foolish one. "I know that," Doro rushed to say. "When I got to the landing, I was getting my key. But I got distracted by a puppy yapping. We've been trying to catch it and bring it inside, since the weather is getting colder. Anyhow, I accidentally dropped my purse. When it hit the ground near the dog, it ran off and I lost my key." She gestured to the sidewalk below.

"I see. I'll get it for you." With that, he climbed down the stairs and returned, bag in hand. "Here you go."

"Thank you."

"I'm happy to help." Mallow glanced back at the ground. "What direction did the puppy go?"

"Over toward the bushes. We've seen him or her in them a few times, but when we get close...off the pup goes again." She followed his gaze as she spoke. "It's a darling dog."

"How long has it been hanging around?"

As he spoke, the pup again came into view. "There it is." Doro extended her hand.

"Let me see if I can capture the little one." Before the words were out of his mouth, Mallow swung from the landing, to the stairs, and on to the ground. This time, he moved much more quickly.

Doro watched in amazement at his grace and athleticism. Obviously, he'd healed well. Once he was on the sidewalk, he reached into his pocket, squatted down, and extended one hand. When he spoke, his voice was low and cajoling. His words did not carry to Doro, but she continued to survey the scene before her. Her surprise increased when the little dog ate from one of Mallow's big hands. Exactly what food, Doro couldn't tell. With the other hand, he gently petted the coat. The little body wriggled against the long fingers. After a moment, Mallow scooped up the furball and cradled it against his chest. As he looked up at Doro, a grin curved his mouth. "I've got her. Do you want me to carry her to you?"

Delight filled Doro. "Yes, please." She watched as Mallow carefully climbed the steps with the puppy tucked inside his jacket. When he reached the doorway where Doro waited, he slipped the dog out. Doro reached for her, but the officer kept his hold.

"She'll get mud on your party outfit. Maybe I should take her to my place for a bath. It looks like she's been roughing it for a while."

A glance revealed he was right. Up close, the pup's filthy coat was obvious. Doro glanced down at her fancy dress. As much as she wanted to cuddle the dog, Doro knew changing first was best. "I can put on other clothes, if you'll wait here with her."

His brow furrowed. "Can you keep her in the faculty residence?"

"Several of the women have cats. One had a dog, but he died a couple of years ago. Old age." When Doro put her hand out to pet the soft ears, the cleanest part, the pup turned to lick Doro's hand. "You're a sweetheart."

"I think she's happy to get attention," Mallow observed.

Doro studied the puppy. "She has to be a couple of months old, at least. I wonder where she came from. We've been trying to get her for days, but none of us has seen other puppies or a mother dog."

"Just yesterday, I heard about a litter of pups and a mama in the woods behind the football field," he replied. "I looked over there several times since then. Never saw any of them, but I'm guessing this little girl came from there. You're probably right about her age, because she must be weaned or she wouldn't have eaten out of my hand so easily."

"She loved whatever you gave her."

Mallow smiled again. "When I went through the dining hall earlier, the cook gave me several sugar cookies. I only had one left, and this baby got most of it. Not the most nutritious food, but I'll make sure she gets fed right."

"Have you had dogs?"

Mallow nodded. "Several while I was growing up. How about you?"

Doro grinned. "I grew up with dogs, too, so I miss not having one. When my mother went to Colorado, she took Baxter—our family pet—with her. She couldn't have him at the sanatorium, but my uncle—her brother—kept Bax, who got to see Mother. His visits lifted her spirits. After my dad moved out there, they took him back. Baxter is elderly now. When I visited this past summer, he still knew me."

"Dogs never forget the people they love."

His soft tone echoed inside Doro. "You don't have a dog now."

He shook his head. "When my sister married, she took our family dog with her. I don't get a chance to visit often, but Roy always remembers me. And I think of him a lot. Maybe now that I have more regular hours and a real home, I'll get another dog."

"Real home?" The phrase puzzled her.

Dark color swept into his lean cheeks. "I rented a room after my ma died and my sister married. No dogs allowed. Not that I had time to spend with one, working the hours I did."

Over the past week, Doro realized she had misjudged Officer Mallow. His actions and words today put an exclamation point on that understanding. She looked again at the puppy nestling in his arms. While Doro would love to have the dog, she saw major obstacles. "My boss is a lovely person, but he's allergic to everything with fur, so I couldn't take her to the library with me. I'd hate to leave her all day."

Mallow looked aghast. "Allergic to fur? I've never heard of such a thing."

"Hardly anyone has, but he grew up on a farm. Evidently, he had a runny nose and itchy eyes often. The town doc only figured out the cause when Mr. Quartine went to visit his grandmother in the city for a month and had no problems."

"Wow. I guess that's why he became a librarian and not a farmer."

"Pretty much," Doro replied with a smile. "Anyhow, I would love to have her. But she might be better off with you. I could run home at lunchtime, of course." She scratched the small ears as longing rippled through her. How Doro missed Baxter.

Several seconds of silence passed before Mallow spoke again. "Maybe we could share her. I'm sure there will be times when I'm busy and can't walk her and such."

The sincerity in his tone and expression echoed inside Doro. When she looked at the pup again, the dark eyes seemed to plead for Doro to agree. "All right."

A fresh grin kicked up the corners of Mallow's mouth. "Great." He ruffled the soft fur. "Hear that. You're not homeless anymore. You've got two homes." A low hum left the puppy. "I think she likes the idea."

"I believe you're right." Some people said dogs didn't smile, but the little furball seemed to be pleased.

"I should let you go," Mallow put in. "And get her home for a bath and a proper meal."

"Good idea," Doro replied, although she wasn't ready for the pair to depart. Correction: she was not ready for the dog to leave. Mallow was simply a new co-worker. And the pup's new co-parent. Strike that. Co-owner. They weren't the little critter's mother and father, for goodness sake.

He shifted from one foot to the other. "I suppose I'll see you at the party."

After inserting the key into the door and stepping inside, Doro turned back to him. "I'm sure you will."

He glanced away for a moment before speaking again. "We didn't get off to a good start, and that's a lot on me." His voice lowered a fraction. "Mostly on me."

The admission further eroded Doro's initial reaction to him. "You had a job to do, and I should've understood that right off."

Mallow nodded. "I wanted to make a sound first impression, since Winwood and his buddies expressed their concern about hiring someone inexperienced." He cleared his throat. "Most campus security officers are retired cops. They made it clear I had to prove myself..." His voice trailed off.

"And a murder before you'd even left your old job put pressure on you." Despite her intention to remain aloof, Doro's sympathy was engaged. How could she push away a man who loved dogs as much as she did, and who had offered to share a darling pup with her? Impossible.

Ev's expression remained solemn. "But that's no excuse for badgering you or anyone else. I hope people don't think I was taking sides with Winwood and the others. Finding the killer was my goal all along. You and Miss Darwine didn't need to help me. You two probably could've solved the case on your own, but you agreed to work alongside me—even after I suspected both of you. I was rude and dismissive that first day."

For several moments, Doro studied his earnest expression. "Everyone realizes you were in a tough spot. Me, included. President Winwood was your boss, and who would've thought he was the guilty party?"

"You suspected him."

"Not right away. He and Professor Corlon seemed close." She shook her head. "I didn't know Corlon was backing off their plan to make the school all-male again."

A half-shrug lifted one of Mallow's shoulders. "I spoke with Corlon's sister this morning. She said he could be tough, but her daughter was the apple of his eye from the time she was born. He would've moved heaven and earth for her."

Sadness filled Doro. "She won't want to come to Michaw College now."

"Probably not, but other girls will enter the school. Many others over the coming decades."

"I hope so." Doro loved the college, and she hoped other young women would avail themselves of the opportunity to get degrees.

"As do I."

For a long moment, she studied his face. "You really feel that way." Although made as a statement, Doro wondered if Mallow was stating his genuine opinion or expressing the prevailing campus sentiment. Despite her improved view of him, Doro wasn't sure. Many men thought a woman's role was as a housewife.

The glitter left his gaze. "Evidently, I have more work to do in order to gain respect from the entire college community."

His obvious dismay put another dent in Doro's skepticism. "You have time."

A chuckle rumbled out of him. "I suppose so."

After a few seconds, Doro grinned. "I better get going before anyone else happens along. I'll see you Saturday night, Officer Mallow."

"Ev," he corrected. "My name is Everett, Miss Banyon, but my friends call me Ev."

Warmth softened her heart. Another friend was always welcome. "My friends call me Doro," she replied.

His grin resurfaced. "Please save me a dance, Doro." When she didn't immediately reply, he patted the puppy's head. "I can bring you up to date on..." His voice trailed off. "She needs a name."

An idea popped into Doro's mind. "I love mysteries."

Again, he laughed. "That's not a secret. I love them, too, but what does that have to do with naming the dog? Is there some wonderful whodunit with a doggie detective?"

Warmth spread from her heart to her cheeks. "None that comes to mind, but I adore Agatha Christie's books. I've read every single one, and I look forward to her writing more."

"I do, too, but surely, you don't want to call this little bundle Agatha. After all, that's your best friend's name."

"Not Agatha," Doro replied. "How about Christie?"

"Hey, Christie, what do you think?" A small woof was the dog's reply. Ev winked at Doro. "She likes it. Maybe Tee, for short." The pup barked again, and he laughed.

Doro stroked the soft fur. "She seems to like the nickname even better. You be a good girl, Tee." She met Ev's steady gaze. "Let me know when you need for me to walk her or such. I'll be wondering how she's doing."

"You'll see her around campus with me." Ev paused. "What about saving that dance?"

He looked and sounded like a shy schoolboy, which surprised her. "I will do that, Ev." Doro let her hand drop to her side as she stepped back.

"Tee and I will see you soon." After putting the pup back inside his jacket, Ev put one hand to his cap and gave a slight bow. As he descended the fire escape, a jaunty tune, whistled slightly off-key, followed in his wake.

Doro hummed under her breath as she continued toward her best friend's apartment. Maybe having a security officer on campus was a good idea after all. Possibly an excellent idea. And having a new friend, one who loved whodunits and dogs, was better than good. It could be great. When her pulse accelerated, Doro blamed it on anxiety over being caught in her costume...could there be another cause?

Only time would tell.

Thank you!

Thank you for reading _The Catalogued Corpse!_ I hope you enjoyed it. If you have time, please rate or review it. Comments from readers are helpful and appreciated. I am on Goodreads and BookBub. Most retailers also accept reviews.

https://www.goodreads.com/author/show/21325652.D_S_Lang

https://partners.bookbub.com/authors/6026727/edit

For more information, please go to my website or Facebook page.

https://www.dslangbooks.com

https://www.facebook.com/profile.php?id=100064024056297

You can sign up for my newsletter on my website. I share other authors' work, news about my books, a peek into the writing life, *historical tidbits, and more. Your email will never be shared, and you unsubscribe at any time!*

About the Author

D.S. Lang started making up stories to entertain herself as an only child, and she is still making them up. Now, she puts them in writing. Her mysteries are set in small town America during the 1920s. The amateur sleuths are young women dedicated to cracking cases with a colorful team of characters. The Doro Banyon series is set near her own hometown, Sylvania, which is mentioned in the books.

After earning Bachelor's and Master's degrees in education, D.S. worked as a golf shop manager, teacher (junior high, high school, and college), program manager, tutor, and mentor. She has a lifelong love of history and often gets sidetracked on research when she should be writing.

When she is away from the computer, D.S. enjoys reading, swimming, spending time with family and friends, and walking her dog Izzy.

Books in the Doro Banyon Historical Mystery series

The Doro Banyon series has a cozier tone than the Arabella Stewart books. History and mystery still mesh as amateur sleuth Doro solves whodunits with her best friend in smalltown America during the 1920s.

Prequel-The Lost Exam

Book One-The Catalogued Corpse (Release Date: August 2023)

Book Two-The Murdered Matron (Release Date December 2023)

Book Three and more are coming in 2024!

The prequel is not available for sale, but it is free to my newsletter subscribers. You can sign up at: https://www.dsla ngbooks.com

Books in the Arabella Stewart Historical Mystery Series

Book Eight-<u>An Uncertain Ceremony</u>

For more information on the series, please visit https://www.
dslangbooks.com